THE DRAGON CONSTELLATION

James Voorhees

Bonfire Books

Copyright © 2024 by James Voorhees

The characters and events portrayed in this book are fictitious. Any similarity to real persons, living or dead, is coincidental and not intended by the author.

Cover Art © 2024 by Jose Ramery

All rights reserved.

No part of this book may be reproduced, or stored in a retrieval system, or transmitted in any form or by any means, electronic, mechanical, photocopying, recording or otherwise, without the express written permission of the publisher except for the use of brief quotations for a book review.

ISBN: 978-1-9642126-10-4 Hardback
ISBN: 978-1-9642126-11-1 Paperback
ISBN: 978-1-9642126-12-8 Ebook

Printed by Bonfire Books LLC, in the United States of America

First printing edition 2024.

www.jamesvoorhees.com

To the one who inspired me to believe in magic

and to everyone who came alive in that magic.

PROLOGUE
City of Witches

The rain came down hard in the City of Witches. The hooded figure made his way through the wet streets. He was being passed by a parade of people wearing black. His navy hood and robes would have stood out on a sunny day, but not today. He was soaked and the wet fabric appeared darker.

He moved with purpose. His path was direct. He looked up to the windows of the top floor and saw her. Entering the Art Nouveau styled building through the golden doors, he was surprised to find that as he crossed the threshold into the lobby, his clothes became dry. *But after all, this is the City of Witches,* he thought. There was a slight feeling of water residue on his face. As he thought of it, he touched it and smiled.

He stepped into the open elevator, and it maneuvered itself without him hitting a button. The elevator took him up to the top floor, where the gates slid open. The room was dark from the storm clouds. No lights were on.

"Is my commission coming along?" a feminine voice asked with a subtle raspy quality in it. "Bellver can be…" She paused for the right word. "Difficult."

The monk stayed in the elevator. He was still distracted by how his clothes were dry.

You have no idea, he thought to himself, afraid to speak the comment.

He relived the pain of traveling back to the year 1877 to check on the sculpture that the Witch had hired Ricardo Bellver to create.

"He argued but made the changes that you requested," he reported..

"Adding the hair gives a stronger feeling of *The Fall*," she added with pride.

"He disagreed," the monk told her.

She raised an eyebrow.

"But he gave in."

She lowered her brow into its relaxed position.

"Take this," she said as she stepped out from the shadows.

He had still not stepped out of the elevator.

"As promised," she said. "A Witch's trinket."

She handed him a gold woven necklace. The monk thought that he saw movement in the links and blinked. He found that the links were still.

"Keep it concealed and do not lose it," she instructed. She turned away from him.

"What is it?" he asked as he moved and examined it.

"You're bright enough to figure it out," she told him over her shoulder and walked off.

He nodded and backed further into the elevator. He placed it in his pocket for now. Again, without having to hit any controls, the elevator moved and began to descend back to the ground level.

As it descended, he relaxed his mind. He focused on the feeling of the remnants of the rain drops, still on his cheeks. And again, he smiled. The elevator touched the ground softly. He heard the smooth sound of the well-oiled metal gates opening. He stepped out and walked through the lobby with that same sense of purpose in his step. The golden door opened itself, and he found that he was again in the rain. He headed back the way he came, his gait strong and rivaling that of any Witch strutting through the wet streets. He marched on with a true sense of direction. It seemed as though nothing could divert him from his course.

Soaked again by the rain, he giggled. He exited the city through the main gate but then avoided the road and walked through a field of lavender. He removed his gloves and let his hands play on the purple flowers, wet from the rain, releasing their charmed aroma. Holding his hands to his nose and inhaling their relaxing scent, he continued and entered the surrounding forest.

CHAPTER 1
Monastery of Naa

It was the twenty-fourth of December, 4007, and the first night of the Blood Moon. Everything appeared crimson beneath its glow. Moonlight flickered on the rough waves that crashed hard against the rocky coast. As they pushed against the shore, the appearance of red and pink crests showed themselves with an eeriness that made it look like the water had been turned to blood.

During the time of a Blood Moon, the cracked moon turned red and took on the appearance of a heart, The celebration of love commenced, and conflicts and wars were suspended for three full days and nights. The Blood Moon did not occur annually. However, when it did appear, it showed itself around the same time of year, at the time of the ancient celebration of Christmas.

The Monastery of the Order of the Brothers of Naa sat high atop white cliffs. It would take a skilled climber to ascend them from the beaches below. The monks, however, used these cliffs as a covert military training ground.

However, their training was only quietly advertised to the rulers of near and distant kingdoms. It had been speculated in regal courts that the Brothers of Naa doubled as hired mercenaries who had assisted in the successful efforts of kingdoms rising above their adversaries. However, that was never confirmed. Yet, somehow, the monks maintained healthy financial holdings in many private companies and in real estate that spanned many lands. This also added to their influence in politics, the recording of history, and the outlawing of magic in many kingdoms.

The monastery and its lands sat on the cliff high above the western wall of the harbor. The sea below was lined with sharp boulders that, over time, had caused a vast quantity of ships to sink. More destructive than the stones that were visible above the water's surface were the razor-sharp edges below: these could slice through the bilge and the hull of any ship.

Urban legend claimed that what made these rocks and their edges so destructive was that they were actually dragon bones, tinged with Mermaid blood. The sharp boulders formed a magical border that protected the Mermaid burial ground in these waters.

Mermaids had been among the Immortals: those sent to this world with a particular destructive purpose. Their entry into this world had occurred so long ago, and since then, the recording of their history had been obscured. However, the legends do agree that their purpose was to cleanse the seas. In achieving their given purpose, they were gifted with mortality and were now able to pass on to the next dimension and find peace. However, at the time of their death, they left behind that exquisite remembrance of themselves.

It was well known that Mermaid bones were filled with gem particles which, at the time of death, altered their structure to solidify. The entire skeleton of a deceased Mermaid was turned into a pure solid-gem sculpture at the bottom of the sea.

Many pirates, private collectors, and eager entrepreneurs tried and failed to retrieve those sculptures. Some lost their lives by drowning; others were attacked by a Mermaid visiting or guarding the burial site. Still more fell victim to the monks who protected the area from the cliffs above. The Brothers of Naa had sworn to protect these burial grounds. This also added to the speculation about how they obtained their wealth.

Following their philosophy that no mortal is perfect, the Brotherhood of the Order of Naa were allowed to repudiate one vow and never impart his choice. Many of them chose not to take their vow to abstain from wrath.

Most went along with allowing themselves to train and fight and when called to, kill in battle; All for the good of the Enlightenment.

Fewer abstained from the other sins: pride, gluttony, lust, envy, and greed. Rarely, did a monk abstain from sloth. However, regardless of the untaken vow, the silence associated with it was the final and Holiest of the vows. The silence bound them to the faith and to servitude towards one another. Only the monsignor and any others he allowed were given the right to speak. The number of verbal brothers had increased under the current monsignor, but even they were ordered to remain silent in his presence.

The time of the Blood Moon was a cause for celebration. Yet, at the Monastery of the Brotherhood of the Order of Naa, this night was quiet. There seemed to be an uncomfortable energy in the air, the silence adding to the eeriness. The reddish hues of the moon's reflection were accompanied by intermittent sparks of white light in the air. It appeared as if lightning bugs were presenting themselves in a mating ritual. This softened the mood of the only monk who was presently in the monastery; This monk had chosen his allowable sin to be *sloth*.

He looked out the open door, too lazy to close it and keep out the cold. To his defense, he had made a fire in the entrance hall of the main building. He peered at the Blood Moon and then to the open landscape that ended at the cliff. The high grass blew in the wind. He had attempted to cut it earlier that day when the red moon appeared in the sky, but needed to prepare a feast and did not have time to finish it. He knew that he would pay for that when the others returned. To avoid seeing it, he dragged himself over to the door and closed it. He had more to do in anticipation of the others returning for a Blood Moon celebration.

As the portly monk shut the door, he missed seeing a figure run across the open grass. The figure leapt with all his might and grabbed hold of the inside of a window frame. He quickly threw himself upward and flipped to land atop the narrow perch above the window. He was consumed by the shadow cast onto the building from the windmill that housed the monastery kitchen. He sighed as he took in the crimson coloring of the usually pure white exteriors of the buildings on the monastery grounds.

Inside the monastery, that single monk walked the corridors. "Every night, the same thing," he whined, ignoring the vow of silence. "Climb to the top of the tower. Light the fires. Climb down. And tonight of all nights, rushing to make a feast in case anyone comes back."

The blue-robed monk gazed up from the center of the circular staircase that wound upwards along the walls of the tower. He was able to see the Blood Moon through the glass atrium that exposed the interior of the tower to the sky. He focused on the windows that wound about the tower, but through them, saw complete darkness with an occasional quick spark of light.

At first, he thought the sparks were snowflakes. He gasped as he moved his gaze higher, his hood falling and exposing his disheveled hair to the cool night and the reflection of the red moonlight through the glass ceiling at the top of the tower. He was too lazy to replace his hood, even though the culture of his order required him to remain hooded.

"Then, every morning," he again spoke aloud, "the same thing. Climb to the top of the tower. Douse the fires. Climb down."

As he began his annoyed ascent up the six hundred forty-six steps, the monk's foul mood continued, as he complained more loudly and stomped harder on the steps.

"What was that?" he questioned at the fourth of forty-four windows and lanterns. He peered out of the window, but nothing caught his attention other than the moonlight on the eerie red ocean. He motioned as if he had the chills from the sight of the red reflection on the waves. He caught a metallic odor on the night air and cringed.

"Never a good sign," he said with a sense of seriousness.

However, like it or not, he had a job to do. And he did not know when the others would return. So, he had to perform his duties every day, most of them, despite his laziness. He twisted his body and reached for the lantern and then continued his hapless climb and upon reaching the top, lit the torch that sat on the glass roof of the tower.

Lighting the torch atop the tower always seemed to change his mood and allowed a gentle but only partial smile to come across his face. Then, like every night, he turned his attention outward to the moonlit sea and then to the darkness of the night. Stars illuminated the sky. Some moved at celestial speeds and then disappeared as they fell.

He drew his attention back to the land. Across the harbor, the city of Mortua was alive with color and fireworks. The celebration of the Blood Moon was in full effect. The monk longed for a celebration.

The reflection of the moonlight on the water was intense and lit the tower and the monastery with a cold, crimson light. As he peered out the opening in the tower, he asked the same question he did every night. "Is it just me? Am I the only one left? Why haven't the others returned?"

Every member of the Brotherhood of the Order of Naa had been brought to the monastery as children; orphans with no family to take them in. They were raised by the other monks who had also been left as babies and children to be raised by the previous monks, and so on throughout history. Each generation of monks told this story to the next.

On the rarest of occasions, a monk would make a pilgrimage to search for orphaned children. It was a strange thing when a brother would go on this type of pilgrimage. Orphans were brought to the monastery, yet not one of these brothers had ever returned. However, no one questioned the command of the monsignor. It seemed a death sentence to travel away from the monastery, but the other monks were not sure why. The other option was that they chose not to return. Even though every monk thought it, it was not encouraged to question it aloud when they were permitted to break their vow of silence during initiation ceremonies. Doing so meant that you were sent to find out for yourself. The fear was usually greater than the wish to verbalize curiosity.

Then, four years ago, the monsignor made the decision that monks could make the pilgrimage together. He had argued there was safety in numbers. However, someone would have to remain to caretake the monastery. Of course, the one who refrained from taking the vow against the sin of sloth was the one to raise his hand in excitement.

"For the Brotherhood," he stated to the raised eyebrow of the monsignor.

So, this time, the entire Brotherhood, with this one exception, had gone on a pilgrimage from kingdom to kingdom but had not returned. Yet, since the Blood Moon appeared in the sky earlier that evening and it was a time of celebration, the monk had been cooking a feast in anticipation of their homecoming. He feared retribution for not doing so upon their possible return.

"What makes that smell?" the monk again questioned the unfamiliar stench on the breeze. The sea air blew in an odor that was unpleasant even to the monk, who had not bathed in over a week. He sniffed the air and then himself and his robes. "Oh! That is rancid. Metallic, even."

The monk let out a sigh, as he did every night at the same time in his routine, and with a lighter foot he skipped down the six hundred forty-six stairs, holding his torch aloft and whistling a somewhat joyous tune.

As he neared the lower stairs, the monk thought that he heard something outside a window he was passing. He peered out but saw nothing. He leaned against the chilled wall of the tower and held out the torch to see if that stirred anything, but nothing happened. The curious monk stretched his head further out and scanned left and right, but again saw nothing. He felt dust fall onto his head and face. He sneezed and turned himself to look up.

The monk's attempted scream went unheard as he was viciously torn out of the window into the night air. He kept trying to scream into the blowing breeze, yet he could only gasp. His adrenaline rushed as he felt the warmth of the sucking on his neck. He began to breathe in time with the tensing of the lips and the pull of his blood. He began to feel his whole body tingle. And then, he felt nothing.

The monk had been killed by a vampire. The vampire's pale complexion was beginning to soften into a pink color as he stared off at a tree in the distance.

"So gross. Generally speaking, monks taste terrible. It really is all in the diet. You are what you eat," Vampire concluded as he released the lifeless corpse and let it fall to the ground. He sat perched in the sliver of a window with just enough room for his feet to balance. His hands were gloved as he dared not touch the silver that framed the window. That widely held belief is true: silver can burn a vampire, only temporarily scarring, but still painful.

He jumped and was lost in the shadows of the cool night air. Color had returned to his skin, although the reddish hue of the moonlight hid his still paler complexion.

The vampire now sat in a tree and waited for the other monks to come and investigate. But no one came. He was surprised by the emptiness of the night. The cool, metallic-tinged breeze blew from the shoreline. And then he detected a hint of more familiar but long-lost scents. He jumped from the tree and walked through the partially cut grasses. The aromas of jasmine and crisp citrus mixed with an earthy familiarity and a tantalizing spice activated his senses and a rush of adrenaline ran through his body. He moved with a sense of urgency.

This was Phineas' scent.

Nothing, he thought, as he continued to survey the darkness for movement. *It's gone.* He became frantic. "Did that just happen?" he asked himself. "Or was it my imagination?"

He spied the monastery grounds, still sniffing the air. He commanded the wind to circulate and deliver the current aromas.

No, he answered the question in his mind as he moved closer to the monastery's entrance.

The vampire kicked the locked door of the tower, knocking it off its hinges. The heavy steel was deformed from where his foot struck it and stood bent, embedded in the wall opposite. No response. No defense. He walked through the tower and towards the library. No confrontation. No presence of anyone. Maybe he had not needed to kill that monk. However, he was hungry and feeling a bit undone, so…

He was distracted by the light from the room to his left. He forced open another door, leading into a dining room. The dining room was arranged for a celebration, a feast for the Blood Moon. Smells of the meal wafted through the air. Yet, still no one. The vampire became lost in his thoughts.

There is no way they knew I was coming.

Vampire inhaled deeply. The salty air from the sea was becoming more intense, and with an increased metallic aroma. He had work to do. Vampire began walking throughout the monastery from one oversized room to the next. Fires were lit in the oversized fireplaces. Shelves were straightened with their objects clean and organized with purpose. But still nothing. It was as if the entire monastery had been abandoned by all except that one monk.

"The lazy one," he said to himself. The vampire was surprised at the cleanliness of the monastery, the strict organization of its things, and the smells of the meal.

He entered the adorned library backwards, as if waiting for a shadow to pass. He turned and took in a deep breath. He feverishly examined the volumes of books that filled the six-story circular room, housing its own serpentine walkway with metal ladders on wheels that were locked in staggered locations throughout the levels. The wall sconces that illuminated the library added to the appearance of a grand hall. With the winding walkway and the golden railing that was meant to resemble the tail of a serpent, the vampire had to admit that he was impressed. The staggered ladders and the precious metal bookbinders peering out from the shelves resembled reflective scales and the ceiling was covered in what was made to resemble the wings of a dragon. But as impressive as it was, he was not here for that.

Where is the book?

He glanced at the glistening walls of bookbinders and spotted a point that reflected no light, midway up on the northeast side.

He leapt up the equivalent of two stories and grabbed the fiery gold railing to pull himself onto the suspended walkway. His grip contorted the metal railing. He flipped over it and ran the rest of the way. As he reached for the book, all he found was an empty space. It was gone.

Did Lucifer lie to me? Or could it have been destroyed and gone forever?

A crash came from outside and dust and smoke filled the glowing library. The salty sea air was heavy in sodium content and was suffocating. The toxic salt that filled the air began to react with the candles in the wall sconces and light the open air as if it were filled with mating fireflies.

Or did someone else take it?

There would not be time to find out the fate of the book. He heard cracking glass and went out to investigate. Vampire looked up to the roof of the main tower as the lit torch atop it glowed stronger in reaction to the salt air. The sound of glass cracking became louder. Fire would not be able to destroy him, but it would consume him and damage his appearance if left to burn. Vanity would not allow for Vampire to become disfigured, even if only temporarily.

The thermite in the salt air was aggressively affecting the flame on the top of the tower and caused repeated explosions that loosened the foundation of the roof. The lazy monk had not attended to maintaining the stability of the roof other than to light the fire every night. The torch was dropping fire all over the thick cracking glass and had compromised it enough so that it could no longer maintain its weight. The roof collapsed and the torch was sent crashing down through the inside of the tower.

Vampire dove back into the library as the torch hit the floor outside and exploded. The walls were on fire, and the torches in the windows continued to react to the particles in the air. Each window was blocked by fire and prevented an exit. The library had no windows, and the pages of the books were also beginning to burn. The vampire was trapped.

"Absolutely not!" he demanded of the fire. *Who wants to spend eternity as a rotted corpse without the ability to die? Physically unattractive?* he thought. Not he, nor his pride, nor his ego.

Vampire began leaping through the library. He grabbed at the metal ladders and ripped them from their locked bases along the walkway that wound upwards in the great space. His crushing grip bent the metal at every point of contact. He was throwing the ladders down to the floor of the library and then jumped down to start assembling them into a bridge over the lowest flames of the fire and out the nearest clear opening, door or window.

The reactive air kept up a constant distraction as if he were being bitten repeatedly by vicious insects. Vampire knew that time was quickly moving in the wrong direction, so he continued to work fast, doing his best to ignore the pestering burns. They would heal.

And then he paused. There it was, locked in a glass display. The rose gold of the binder differentiated it from the others. The flames bounced off it like bullies teasing an invincible victim. He knew that he had one chance and, whatever the cost, he had to take it. Vampire jumped into the inferno that surrounded the book. He smashed the glass and grabbed the book by the binder. He quickly opened it and was satisfied to find its pages empty. He waved his hand over the open text and spoke the ancient words. The text began to expose itself. He read the words "Jeweled Dragon" before they disappeared again. He knew that this was the right book. This held the answers that he needed, but he would still need a Witch to bring the words and images forth, not just temporarily. He tucked the book into the back of his waistband and focused on his exit.

As he jumped back to the ladders, an explosion grabbed his attention. There was nothing to secure the ladders in place, so he had to stabilize them.

Vampire began to climb onto the escape route that he had created. The wall around the window on the second floor had begun to fall and showed a larger exit. The flames rose and fell, teasing Vampire to attempt to use it as an exit. He had to secure his ladder to the second-floor window.

"Enough! Time to go, you fool!" He heard the voice in his head. The rungs of the interlocked ladders were hot. Vampire smashed a library chair that had not yet caught fire and grabbed two of the legs to protect his hands from the burning hot metal of the ladder rungs.

Although immortal, he was able to feel the pain associated with the burns on his hands from the fire below and the pesky bites of the reactive sea air on his exposed flesh.

Vampire continued his cautious climb over the loosely constructed ladder frame below him. The structure shook every time he shifted his weight. The legs of the chair protected his hands, but only so much. Vampire peered ahead at the rising and falling flames that tempted him towards that window. He moved in time with the rise and fall of the flames, coordinating his body movements with the dance of the unstable ladders. He continued his slow and steady climb to the second-floor window until he heard a crash coming from within the library.

He turned to see the doorway erupt into flames and push the fire out into the main tower. Vampire took a full leap towards the window and caught hold of its frame with a strong grip. He felt the silver window frame burn his exposed skin, as his gloves had been scorched away. He was struggling to pull himself up and got his elbows and forearms onto the base of the window. The pain was undeniable.

He lifted his head out and saw the night sky. The cool air blew in at him, but it was still reactive and painful as the bites of fire continued to spark on his face and hands. He grabbed the book, tucked into the back of his pants, and threw it out of the window as far from the burning monastery as he could. It hit a distant tree and tumbled to the ground. The breeze blew the empty pages and turned them to expose their nakedness. The fiery bites had no effect on the pages of the book.

Vampire continued to struggle to pull himself up through the window. He spotted a hooded figure in the distance. He was seated under a tree and writing in a journal. The distraction could only momentarily override the pain. Vampire threw himself out the window and into the night sky.

His landing brought him down hard onto the rocky terrain. Vampire looked quizzical and then annoyed. He pulled himself upright and dusted himself off before walking towards the hooded figure.

"Hey!" he began, yelling to the hooded man. "Really? No help? Nothing? None whatsoever?"

He searched the air for that familiar citrusy scent. Nothing.

The man picked up the book that Vampire had thrown. He sat under the tree and turned the empty pages.

"Nope," the hooded monk replied. "I'm busy with my memoirs."

"Planning on dying?" Vampire sarcastically asked.

From behind Vampire, the tower, the library and the structure as a whole came tumbling down in flames.

"Ooh," the hooded man let out, although not with any emotion. He put the book to his side and pulled a knife from his belt. "No," the monk stated blankly. "I just like to keep a chronicle of my life."

"Like that's going to do anything," Vampire said, mockingly.

The monk took an apple from his bag and sliced it with the knife. He continued cutting and eating his apple.

The hooded monk motioned, as if offering Vampire some of his apple. He met Vampire's stare with his eyes still shadowed. He shrugged his shoulders and continued eating. Free of reaction. Free of fear.

"I could have died!"

"You're so dramatic. You can't die."

"I can suffer!"

"We all suffer. Get over it."

The man put his journal that was filled with words and hand drawn images into his backpack. He lifted his bag from the ground. There was a heaviness to it; a weight beyond that of a monk's 'lack of' worldly possessions.

Gluttony, Vampire thought. *That's your unspoken vow.*

The monk stood tall and began walking away into the night as the fire raged behind Vampire and the thermite continued to ignite and bite at his face.

"You just destroyed my home. Go fuck yourself!" the monk yelled over his shoulder. He held his arm in the air and stuck his middle finger up to the night sky. He continued walking off with no added speed and no fear.

Vampire snickered and shook his head. He turned around toward the fire. As he stopped and sniffed the air, he caught the faintest lingering of Phineas' presence. "Nothing has changed. Same inviting scent," he continued. "The time is near…"

CHAPTER 2
City of Witches

The hooded monk returned to the City of Witches. He was again dressed in the flowing, navy robes. However, this time, the day was sunny and dry. He stood out like a tourist with his mustard-colored gloves. His oversized hood hid his identity from the magical onlookers, who passed him along the busy high street.

The Witches' style was reflected in everything from their clothing to their architecture. It was seen in the Art Nouveau street lamps that had survived time; from the glistening benches that lined the walkways of the parks to the way a dinner table would be laid out for a meal and the food presented. Everything in the City of Witches had an air of sophistication.

The City of Witches was a haven for those with magical abilities. In fear of magic taking over their power, many rulers had outlawed the practice and had shunned those with magical abilities. Ironically, a ruler would hire Witches for a hefty price to make sure that their kingdom and really, their own power, was protected. Some even had to go as far as to marry the Witch in their employment, while concealing this fact to save face.

Since the fall of Queen Ileana, most kingdoms began to denounce everything magical, from wand shops to herbs to apothecaries with magical earthly remedies. All of these would be closed indefinitely under the Treaty of the Order of the Green Kingdoms. The Kingdom of Witches was one of the few places where magic was legally practiced; however, the level of magic was still policed.

"Lunch, sir?" offered the eager restaurant host who walked backwards with the menu open and suspended in the air as he waved his fingers above it. It was a simple but enchanting trick that was a go-to for attracting non magical tourists into a shop or restaurant. Yet the monk showed no interest and continued on.

The blue color of his robes defined him as a Brother of the Order of Naa. But it was the gloves that drew attention to him as a non magical type. The palette of a Witch's wardrobe was simple, dark, and neutral. Styled, yes, but the colors were not meant to draw attention. The Witch Council had suffered many setbacks and had finally conceded to attempting to 'fit in', even shying away from the non magical.

Aside from the loss of their rights to perform magic, Witches also suffered a great blow in that their ancient writings and spell books had been burned to ensure that their knowledge could not be passed on. Some lesser books were available. They accounted for the simple spells that every Witch learned like nursery rhymes. However, the texts that included the strongest spells were lost; therefore, a Witch's magic was now used only for entertaining. Those who attempted grand spells usually met with their own destruction. The spells needed to be exact, and without the knowledge of the ancients, many things could go wrong.

Knowing that he was marked as a tourist, the monk walked cautiously, for he did not trust Witches. Neither would a Witch trust a Brother of the Order of Naa. He peered over his shoulder, wary of any interruption to his own thoughts.

The Witches, although somewhat oppressed, had learned to live joyously among each other and to work together. The forces that had driven them to selfishness and greed had disappeared, along with the loss of the ancient texts.

The monk gazed up to the glass rotunda at the top of the triangular building standing at the corner of a five-point intersection. His oversized hood limited his vision but also concealed his identity. However, when he looked up, he was able to spy the figure moving away from the windows. He nodded and cautiously walked across the stone street to the building entrance. His hood and robes gave the impression of flight as they flapped like wings with every step.

The cautious monk looked over both shoulders before entering the building through the golden door. It appeared safe but his caution was valid. His study of the history of Witches left him untrusting of the magical community, regardless of the truce between the two kinds of people.

The elevator had come to the lobby floor and the gates opened. The elevator was for him. He entered and admired how the metal bars and adornments bent like snakes and floated like birds until the gates closed and the elevator ascended. He watched the spiral staircase that wound itself around the elevator shaft. As the daylight reflected off the metal railings and the edge of the steps, the staircase seemed to contain movement within itself. However, the monk believed that the changing sparkle from the gems embedded in the steps reflected the sunlight in such a way as to appear as though something were following him up to the top floor.

Although the Witches had agreed to no longer practice higher magic, they did not accept poverty. They used the small bits of magic that were allowed in the Kingdom of Witches to build riches. They had maintained themselves as a prosperous community. Witches were not allowed to practice higher magic, but they were allowed to sell their limited magical goods. No one who purchased goods from Witches asked how they were produced. They just knew that they were of the finest quality and were willing to pay a higher cost for them.

The elevator came to a soft stop at the top. Had it not been for the monk's visual awareness, he would have thought the elevator had been standing still the whole time. The metal bars and adornments reversed their fluid movements, and the gates opened again.

The monk, as was his usual pattern, took caution in stepping out onto the black and white-patterned floor. The surface was hard under his feet, yet his steps made no sound.

"A simple spell," whispered the feminine voice from over his shoulder. "This way, my guests don't know that I am spying and eavesdropping while they gossip."

The monk held his position and said nothing.

"Did you bring what I asked for?" she questioned, as she slowly extended her fingers in anticipation. Her movements had a feline quality, daylight reflected off her fingernails, revealing their deep plum color. The monk was surprised that they were not true black, like every other witch's nails.

The witch turned her attention to the monk's mustard-colored gloves. "Not exactly fitting in," she said.

The monk, still silent, removed a book with a rose gold binder from his bag. He held it up without looking at her. The Witch wrapped her fingers around it. She bit her lower lip softly. She knew what she now possessed; It did not matter if the monk did. It did not matter what he might think nor who he would tell. She now possessed the ancient text and would be able to complete her work, *The Book of Spells*.

"Thank you," she whispered into his ear and pulled the book from him. She was surprised that she met with resistance.

"Payment," the monk reminded her in a timid voice.

"Ah. Yes." The Witch turned to walk away. The clinking of her heels on the floor was now audible. She stopped in front of an elaborately decorated armoire. She turned to the hooded monk with a sideways smile. "Spells are not meant to last forever," she said over her shoulder, knowing the monk was surprised at the sound of her footsteps. "Well, most of them at least," she added. She drew her right hand to the face of the handsome cabinet. It appeared to have no doors, just metal embellishments in the forms of protruding figures. Humans, angels, demons, and beasts of all kinds had been cast in gold, silver, and bronze. The Witch reached for a copper figure in a top hat. As her finger made contact with the figure, it appeared to come to life. She caressed it with the side of her index finger and stared at the monk. His eyes were concealed, but she knew that he was fascinated by the magic happening before him.

The copper figure tipped his hat and then placed it back onto his head. He clapped his metallic hands with a high-pitched smack that brought the other figures to life. One by one, they reoriented themselves on the face of the cabinet and created two vertical lines. At the top of the panel was the copper figure, who began to lower himself and revealed a line which served as the marker of the now present doors of the cabinet. Each figure turned and moved away, and in doing so, bent the doors from the top until the figures pulled them around the side and left the face of the cabinet open.

Inside the cabinet was a glowing orb. It was small enough to fit into the palm of a hand and glowed white. The Witch reached in and picked it up. It immediately turned a deep purple. She walked towards the monk and held the orb over his outstretched hands. She gently moved her hands away and the orb slowly descended into his right palm.

The monk extended his left hand to offer her the book as he marveled at the orb. Her eyes glowed in anticipation of receiving the text.

"You have an appreciation of magic," the Witch said, and walked out of the room as she thumbed through the book.

The monk said nothing as he stared at the orb and watched it change in color to canary yellow.

"It knows your sins," the Witch spoke from the other room. "And therefore, it knows how to help you escape them. It will lead you where you need to go."

He leaned forward and spied to see if he could catch a sight of the Witch, but no. The monk continued watching the orb in silence. The sunlight caught his eyes. He turned his gaze out the window and admired the sun that now shone its way through the clouds. The color seemed to change. He understood that things were different in the City of Witches, or at least they were perceived differently.

He wanted to stay. He wanted to study and learn. However, he knew that he needed to go. He dared not step forward. He walked backwards into the elevator. He held a finger in the opening to see what might happen. The metal began to move like before. However, this time, it maneuvered around his finger so as not to injure him.

"Hmmm," he joyfully expressed from under his hood. The Witch had reappeared in the direct line of his vision. She nodded to him, and he returned the gesture as the elevator descended. She maintained eye contact until he was out of sight.

She stretched her hand out into the air. The woven gold necklace that she had given to him uncoiled and traveled down his arm and through the air to her. It wound up her arm and created a sleeve. At that moment, she was out of his sight.

"Sometimes confidence needs a little help," she said, as the light reflected off the stone and illuminated her eyes. "I will aid you," she said, "even when you are unaware that you need it."

CHAPTER 3
The Road to Mortua

The bar was crowded and loud as the celebrations of the second night of the Blood Moon continued. Monk and Seer had taken a back table, near the fireplace. Monk had apologized to Seer for them missing out on any festivities of the first night of the Blood Moon. Seer drank with a touch of sadness and a heavy heart. The flames of the fireplace were mirrored in Seer's eyes as they continued to drink heavily. Monk kept a secret smile as he breathed in the scent of the burning pine.

Seer was an exceptionally handsome man. However, he was surprisingly less confident than one would expect for such an attractive individual. His blood-red robes held tight to his muscular form. They were cut in a similar fitted style to the Cerulean blue robes of the Brotherhood of the Order of Naa.

Seer had spent so much of his life in fear, or on the run. His life's journey had left him mentally scarred in a way that made him avoid people as much as possible. The combination of his attractive appearance and his standoffish nature made him even more desirable to some people. He generally kept to himself. He did, however, trust Monk. Through a combination of circumstances that had pulled them in and out of one another's lives for the past four decades, they maintained a close bond akin to family.

Monk, on the other hand, had an air of sensuality in his movements. He gave off an essence of confidence and strength. To look into his eyes was to see into true strength. The light hit Monk's face and exposed the depth of the scar that ran diagonally across it, disappearing into the high collar of his robes. Monk caught Seer staring at it. The look on Seer's face showed the same embarrassed sense of responsibility that it had when Monk suffered the injury as a child. He had been beaten while defending Seer.

"We may have to kill him," Monk whispered to Seer to draw his mind away from his guilt.

"What?" Seer's shock was palpable. Without thinking, he lifted his full mug to his mouth and began to chug his ale. He gulped it down, while Monk watched him with a ruffled brow. When it was empty, he slammed it down on the table.

"You okay?" Monk asked, as he pulled his thoughts back to the matters at hand.

"He's not normal," Seer responded, in reference to witnessing the scene at the monastery.

"Seems not," Monk answered blankly. "But we are?"

"You saw what he did to Brother Jacob," Seer continued, staring at nothing.

"Yes, I did," Monk replied with the same matter-of-fact tone. "Brother Jacob was a lazy sloth."

"Not the point," Seer said and faced Monk with concern. "He's an Immortal."

"A vampire, to be exact," Monk said.

"A vampire," Seer repeated flatly. "And we now have to kill a vampire."

"I said, *may have to*, but yes. It is a possibility."

"How are you planning on doing that?" Seer motioned for more ale. "It takes an Immortal to kill another Immortal. And you couldn't even move when you saw him."

The waitress obliged with two pints and a wink at Seer. Monk encouraged him to follow her.

"Keep it up and I may have to kill you," Seer stated as he gained his composure again.

"Good luck with that," Monk concluded and continued to stare into the distance. "Somehow, I knew him instantly."

The waitress returned with more ale and another wink for Seer. He blushed immediately. She attempted a brush of his hand, but he pulled back before she made contact. Monk caught sight of the exchange but said nothing. He knew that his further encouragement would only cause Seer to panic and become upset.

"He seemed to be searching in the air, like an animal who had caught the scent of something interesting," Monk said, reviewing the events at the monastery.

"Like dinner?"

Monk mustered a laugh. "Yeah. Maybe."

"I told you that something like this would happen."

"Yeah, but you left out a lot of details. I don't know when or where, but I do know that we will meet up with him again," Monk explained.

"And I'm the seer."

"Yes, but—"

"I did not 'leave out' the details. It's just that the 'details' were not available. He's an Immortal. I can't— No one can 'see' Immortals," Seer reminded Monk with a touch of bitterness.

Monk looked off into space.

Seer was now the one to hold his comments as he thought it best not to say any more.

Monk got up from the table and took the last swig from his mug. "Come on," he commanded, already on the move.

"Where are we going?" Seer questioned.

"You're a seer. You should know that answer." Monk disappeared into the reddish glow of the Blood Moon and then the darkness of the night.

"Such a simple insult," Seer whispered to himself as he finished gathering his bag and followed Monk. "I expect more from intelligent people…" he yelled out to Monk. "Maybe the people aren't as intelligent as I think."

"Such a simple insult," Monk joked back.

Seer's retort was quickly curtailed as he peered ahead and saw Monk stop in the middle of the road and the shadowed form that hovered in front of him in the darkness of the night.

"Don't move," Monk instructed.

"Monk?"

"And keep quiet," he added in a whisper.

The shadow was in a constant flux of form. It changed from human into various beasts, including peacock, pig, snake, bear, goat, frog, and dog to undefined variations of shapes, and went from various layers of transparency from complete darkness to seeming gone or invisible. Seer's eyes burned crimson as he attempted to 'see' into the consciousness of what was in front of them.

Monk watched him, anticipating what he was doing. Seer shook his head with a disappointed expression. His inability to 'see' the ever-changing form led them to understand that whatever this was, it was not of mortal consciousness. Monk was cautiously stepping back towards where Seer was standing.

Once he stood next to him, he leaned in and whispered, "It looks like it's trying to figure something out."

Seer continued to glare at the blackness with an added curiosity. Monk caught a glimpse of this growing interest. He hit him in the back of the head to force his words and gave him a questioning nod.

"Definitely an organic form. This is not man made," Seer whispered. "I can feel that there is a consciousness, but I can't understand anything else about it. It's as if it's trying to learn how to be something. Like it's searching deep into itself to remember how to be... how to take form."

"That's a lot of information about something that you can't see," Monk admitted, impressed.

"Monk?" Seer rushed a response as if not listening to him.

"Yup," Monk replied as they watched the form begin to take on a reflective tone and gather itself into a solid sphere.

"Something is happening," Seer said, as he again attempted to use his gifts. His eyes glowed crimson as he focused his special abilities on the form. It was slowly shrinking into a sphere that was no bigger than a child's ball hovering in the air, its blackness shiny and reflective. Monk and Seer saw their altered reflections in the sphere. They became entranced by what they saw, by the distorted versions of themselves. They were unable to look away.

Seer noticed that Monk's reflection became increasingly transparent until he was no longer visible. He saw his own reflection turn and walk away. He saw a progression of different harrowing situations that involved pain and torture. He saw the destruction of the world. He saw cities fall and forests burn. He saw the seas attacking the land. He saw creatures of legend full of rage and at war.

Monk felt as though he were falling. Monk could see only the shiny black sphere that hovered in the night air. Seer, on the other hand, continued to see the added decay of the world that he knew. He saw battles that toppled good rulers from their thrones. He then saw what Monk saw and felt him falling. And then he saw nothing. The sphere gave no further signs, no light, no reflection. It was as if Monk was gone.

Seer gasped and looked to his left: Monk was no longer standing next to him. He turned back to the sphere and saw it still in place. His own and Monk's reflections were again present in it. Taking a quick glance around, he yelled out for Monk. His screams went unanswered.

I don't understand, he admitted to himself. Seer did what he was able and attempted to see Monk and to see his future. The visions were distorted. Monk was going in and out of solid form. It appeared that Monk was made of light, yet there was pain.

Seer had a shred of hope that he would be able to find Monk through his visions, but the feeling was so painful that he got no relief from seeing his image. And then the most painful rush of loss came to Seer. It was so strong that it forced him to his knees in anguish and knocked the air from his lungs. He was down on his hands and knees when he felt someone attempting to help him to his feet.

The sensation of someone touching him added to his fear and he reacted by pushing whoever it was away and toppling onto his back.

"Seer! It's me — Monk."

"Monk? Where the hell did you go?"

"I have no idea. All I know is that wherever it was, it hurt so bad. I still feel my body burning."

"Monk… I saw… not very good things for you."

"Well, just be glad that you only had to see them. I had to experience them," he said, helping Seer to his feet. "But on the bright side, that thing is gone. It was odd. I felt like I was flying."

Seer immediately gazed into the air where the black sphere had been and saw that it was no longer there.

"Flying? I saw you falling," he told him, as Monk waved through the air to make sure that the sphere was not just transparent.

"Like I had wings. The air smells very different up there; like— well, like everything you ever enjoyed smelling all at once."

"That could be a bit..."

"In a good way," Monk continued.

Seer looked around, and although he saw nothing, he was still concerned about their safety.

"Monk?"

"Yeah, I agree. We should get out of here. We can come back at daylight and scan for evidence of whatever that might have been."

CHAPTER 4
The Road to Mortua

"This is where it happened," Monk reminded Seer.

"I don't get it," Seer whispered, as he looked around for evidence of the previous night's events. "Nothing," he continued, pushing the fallen leaves with his foot. He reached down and grabbed a handful. He threw them into the air and watched them fall to the ground in the most simple and normal way. "I don't even think that a single leaf has blown in this area since last night."

"That is peculiar," added a voice in a shy quiver.

They turned to see a slender young man guiding his horse-drawn cart.

"Tink! You're back," Monk stated as he ran over and threw his arms around his young friend. He held his slim frame tightly and breathed in his spicy scent. He squeezed harder and lifted him into the air. "We missed you."

Tinker stared at the scar across Monk's face. He, as always, felt saddened by Monk's disfigurement. Monk gave him a friendly slap on his cheek to remind him that it was not his fault. He grinned and winked. Tinker returned the gestures with a smile of his own.

"Come on, man," Monk told him with pride, as he ran his fingers along his facial flaw. "It's sexy."

Tinker laughed with him, but this time not out of pity. "To be honest," Tinker said with a shrug of the shoulders, "it kind of is."

"Hello, Tinker," Seer added, offering a handshake, as Tinker was still wearing his riding gloves.

"Hi," Tinker replied and quickly dropped his glance to the ground.

"He can't read your mind, Tink," Monk jested.

"Shh," Tinker replied. Monk rolled his eyes. "You don't really know that," Tinker added in a whisper.

Tinker had always been frightened to look Seer in the eyes, out of fear of him reading his thoughts, seeing some horrible death in his future, and worst of all, stealing his knowledge and leaving him without thought and logic.

"Even if I could, I promise that I would not steal your knowledge," Seer said.

"Thank you," Tinker replied withquick, nervous eye movements.

They all began to walk back to where Monk and Seer had stood the night before.

"Wait a minute! How did you know that?" Tinker asked Seer.

Monk and Seer glanced at one another and then back to Tinker, who stood more nervous with his arms tight across his chest. He maintained his stare at Seer until he realized that he was staring into his eyes.

"I told him," Monk responded, as he and Seer had a laugh.

"Ha, ha. You're both very funny," Tinker said.

"So funny that you were almost taken up by some sort of portal."

Monk and Seer immediately stopped laughing and moved closer to Tinker.

"How do you know that?" Monk questioned Tinker, still staring at Seer who returned the concerned expression.

"How do you not know that?" Tinker replied as he took the upper hand and stared into Seer's eyes with a sneer. "It's right there." He walked past them towards where the black form faintly hovered, stopping directly under where the sphere had altered its form the night before. "There is a remnant of a portal," Tinker said, motioning its position in the air with his hands.

"We've searched," Seer told him. "There is nothing."

"Amateurs," Tinker said, with judgment.

Tinker pulled a shimmery metallic powder from a vial that was attached to his belt. He threw it into the air and the golden flecks lingered and glistened around what otherwise looked like air. There was no movement in the form. It appeared dormant. Tinker ran his hand over, under and through the now-exposed form.

"It's closed now, but I can see that it was here," Tinker told them.

Monk and Seer glanced at one another, knowing there was no need to confirm that.

Tinker continued. "It's still sticky."

"Why was it changing forms?" Monk asked.

"It was trying to make out your form, your physical and spiritual makeup," Tinker told them.

"We were standing here and then Monk was gone. But I still saw him in the form…our reflections…but they were distorted," Seer explained.

"And then he came back," Tinker reminded them.

"Yes."

"It was attracted to something about you, Monk. What did you see?" Tinker uncorked a jar and allowed the mist that came from within to rise and surround the area under question.

"I was flying, and my back was burning when I got back," Monk reported, as he too waved his hand through the void.

"Did you know what was happening? I mean, did you know that you were taken up by the portal?"

"I don't recall thinking about it. I only remember flying and then the burning pain."

Tinker continued to search the area. "Are you sure that you studied at the monastery? The library is, I mean *was*, full of all of this information."

"Maybe I'm just making sure that we are thinking alike, and that Seer gets a full view of it all," Monk answered, with a joking face towards Seer. "And you were five when we left."

"I broke in and read on occasion," Tinker confessed. "Often really."

Monk realized what Tinker had just said. "What do you mean, *was?*"

"Apparently, it was destroyed," Tinker told them without remorse.

Monk looked at Seer, who shook his head to acknowledge that he was unaware of the monastery having been destroyed.

Tinker was quick to get back to explaining portals to them. "You see there are — how do I get you to understand — 'roads' that can bring you from one place to another. The difference between regular physical roads and the one that you experienced last night is that the regular ones keep you in the same dimension and are bound by generally understood laws of mortal and non magical physics. The others, for example portals, enable you to travel through time and space, to different dimensions. They have a broader range than even the Leprechauns' Rainbow Network. But you need someone with the ability to open one to be able to conjure it, like a Witch or sorcerer… something magical."

"So, what did I experience last night?" Monk questioned.

"Not sure. Maybe another dimension? Do you remember any specifics about the place?"

"No. Aside from the burning."

"There is no proof of the existence of portals that allow traveling to the future. Some theorize that the past, present, and future all exist at the same time. I have not seen proof of the future playing into multidimensional experiences. Not to say that it's not true; just that the evidence is not yet there."

"From my experience," Seer began, "the future is a tricky thing. The potentials are there, but so many things have to fall into place for a clear path to develop."

"Unless…" Tinker said.

"Maybe, what you experienced last night is part of your future," Seer deduced.

"Is the burning part of this experience?" Monk asked.

"Is it still burning?" Seer asked.

"Yes, but not as bad. More like stinging now," Monk admitted.

"No idea," Tinker replied with growing interest. "Did you look at it?" Monk shook his head. "Is it scratched up?" Tinker questioned as he rushed to Monk and started pulling at his Cerulean blue robes.

"Tink? What are you doing?"

"It's still burning, and you haven't seen it?" Seer begged as he, too, was pulling at the layered fabric.

"I drank too much and passed out last night…" Monk admitted.

"As did I, but I wasn't the one who was burning," Seer scolded.

They managed to expose Monk's torso and stood behind him in silence.

"What is it?" Monk questioned.

Tinker and Seer looked at one another with concern.

"Monk?" Tinker questioned with caution.

"Tink?"

"Two questions… Simple. Direct."

"Ask."

"When did you get this tattoo?'

"I don't have a tattoo."

Tinker and Seer again glanced at one another.

"Would you mind if I put a salve on your back to stop the burning— I mean, stinging?"

"What?"

"Answer the question. It's going to hurt."

"It already hurts."

"It's going to hurt more but just for a minute."

"Can you explain what's happening?"

"Answer my question," Tinker demanded as he grabbed a soaked cloth from his cart.

"Fine. Do it."

Tinker was already pushing forward and rubbed the salve-drenched fabric onto Monk's glowing back.

Monk screamed in pain and fell hard to the ground. Tinker pressed the cloth over the flesh until Monk stopped expressing pain. The pain was gone, and Monk was face down in the dirt. His breathing slowed back to normal. Seer examined Monk as Tinker went to get something from his cart.

"From the looks of Monk's back..." Tinker began and handed Monk a mirror.

Monk stood and held it in front of himself as Tinker held a second one behind him. Monk adjusted his mirror until he was able to see the reflection in the mirror that Tinker was holding.

"I wasn't that drunk. I would have remembered getting this done," Monk joked as he admired the intricate details of the glistening markings on his body. He saw the outline of wings that appeared like a tattoo across his back but felt as though the reflective lines were branded into him. The outline continued below the belt line. He stripped completely down as they all stood in awe of the precise artwork that spread across his back and over his shoulders. The lines went down the back of his legs to his knees and around the sides of his torso.

There was a sound like a distant gasp. Monk faced Tinker who shook his head 'no'. He turned to Seer.

"That wasn't me," he said, with his hands in the air as if in surrender.

"It was someone," Monk said as he scanned the trees to see who was there. "We need to go."

"Yeah, but maybe after you pull your pants back up," Tinker joked as he pointed out the obvious. "Tonight is the third night of the Blood Moon," Tinker reminded them.

"Then, it's a good thing we will be in Mortua," Monk said, with a smile. "Feels right."

Monk's favorite day of the year was the first day of the Blood Moon. *Full of hope and magic*, he would always say. They had missed a real celebration.

"I promise to make it up to you," Monk told them, feeling bad that they did not celebrate the other nights as a family.

Tinker looked at Seer and grinned. They said nothing. Seer put his gloved hand on Monk's shoulder and squeezed in reassurance that everything was all right. Monk smiled and put his hand over Seer's as he pulled Tinker in for a playful hug and a kiss into his full head of hair.

Monk continued to smile as Tinker went back to educating them in the ways of theoretical physics. He led his horse, who was pulling his cart filled with gadgets and books.

"Not sure that I understand," Seer said.

"And that is why you are pretty," Monk told him. "You don't have to be as smart as Tink," he joked.

Tinker brought his lecture back to the previous night's events.

Seer argued, still trying to make sense of the conversation. "But regardless of what happened, I still saw Monk in the black sphere even though he was not standing next to me."

"Nah, you saw a marker. That's just a homing device so that he could find his way back." Tinker's eyes widened in amazement. "Really? No reading whatsoever?"

"It's why we keep you around," Monk joked. "We are men of action while you filter through all of the theory behind what we are already rushing towards."

"And warn you against."

"Exactly."

"But there was a time when Monk was gone from the sphere," Seer continued, "It seemed like he was falling and then disappeared into the blackness. Everything was gone. There was no reflection at all, not even light. It had lost its shine."

Tinker stopped walking and started taking mental notes on what Seer was reporting. He was puzzled, but nothing came to him. He was also distracted by something else.

"I believe that that is when he went to the future," Tinker told them.

"And got tattooed," Seer added.

"You mean branded," Monk countered.

They hit the pinnacle of the hill they had been traveling up and got a view of the seaside kingdom from above. The stone road led down the hill to one of seven bridges that connected the tidal island to the mainland.

"Gentleman, welcome to Mortua," Tinker announced.

"It is beautiful," Seer said, gazing at the rooftops glistening with their golden tiles, the crisp white structures that held up those roofs, and the various blues and greens that balanced perfectly in the waters of the harbor and further out into the sea.

"I do love this view. The sea goes on forever," Monk said. "But we had better hurry. The tide isn't going to wait for us.""Welcome home, Tink," he said with his hand on his shoulder.

CHAPTER 5
The Taverne Ayer, City of Mortua

The city of Mortua had earned its reputation as a must-see for anyone who had the potential for travel or relocation. The city was a tidal island, surrounded by walls illuminated on the exterior by Mermaid art; the art being visible only at night, for the moonlight was what captured the Mermaids' glow of bioluminescence.

After the moon had cracked all those years ago, the tides had also been disturbed. Here, they would rise to their peaks at night. The walls of the city were built to keep out the tides and add to the protection of the city through a truce that had been established eons ago. The truce involved the human king and the Mermaid queen producing an heir. The seven bridges that connected Mortua to the mainland were covered and unpassable at high tide. Boats were the only form of transportation in and out of the city until the tides receded in the morning.

The Mermaids were able to create the art on the outer walls of the city at high tide when the bridges were under the water line and the water encircled the walled city. When the tide rose, the Mermaids swam freely around the city and created their wall art, along with luring men with their siren song.

The existence of Mermaids, formerly Immortal creatures, had been recorded in the time of man for thousands of years. Seafarers had described them for as long as men had taken to the sea. And yes: they were as alluring and beautiful as described. Vicious? Only when necessary. Interested in human men? Just for fun; occasionally for purpose. When the original Mermaids were sent to cleanse the seas, they called to drunken sailors to impregnate themselves and create new Mermaids.

For generations, that offspring was always a beautiful, female Mermaid, as Mermaid traits were dominant over human traits. For centuries, the father would always die after intercourse. So yes, the human king died for his kingdom, and his daughter was a Mermaid. His sacrifice was seen by the Mermaids to be truly selfless, and because of it, they chose not to destroy humanity as they cleansed the seas. The Mermaids practiced their free-will and allowed humanity another chance.

This decision was seen as a favorable choice by the Enlightenment, and the Mermaids were rewarded with mortality, for they had fulfilled their true purpose. The king's sacrifice preserved his city in peace and beauty and unbeknownst to him, saved all of humanity.

As evolution would have it, the daughters of the Mermaid-human bonds began to produce not only descendants with more human characteristics, but also male offspring. The present rulers of Mortua were siblings, triplets, a queen and two kings, sharing equal power.

The queen, Sharon, was a Mermaid but able to live on either land or in the water. She had a strong character, was analytical in nature, and was the general of the most feared armed forces. Mortua was famous for its war strategies and success on any type of battlefield. Queen Sharon commanded the army of humans and the navy of human and Mermaid forces.

Her brothers, King Charles and King Jax, were the first males born to a Mermaid. King Charles, the more rebellious of the siblings during their earlier years, was now the rock on which the crown sat. He was a solid and stable sounding block with an objective political view.

King Jax had always been a quieter force. He was fair and strong-willed. However, once crossed, he was the most likely to destroy anyone who took that chance, without an ounce of regret.

Both King Charles and King Jax were more human than their sister. However, King Jax had Mermaid characteristics; alas, he was born sterile and unable to produce an heir. In their youth, King Charles would kid him, wishing that he was "... as lucky. I would bed every beauty who came my way if I didn't have to worry about marrying them all." King Jax was confident that an heir to the throne would come from one of his siblings.

All the men of Mortua were raised to be wary of the Mermaid's call. The Mermaids had no need for human men, other than to procreate and to produce the next generation of Mermaids. The Mermaids would consume the men who did not 'rise to the occasion'.

AZ was one of those Mortuan men who knew better than to answer a Mermaid's call. He had his eyes set on someone else — the Princess of Mortua. The Princess was the daughter of Queen Sharon.

And although the princess was a Mermaid, she shared only some of the Mermaid characteristics. She was able to stay under the surface of the water for extended periods, more than one would think for a human. However, she could not breathe nor live underwater. She did still hold the charms of the beauty of the Mermaids, but she was not able to lure men to their demise. Many gossiped, in her favor, that it was her choice not to. She and the rulers were greatly favored amongst the people.

AZ's constant and public sighs for her were the cause of repeated head shakes from his friends, dreams from his mother, and snickers from his father. But his lack of a sense of responsibility also caused angry arguments with his father, 'tsks' from his mother, and drunken 'cheers' from his friends. But AZ had a plan. Handsome? Yes. Charming? Yes. Rich? Yes… well, sort of: his parents were. So, by default… Yes!

"That's your plan?" AZ's friend, Harvey, questioned with a shake of the head as he poured himself another mug. "To be a handsome… rich… charming guy?"

"Ummm, yes. You have a better one?" AZ replied, shocked by the thought that his plan would not work.

"Yeah! Get a job. Get some responsibility. The princess is not interested in a useless pretty boy. If she were, she would marry Estab! He's much more handsome than you!"

"Really? You think that he's better looking than me?" Comparisons to Estab had always upset AZ.

"Okay," Harvey laughed with a shake of the head. "Good luck with your plan. I have to go. Even though it's the Blood Moon, some of us have work tomorrow."

"No, no, no. Don't go yet. One more round. On me."

"Good night, AZ. You're my best friend, and I love you regardless of you being— well, you. But I have to go. I'll see you tomorrow. After work!"

Harvey gave him a big hug before making his exit from the Taverne Ayer, still shaking his head. AZ, like always, ignored his friend's comments and thoughts that mimicked those of his parents and teachers and— well, everyone except the other rich, lazy, pretty boys. He sat back into the booth as the barmaid brought another pitcher. AZ continued to refill his mug with ale over the next few hours as he consorted with the testosterone-filled young male Mortuan society. He continued to laugh with locals and visitors and bought rounds for the whole bar with many a gold coin. He became, not surprisingly, very drunk and did not notice the spying eyes that had been on him all night.

Seated in the shadows of the back corner of the Taverne Ayer was a figure with a hood drawn over his head. This was not a curious look. Wearing a hood told the Mermaids that you were not available. They respected your allegiance to another person. The high collar of his shirt covered his face as he sat drinking from a silver goblet. As he lowered his collar to drink from the goblet, the shadows continued to cover his identity.

The hooded man slowly looked up, with a tilt of his neck, as the door opened, and the bar continued to fill with those celebrating the third and final night of the Blood Moon. As the still-red moonlight entered the tavern through the open door, it showed the hooded man in a rich color that appeared not to be black, as it had in the darkness of the shadows. The light also gave a hint to a scar that cut across his face from below his right eye slicing diagonally and across his lips.

AZ continued with his dice game as more travelers entered the bar.

The door opened again, bringing a chill inside the tavern. As he walked in, the stranger with salt-and-pepper hair and a smoldering intensity in his greenish-brown eyes glanced up and over to the hooded man. He took in a deep breath and smiled, as if a great memory had just come into his thoughts. He smiled.

Monk hid his concern regarding the man not casting a reflection into the mirror behind the bar. Vampire did not see his own tousled hair. He did not see the glow in his own eyes. He looked into the mirror and saw not his reflection nor the action taking place around him, but something different. He was watching the actions of a different plane of existence. The beasts that he saw did not exist in the place where he was standing, yet he was not drawn into it. He turned his immediate attention and charms onto the drunken AZ.

"A battle of wits," Monk whispered into the air and took another sip of wine.

Vampire put his arm around AZ's shoulder and handed him a drink. His deep-violet, formal coat drew AZ's attention as AZ felt the fabric and was impressed with the high quality. With a nod of the head, AZ agreed to what was offered. It seemed to be a game of darts. Monk could not hear the bet. However, he knew, instinctually, that AZ was in over his head.

Vampire continued to persuade AZ by showing him his shoes and pulling money from his belt. AZ became even more impressed with the man because of what he possessed. More of AZ's friends had also come in, as Vampire, a stranger to them, was now buying more pitchers of ale and shots of stronger spirits for the pretty young men of Mortua.

Another unfamiliar guest entered the tavern. It was a regular occurrence for tourists to mingle with the locals. The man was dressed in a cape that was lined in a rust-gold color. As he entered the tavern, he tipped his hat to Vampire. He walked away from him but kept a cautious eye out and gave a sniff to the air. He seemed to sense an unknown force but was unable to acknowledge the presence. Vampire continued to loiter close to AZ and entice him with more alcohol. The caped man was positioned at the bar and continued to linger.

AZ was in mid-laugh when the door opened again. The sweet smell of lavender entered, along with three hooded women. He recognized the scent immediately and turned his attention to the door.

The young ladies removed their hoods. Vampire continued to talk, but AZ did not even know he was there. She was there. Princess.

The visually intoxicating young woman was the Princess of Mortua and the ruler of AZ's heart. She was laughing with her friends as one of them waved to a group across the room. She turned and saw AZ stand a little straighter with a twinkling excitement in his drunken eyes and gave him a shy grin. He was still completely unaware of Vampire's continued presence and entirely focused on her as she moved. To AZ, it appeared as if she were floating through the crowd of local rich drunks, tourists, drug dealers, prostitutes, and their callers. Princess playfully put on a pair of her friend's dark glasses.

The drunken AZ began to walk away from Vampire as he continued his conversation. His senses were also drawn throughout the room.

He had come here tonight to convince AZ to help him with his quest. Yet, he repeatedly glanced back at the hooded man and smiled.

AZ was being told something funny by a friend, which caused him to bend in closed-eyed laughter.

Vampire lost his patience. Fangs grew from his teeth as his eyes turned to pure light. He grabbed the nearest body, pulling her to his fangs, as if he would suck the life from her. The attack grabbed the attention of every patron in the tavern, as it was meant to.

"Damn it!" exclaimed the gold-caped man who threw a powder into the air. "Alzicatralis!" he screamed, and a blinding light took over the tavern. The dark glasses protected Princess' vision from the pyrotechnics. AZ was laughing with his eyes closed as he too escaped the dazzling light that dulled the vision of other patrons. He stared at Princess who stood with a defensive posture and moved to protect her. He ran to put himself between her and Vampire, but tripped. Princess was struck off balance as AZ knocked her to the ground.

"I have you," he reassured her.

They stared directly into each other's eyes as the dark glasses were knocked from her head and AZ maintaining his protective position atop her. He was blinking, for although he was spared the blast of the intense light while he was laughing with his eyes closed, he had taken in enough of the magical distraction to not see clearly. Princess' look of favor lingered, but then turned to anger. A force stronger than gravity pulled AZ off her and lifted him to his feet.

AZ was released and searched for the force of the pull. The blinding light had subsided, but he still had difficulty making out details. He saw the blue color of the hood and somehow felt a sense of safety.

The crowd was running and screaming in fear of the vampire. Most were still unable to see clearly as they knocked into each other and pushed people to the ground to save themselves. The occasional scream of a name was heard as a few of the patrons were looking to be sure that a friend or loved one was safe.

Vampire watched with no interest in attacking. The gold-caped man stood by his side, but he kept a cautious eye on the princess.

AZ's vision was improving. He realized that the man who had lifted him off Princess was a monk. He saw the thick scar across his face and scanned down to see his armored belt. He immediately grabbed the swords from the holsters on his newly trusted compatriot and turned to find that the vampire was upon him.

"No!" AZ screamed with his arrogance turning to fear.

"Yes," replied Vampire, holding him by his shirt. "You're coming with me. I need your Cez stones."

"No," demanded Monk, not reacting to what he had just heard and holding a silver dagger close to Vampire's throat.

"No — no!" answered AZ, realizing that he was between the two men.

"Yes," Sorcerer whispered into Monk's ear as he came up from behind and forced a dagger across the front of his neck. Sorcerer threw his gold cape over his shoulder.

"I believe he said *no*," Princess spoke with confidence as she stood in front of the group, with her swords pointed at both Vampire and Monk. "I'm only looking to maintain order, but do not worry, I will be quick enough to finish you, too," she assured Sorcerer, as his mouth wrinkled in frustration of her interference.

The tavern appeared empty. "That was quicker than I expected," he said, casually.

"Not me," replied Monk.

"I was just hoping to have another drink first," Sorcerer finished.

"If necessary, I will still kill you," Princess said as she was confused by the casual conversation of the three men.

"So unlady-like," flirted Vampire, "your majesty." He bowed to her.

"Your presence in Mortua seems to always come with a bit of chaos, Vampire," Princess said. "I'm sure my mother will be happy to hear of your arrival."

Vampire moved faster than light and was in front of Princess before she could realize that he had released AZ. The release of his counterforce on AZ knocked the others slightly forward as they all released their grips.

"My reasons for being in Mortua are because of the chaos, Princess," he told her.

"No!" screamed AZ, worried that Vampire would attack her. "*That* is a vampire!" acknowledged AZ.

"Yes." Sorcerer finished the pint and reached for another mug, only to find it empty. He threw it aside and took another.

"It was you," Monk stated, thinking back to the monastery and to when he showed Seer and Tinker his tattooed wings. "These mirrors. No reflection."

Vampire said nothing.

"Why are you following me?" Monk asked.

"I'm not following you," Vampire told him. "I'm following him," he added and pointed to AZ.

AZ attempted to grab Princess and escape. His efforts were thwarted before his third step, as Vampire pushed him back into a chair. Monk and Sorcerer gave each other a disapproving look.

"Your fault," uttered Sorcerer, holding his mug in salute before chugging the contents.

"My fault?" Monk asked.

AZ attacked Vampire's knees to take him down. Vampire did not move and kicked AZ to the ground.

"Yes. Your fault," Vampire spoke through his disgust. Vampire kicked AZ. "Get off me, you fool." He walked over to where Monk stood. "You see, you and I have a particular history and if only you had been in the right frame of mind, we could have sorted all this out without any of these theatrics."

Monk rolled his eyes and offered a gentlemanly hand to assist the princess from her seated position. "You know that he won't hurt you, your majesty."

"Really?" AZ asked. "So, what happens if I don't believe you?"

Monk snickered. "I didn't say that he would not hurt *you*," he said to AZ. "Apparently, you can find Cez stones. I too can use someone like you."

Vampire turned and walked over to the bar with Sorcerer. "For what?"

"A life on the run is growing less interesting," Monk replied. He looked back at AZ. "A Cez stone will afford me some peace and quiet."

Monk walked over to Sorcerer. "I expected that when we met again, you would be in better company." He kicked a mug out of his way. "How's the fox?"

"As feisty as ever," Sorcerer replied, giving no explanation to Monk as to how he and Vampire had become cohorts nor to Vampire as to how he and Monk knew one another.

AZ and Princess were following the conversation like spectators at an exciting tennis match. Their eyes watched the verbal ball as it bounced from Monk to Vampire to Sorcerer.

Monk shook his head. "Come on, kid," he said to AZ. "You and I have some work to do."

"I can't let you take him," Vampire said and moved closer to Monk. He stroked Monk's scar.

"Good luck stopping me," Monk retorted as he felt the rush of energy. He pushed a silver goblet to Vampire's neck. He held it tight as Vampire yelled out in pain.

AZ and Princess ran for the door. Sorcerer blocked their path with his sword held aloft. Monk rushed Sorcerer from the side and tackled him to the ground. Sorcerer was quick to his feet and grabbed Princess by the wrist. He pulled her back into the tavern.

"Monk!" Vampire screamed as he fell to the floor in uncontrollable pain. The silver goblet had caused him excruciating pain and burned his neck.

Monk held AZ, but AZ resisted as he attempted to grab Princess' hand. Monk swung the goblet and hit AZ hard on the head, knocking him out and throwing him over his shoulder as he ran out the tavern.

CHAPTER 6
City of Mortua

Everything was quiet. The revelers had all gone home from the third and final night of the Blood Moon celebrations. Monk stood in silence and watched through the open spaces of the barn door. There was no movement in the street. The flames from the streetlamps gave him the ability to see shadows approaching from all four directions on the corner. The disadvantage of his position was that he could not see most of the roofs. However, he knew that he would hear anyone climbing on the metal that covered his hideout. But a vampire could be light-footed, he thought. That was a concern.

AZ was beginning to come to, and felt the pain on his head from Monk's blow. He quickly remembered what had happened and saw Monk standing in front of him. AZ rose in an attempt to attack, but his balance was still off, and he fell into Monk as his knees buckled under him. Monk assisted him back to the ground.

"Easy, my friend."

"I'm not your friend!" AZ exclaimed. "We have to go back. "The princess…"

"Is fine. Safe at home in the castle by now. They would not hurt her. It was you that they were after," Monk whispered and held his hand over AZ's mouth to keep him from screaming again. "Now lower your voice."

As Monk removed his hand from AZ's mouth, AZ took his sleeve to his nose and mouth to attempt to block the foul stench of barn animals, wet hay, and feces. Monk handed him a scarf, which he wrapped around his mouth and nose. AZ took note of the scar and lowered his gaze. Monk kept monitoring and took breaths from the openings between the wooden planks of the barn wall.

They stayed silent as Monk continued his lookout and AZ focused on how to stop the foul stench from entering his nostrils.

"It's funny," Monk whispered as he continued to scan the quiet street. "All the people in my life look at me with pity because of this scar." He turned and faced AZ. "And they all feel responsibility for it, like they never saw it until they did something to cause it." He felt along the diagonal path of the deformity. "It's just a scar."

"How did you get it?" AZ asked, cautiously.

Monk turned but paused before smiling, saying nothing.

AZ undid the scarf from his mouth and nose and walked over to Monk.

"You're better-looking with this on," he said and handed him the scarf.

Monk kept his eye on the street, on the intersections, buildings, and roofs outside.

"So?" AZ said as he cautiously copied Monk's spying to see if there was any activity outside.

"What?" Monk shot back as if to say, 'not interested in talking'. Monk turned angrily and whispered through clenched teeth. "What were you going to ask?"

"There's a real vampire?" AZ cautiously offered.

"You live in Mortua. You know about Mermaids. So why not vampires?"

"I know. Just never knew that it was true." AZ maintained a lost expression. "How do you know that he won't hurt the princess?"

Monk drew his attention back to the silence of the street outside. "Time to go," he said to AZ.

"I'm not going anywhere with you," AZ resisted.

"Fine then. Enjoy the smell. And good luck when Vampire finds you."

Monk kicked open the barn door and walked into the now-pinkish moonlight. AZ cowered from the loud noise. The moon was slowly returning to its normal white glow. The Blood Moon was coming to an end.

"Shhh!" AZ urged. He watched as Monk continued to walk away. AZ heard a 'bang' from inside the barn. He quickly turned in fear and ran out to follow Monk. A goat had awoken from a bad dream and rammed the wooden pen.

"Hey," AZ whispered. He looked around in fear to make sure he did not alert Vampire and Sorcerer to their position. "Hey," he again whispered to Monk. He ran in front of him and stood in his path.

"What?" Monk asked.

"No! My turn to ask questions," AZ demanded. "What the fuck is going on?"

Monk shook his head and made a displeased snicker. "More than you are able to comprehend at this point."

"I hate you already," AZ told him with a sour tone.

"I get that a lot," Monk confessed. "You'll get over it." Monk walked around him and turned the next corner.

AZ stood in anger, allowing it to build and increase his adrenaline. He turned and ran after Monk again and blocked his path.

"Damn it!" Monk whispered harshly. "Is this going to go on all night? I have things to do."

"Yeah, well — so do I. Where is Princess?"

"I already told you. Home in the castle by now."

"You said that they wouldn't hurt her."

"And that was true."

"Why is the vampire so interested in me?"

Monk stared into AZ's eyes.

"He wants your Cez stones. You're the Perculfilus kid." AZ's eyes widened as he gasped. "I am in Mortua looking for you as well. I got a lead on the general location of a stone and need you to find it for me."

AZ exhaled and relaxed. "Nope. Not me."

"Yes. You. You will find the Cez stone," he told him. "And I'll make it worth your while. We can split the value of this one and you will be set for life."

"Sorry, buddy," AZ shot back waving his arms in the air. "It was my brother, Saric, who was able to find them. Looks like you're shit out of luck."

AZ was startled when another man walked over and joined their conversation. "Hey," Seer whispered. He glanced at AZ. "Your screaming is starting to draw the wrong attention."

AZ recoiled and dropped coins from his pocket. Seer bent over to pick them up and hand them to AZ. Seer quickly pulled back, being sure not to touch his hand, and stepped away. AZ saw Seer's nervousness.

"And who's this?" AZ asked. "Another one of your crazy acquaintances?"

"Oh, no. No. I am not crazy," Seer said quickly, as if he were crazy. "I understand why you say that," he continued, with a nervous giggle. "Monk does seem to associate with various types."

"Yeah," AZ replied, with a cautious tone. "Various. But as long as you're not crazy." He began to back away.

"AZ?" Monk questioned.

"What? What do you want?"

"To help you."

"No. You want me to help you find a Cez stone. Again… Sorry. I don't have that ability and have spent my entire life trying to get out of my dead brother's shadow." Monk and Seer looked at one another. "No thanks. I'm good," AZ said, and turned to walk away again.

"A princess, AZ?" Monk asked. "The princess, AZ? Is she really going to be interested in who you are? If she is what you want in life, you're going to have to do much more than use your parents' fortune to drink until you pass out to get her."

AZ angrily rushed right up to Monk. "I have a plan. I'm not what you think I am."

"Well," Monk began and turned his attention to Seer.

AZ followed Monk's gaze and saw Seer with his eyes closed and fire-red light coming from behind his eyelids. AZ was horrified. Monk took AZ by the shoulders and pushed him back to arm's length.

The red light went out and Seer opened his eyes. "Nothing," he said.

"Nothing what? You're a seer," AZ said.

"I am. And I see nothing positive in your future with the princess."

"Look again," AZ demanded.

"Not exactly how it works, kid," Monk told him.

AZ's expression demanded that Seer try to find something hopeful. Seer shook his head.

"Sorry," he said, with his eyes cast to the ground.

"But maybe I have an opportunity that can help you out," Monk said.

"What? Some crazy bullshit that involves me risking my life with you and your band of lunatics?" AZ looked at Seer. "No offense."

"None taken," Seer replied.

"No," Monk began. "But kinda, yes."

AZ glanced at Seer.

"It could be a successful path," Seer told him.

"Well, look and see," AZ demanded.

"Again. Not how this works," Monk told him.

"You have to actually be on a path for me to see the possibilities," Seer told him. "The more committed you are, the clearer and the further into time I can suggest."

"Suggest?"

"Each step changes things. Every decision has an effect. That's why, the more committed one is to a path, the clearer the future becomes."

AZ stared at Seer with a growing nervousness. He began to fidget and then turned to Monk.

"I don't want to be bait for that vampire, though," he told Monk flatly. "He is scary."

Monk faced Seer. Seer closed his eyes, and the red light began to glow behind his eyelids again.

AZ looked on with anticipation.

Seer began to smile. The light diminished and he opened his eyes. "That is definitely a positive step," he told them. "Asking what you need to do just opened up a path towards the princess for you."

AZ smiled with excitement. He focused back and forth from Seer to Monk. His smile was so wide, it looked as though he were frozen into position.

"Meet me here at sunrise," Monk told him.

AZ nodded rapidly. "Sunrise. Here." He seemed in a trance from the simple idea that he could have a future with Princess.

"Get some sleep," Monk instructed. "I don't know when you will get it again after tonight."

"Sleep," AZ repeated and continued nodding.

"Go," Monk added.

AZ continued his nodding and backed away until he almost tripped. He turned and ran across the plaza.

"For love," Monk said, with kindness in his voice.

"It could kill you," Seer added.

"Did you see his death?"

"No. But he will be tested," Seer told him. "His path is short."

"Meaning?"

"He will be indecisive."

"And then?"

"Can't see yet. He has to decide."

"Then I'm going to need to continue to dangle that carrot, the idea of him being with the Princess, in front of him."

"Sounds manipulative," Seer said.

"It is. But it's necessary," Monk said, as he continued to watch AZ run across the plaza and out of sight. "If he can find a Cez stone, there will be no more running and scraping for us. Our lifetime of struggle will be behind us."

"Those are invaluable," Seer said. "And what of the vampire?"

"You tell me," Monk replied with a laugh.

CHAPTER 7
Caves of Waku

Monk and AZ had met at sunrise as planned. Monk was surprised to find that AZ was early. AZ was surprised to find that he was early too. They had left the city to the northwest and walked away from the sea. As they hit the peak of the third hill, Monk led AZ off the road and through the high grass.

"It's so hot!" AZ complained, as he and Monk continued their trek out of the city to the Caves of Waku.

"But it's a dry heat," Monk joked as he pushed through the brush with his staff. "And besides, it's nice and cool in the caves."

"You can't enter the caves," AZ reminded him. "This whole thing is pointless. Where's that seer, anyway? He should be guiding us."

Monk was a patient man; however, AZ's constant whining was becoming more than an annoyance. Once they had left the road,

Monk had taken his anger out by clearing brush with a machete. But now he had had enough.

"Listen!" Monk turned and held AZ by the collar before AZ could realize what had happened. "You want the princess? I can help you."

After his initial shock, AZ regained his arrogance. "Are you done?" he asked, and Monk let go. "Is that your thing? Promise people what they want and then use them to get what you want?"

"Yup," Monk admitted as he started walking again.

"Then, you really are an asshole," AZ said as he held his position.

Monk continued walking. AZ saw movement in the high grass behind him and he quickly started to follow Monk again.

"But really," AZ continued. "What are we doing? There is no way into any of the caves. They've been sealed up forever."

"Gates," Monk said.

"Inaccessible. Locked by magic. Everybody knows that."

"Oh, AZ," Monk tutted. "You accept so many limitations. That is what limits you."

"Again, with your self-righteous bullshit. Okay, Mister Know-It-All! Tell me! Tell me everything that I'm doing wrong so that I don't have to listen to anything else from you."

Monk stopped and let out a deep sigh. AZ stopped and held a defensive posture. He did not expect Monk to be listening to him.

"AZ," Monk began as he turned and looked at him. "You have so much potential. I believe that you — I'm shocked by it as well — have a very special gift. But it is useless if you keep acting like a spoiled prick."

AZ's expression went from appreciative to angered with the word *prick*.

"I'm a prick?" AZ yelled out.

"Yes," Monk said, as if the answer was obvious.

"And you?'

"A sanctimonious know-it-all," Monk answered in the same tone. "However, I'm not the one who has to impress the Princess of Mortua. Am I?"

AZ searched for a witty remark but knew that Monk was right.

"Seer already told you that you are on that path. He would not lie to you," Monk said. "I would," he admitted. "But he would not."

"Finally," AZ said, "I can believe something you say."

Monk said nothing as he led AZ through the brush on the hills above the city. The vegetation thinned out and the terrain was more dirt and rock. The city was no longer in sight as they were now on the other side of the hills.

"There they are," Monk announced, still ignoring AZ's comments. "The Caves of Waku."

"Where no one is supposed to go," AZ stated in a mocking voice. "What's in there, anyway?"

"Lots of things," Monk replied, as he started walking again. "But we're here for a Cez stone."

"Excuse me," AZ said, disingenuously. "What I meant to ask is…what is there to worry about in the caves? I cannot find Cez stones. So, that is all up to you."

"There are many things to worry about in these caves," Monk answered.

"Like?" AZ asked through clenched teeth.

"Wolves."

"Regular ones or some kind of supernatural werewolves?"

"And then the spiders."

"You didn't answer my question."

"Does it matter?"

"Yes," AZ said, in a concerned voice.

"No."

"Ummm, again, yes!"

Monk cracked a smile. "A werewolf is a wolf that has been bitten by an Immortal. But then it can propel the transformation of its entire pack by biting them as well. They are there. Yes. And then the spiders. Any type of dark creature has the possibility of being housed in those caves. Oh, I almost forgot. If you find water, dive in. Holy water will protect you from all these creatures.”

“How do I know it’s holy water?”

“I blessed it last time.”

“Last time? What? This is like a trip to the country for you?”

“To be fair, I was a bit drunk.”

“I’m becoming even more uncomfortable with this whole field trip,” AZ admitted.

“And I’m becoming completely clear about it. Ironic.”

“Is there an expiration date on holy water?” AZ asked, ignoring Monk’s comment.

“No, I don’t believe so.”

“See. Your failure to commit is not helpful!” AZ yelled out in frustration.

Monk came to a stop and took in the view below the mounds of sand and rock that formed the openings of the Caves of Waku. “Not a very inviting place, is it?” he asked.

“We are finally in agreement,” AZ replied.

The Caves of Waku were made up of sixty-five entrances that were spread throughout the Valley of Kaar. The entrances were shaped like descending tubes with a magically locked gate deep within each of them. The Valley of Kaar was formed in a crater. The walls of the crater allowed limited access into or out of the valley.

Originally, the caves were created to aid in keeping humanity safe during times of worldly destruction by allowing people to live underground. However, since humanity had returned to the surface, the caves now functioned as a prison. The prisoners were creatures that posed a threat to humanity. As Monk and AZ surveyed the entrances, they saw that several of them had smoke coming from within.

"Is someone cooking?" AZ asked.

"No," Monk replied, seriously. "But someone was here."

"Was or is?" AZ asked, and reluctantly followed Monk down into the valley.

"We may find out," Monk replied and moved closer to the first caves. AZ followed with caution.

"Stop!" yelled a voice from behind them.

AZ jumped to the side and hit the ground. Monk stopped where he stood.

"Tink?" Monk yelled.

"There are holes throughout the valley!" Tinker yelled out. "I need to scan it first to make sure where the ground is stable."

Monk pulled AZ up to his feet.

"Open one of those holes," Tinker said, "and you open another entrance."

"Or exit," Monk said.

"Or exit," Tinker agreed.

"But without a gate," AZ added.

"Exactly," Tinker agreed. "Do I know you?"

"There are more of you lunatics?" AZ asked, in a judgmental tone.

"Apparently," retorted Monk. He leaned in for a friendly hug with the tall slender man. "You good?" he asked.

"Yeah," Tinker responded. "Can use a bit of sleep but, you know… all good."

"Well, he's not sure when you're gonna get any," AZ told Tinker, referencing Monk's order to him the day before.

AZ stared at the darkened bags under the young man's eyes. He looked years older than he was because of his lack of sleep.

Monk continued smiling at him and pulled him in tight again. "Good to see you, my friend."

The man glanced over at AZ but said nothing.

"Oh. My apologies," Monk offered. "AZ. This is Tinker. Tink. This is AZ."

"What kind of name is Tinker?" AZ asked.

"What kind of name is AZ?" Tinker said, mustering the energy to argue. "Yes. I do know you."

Angry silence followed.

"Okay." Monk finally broke the silence. "I can see that we are off to a great start. Let's put our penises away — because let's face it, mine is the biggest — and get to work."

"I'm sorry," Tinker apologized to AZ. "I am really tired."

"I know. I know, my boy," Monk comforted his exhausted friend.

"I'm… I'm sorry, too," AZ apologized. "I guess, I've had a bit of stress lately."

"Hanging around him," Tinker jested. "Oh yes! I'm sure that you have."

AZ and Tinker shared a laugh at Monk's expense. Monk joined in.

"Probably true," Monk added.

"Probably nothing. Definitely," AZ added.

Tinker placed his gadget, a *Holocator*, on the ground. He pressed a button on the top and it began to spin. AZ watched it separate in the middle, while a beam of red light emanated from it horizontally. It covered the ground up to one hundred feet in all directions. The red light faded in some areas, while remaining in others.

"Avoid the red spots, AZ," Tinker said. "Those are the holes; the unsupported ground you could fall through."

AZ nodded. Monk walked forward and examined the cave entrances.

"Stop," Tinker demanded. "Let me move the Holocator so we can be safe."

"That's called a Holocator?" AZ asked, laughing.

"I give all of my devices names that correlate with their purpose."

"Makes sense," AZ admitted. "Hold up! You made that?"

"I make all of my devices," Tinker said.

"That's amazing," AZ said. "Why don't you have more friends like him?" he asked Monk.

Monk ignored AZ and looked down the tubelike entrance of one of the caves. He saw that the gates were intact. He continued on and examined several more openings.

"Tink?"

"Yes?" Tinker answered while he searched for a light in his knapsack.

"Did you go in?"

"Are you crazy? No," he replied, sounding concerned.

"Well, someone did." Monk pointed into the darkness.

Tinker grabbed the light and flashed it deep into the cave entrance. The gates were too deep within for the light to show them. Monk grabbed it from him and walked a few steps into the darkness. The light went out.

"I can't tell," Tinker said, squinting and pulling a pair of goggles with yellow lenses from the inner pocket of his jacket. "It's solar powered," he said of the light. "Sorry. Guess it needs a charge," he admitted as Monk handed the light back to him.

AZ walked over and peered into the darkness. "I don't see anything."

Tinker handed him a similar pair of goggles. AZ handled them with caution, due to the sharpness of the frame edges, but put them on to see what Monk was talking about.

The lenses gave him the ability to see through the darkness of the cave. He was able to see that a metal gate, deep in the cave, had been destroyed to allow entry.

"It's pulled out," AZ mentioned.

"Yeah. Someone got in," Monk added.

"Hopefully, no one got out," Tinker said, with an air of concern.

"Hopefully," Monk agreed. "There's magic in the air."

"I can feel it," Tinker agreed.

"Hey," AZ questioned Monk. "How is it that you can see the gate in the darkness?"

"Oh, he's full of tricks, this one," Tinker answered for him.

Monk walked back into the daylight and looked to the sky. He blocked the sun's glare with his hand.

"We definitely will not have time to get out of there tonight," he said. "It was almost a full day's walk to get here."

"Out? Why would we even want to go in there to begin with?" AZ asked. "Can't we just fix the gate and leave whoever got in, in there? Whoever it was, he—"

"Or she," Tinker interrupted.

Monk turned and nodded at Tinker but said nothing.

"Or she… got where he or she wanted to go," AZ added, hoping to dissuade further investigation.

"You're sure that you didn't see anyone, Tink," Monk asked again.

"No one," Tinker said, which satisfied Monk's question. He knew that Tinker would not lie to him.

AZ glanced over and saw that Monk was standing with his eyes closed and with his palms facing the cave entrance. He was taking irregular breaths. AZ looked to Tinker, who shrugged his shoulders.

The surprisingly warm breeze that was blowing from inside the cave brought with it the sweet smell of orange and vanilla. Monk had learned through his studies that both mortals and Immortals held an essence in the specific frequencies that they emitted. Those personal frequencies were able to demonstrate visual auras and specific aromas. The aura was able to be seen in the presence of the individual. However, the aroma could linger in the air even when its bearer was gone. Each individual was unique. Some were similar, but still, each one was distinct. Monk had spent years with ancient texts and had mastered the ability to decipher particular scents and read auras.

"It is safe," Monk told Tinker and AZ.

AZ faced Tinker and pulled on his arm.

"He's never been wrong before," Tinker told AZ, to ease his concern. He threw his sack around his shoulders and moved forward.

"Never?"

"Well, never as long as I've known. Who knows what happens when I'm not with him," Tinker said, as he was consumed by the darkness of the cave.

AZ tried to think of an excuse not to go with them.

"AZ!" Monk yelled from inside.

"Coming. I had to pee," he lied and lifted his pack. "I'm so going to regret this," he told himself and adjusted the goggles as he, too, entered and was consumed by the darkness.

After climbing over the mangled metal of the gates, they walked for what seemed like hours. The constant tripping over the loose rocks and gravel and pebbles that made up the floor of the cave kept them at a slow pace.

"Hey, Tinker," AZ asked in the darkness. "I know I asked before but, how is it that he can see in here? It's completely pitch-black."

"There are many mysteries that surround Monk. I have stopped asking and, in most cases, just given into faith that he knows what he is doing."

"You make it sound like you're saying that to remind yourself of it."

"I am. And I have to do it… a lot!"

"Yeah. That's not helpful right now."

"Shhh," Monk ordered them, and stopped moving.

The cave went silent. The sound of their footsteps had accompanied them, thus far, but now that they were not moving, that sound was gone. No sound was heard. No breeze was felt. Only cold, the cold of the cave air. And the smell. Monk continued to occasionally catch the orange and vanilla in the air, but for the most part, it was just the mustiness of a damp cave. AZ and Tinker each kept their mouths and noses covered with linen scarves. Monk did not. He needed all the sensory information that would allow him to find his way through the darkness.

Through his goggles, AZ saw that Monk had squatted down. He saw him touch the floor of the cave and he gasped as he saw the floor ripple and move. "What is that?" AZ asked, fearfully.

"It's called…" Monk spoke cautiously. "Water."

"Water? Like water?" AZ asked, this time with a slight attitude. "Holy water? Oh right, the holy water that you blessed last time you were here, but you were drunk and may or may not have actually done it. Holy water. In this Hell?"

"Sounds about right," Monk said.

"Sorry but that doesn't help either," AZ said. "How can you be sure that it's holy water? Maybe your holy water evaporated, and this is just plain old water from some putrid underground spring."

"I can always bless it again," Monk said.

"Well, if anything comes, get in the water," Tinker told him and squatted down to touch the surface of the water. "Nothing that lives in here can see but they 'feel' your presence and react to smell and sound."

As Tinker was explaining, Monk had taken a step and the sound of the gravel under his foot panicked AZ, who became so frightened that he dove into the water. AZ lay flat on his stomach with his face in the one-inch-deep puddle. He did not move from embarrassment. Tinker leaned over and lifted his face out of the water.

"But you only have to stand in it. You see it's only about one inch deep…"

"Thanks for telling me that," said AZ, as he lay soaked on the cave floor.

"The holy water blocks your natural scent and the 'feeling' of you being present. Nothing mortal or Immortal can tell that you are here."

"Got it," AZ said, through his humiliation.

Tinker and AZ were doing their best to stay quiet, more so out of fear. They kept the goggles on so that they would be able to see movement in the cave. They were seated back to back for better coverage of the tunnels.

Monk had gone ahead to investigate.

"Something about Cez stones," Tinker told him which raised his interest but not enough for him to say anything further. AZ distracted himself with the goggles to remain quiet which made being in the caves less unbearable.

"Absolutely amazing," AZ whispered, seated in the holy water.

"Thank you, AZ," Tinker said, proudly.

"You heard me say that?" AZ asked. "I thought that I just thought it." He continued to take the goggles on and off and turn his head in different directions.

"It was probably just a whisper, but we are in a cave," Tinker reminded him. "Voices carry."

"I guess they do." AZ turned to face his left and put the goggles back on. "Ahhh!" he exclaimed and pushed back into Tinker.

Monk had snuck up on them in the dark and was directly in front of him.

"Don't do that," AZ said, angrily.

"Aren't you supposed to be looking out?" Monk whispered with a serious tone.

"We are."

"Then keep the goggles on," he ordered and tapped AZ on the shoulder. "I saw nothing of real concern up ahead."

"Ummm… Nothing of real concern?" Tinker asked.

"Again," AZ said, "A failure to commit. Maybe that's your problem with the vampire."

Monk shook his head. AZ saw now that his goggles were back on. Tinker was surprised to hear that the vampire was back in Mortua.

"Just the usual," Monk told them in reference to what he found ahead in the caves. "Nothing more than that."

"And by the usual," AZ asked, "you mean what, exactly?"

"Werewolves. Spiders that are a bit larger than *usual*. You know. That sort of thing."

"Oh yeah… That sort of thing," AZ said. "I am beginning to understand that your usual and my usual are two totally different usuals."

"Nothing truly evil," Monk said, adding to AZ's confusion.

"AZ," Tinker said, calmly. "The spiders are large. Yes. But they have no interest in us. Our blood is nauseating to them. They will not attack us unless provoked. But the werewolves…Well, the werewolves are the reason for the holy water."

AZ cautiously moved himself to the left and squatted. He splashed more holy water onto his arms and face. "Explain to me again why we are here," he said.

"Cez stones," Monk informed him. "You're going to find me one."

AZ shook his head. "My brother was the tracker."

"You have a very valuable gift, AZ." Monk told him, ignoring his words.

"Not that any of this matters," AZ added. "My brother died when I was a baby."

"Who told you that?" Monk asked.

"Well, my parents," AZ offered.

"Are you sure that they have told you the truth?" Tinker asked.

"Why would they have lied to me?"

"To protect you," Monk told him.

"From?"

"From someone wanting you to find stones for them," Tinker said.

"You mean like you're doing right now?" AZ asked.

A distant scratching noise drew everyone's attention. They all went silent for a moment.

"Believe it or not, I have never told anyone else about this," AZ whispered.

"Really — you haven't told anyone else?" Monk asked.

"I was never to talk about it."

"And you haven't?"

"Til now."

"No offense, AZ," Monk interrupted, "but you do have a—"

"Big mouth?"

"I was going to go with a big ego," Monk continued in a whispered tone. "I recall someone else whose big ego recently got in his own way. But yes. You have a big mouth. I can't understand why you wouldn't have blabbed on and on about your family's Cez stones."

"My parents use them for business and have gotten rich off them."

"So why are you talking to us about it?" Tinker asked.

"I don't know. I felt like you should know. Like here, in the dark, the secret is safe with you."

"It is," Tinker whispered.

"It is," Monk agreed.

AZ felt relieved.

"It doesn't mean that we're not going to use you to find more. We need them," Monk told him.

"You're wasting your time, but that's okay. I don't mind. It feels good to be part of something."

They heard a distant explosion which echoed through the caves. They had no idea where it came from. Then, the howling and roaring began. It continued and seemed to be growing closer. Again, they were unable to tell from which direction it came.

Tinker reached into his bag and pulled out a device, a *Proceeder*. He wound it up and a spark reached across from one antenna to another. He held the device aloft and moved his arm in different directions as the roaring continued.

"Should I even ask?" AZ said, sarcastically.

"I am trying to discover the direction of the sound."

"And?"

"And…it seems to be coming from… everywhere," Tinker concluded with concern. "Monk?"

"Yes, Tink. I know."

They remained silent as the roars changed to desperate howls. The harrowing screech of claws against hard rock was painful to their ears. The sounds were louder and were coming closer.

AZ, who was still standing in the holy water, was gently shoved to the side as Tinker joined him. Monk was thinking, but he was now able to see the movement in each of the tunnels.

"Monk!" Tinker motioned for Monk to join them in the holy water.

"We'll need more than that," Monk said. "There are too many of them. They are running from something and are going to start swinging in the dark. Inevitably, we will be discovered when their claws pierce our flesh."

"Monk! Get in the water," AZ said.

"Soak yourselves," Monk ordered. "Splash every dry inch of each other."

They kneeled down and did as instructed.

Monk removed a thin chain that he had concealed within his robes, looped repeatedly over his shoulders. He tugged on it and released tiny razors. AZ and Tinker were temporarily blinded from the intensity of the sparks that it emitted as the tiny razors were released from between the links Monk held.. AZ quickly removed his goggles to avoid further torture but was still able to see the sparks. Tinker kept on his goggles but closed his eyes.

Once he had released the razors from the chain links, Monk threw the chain so that it would adhere to the rock walls of the cave at waist-height level and crossed each of the seven tunnel openings.

The horror of the werewolf howls and roars, and the scraping of their claws against the metallic rock, added to the stress of the moment. There seemed to be no escape from what was now rushing their way. The aural pain intensified as the sounds echoed through the tunnels.

"Goggles off!" Monk screamed, jumping into the puddle with the others and holding them tight.

The sounds were directly in their ears now and Tinker and AZ held increasingly tighter to Monk for stability.

The werewolves continued their approach. The most reckless met the chain that Monk had adhered across the entrances. The ones running on their hind legs were sliced through the middle and the ones running on all four legs were sliced in half through their open jaws, necks, eyes, or straight through the centers of their bodies. With every point of contact, the chain ignited with sparks that set the fur of the beasts aflame. The fire rose quickly and pained the eyes of the werewolves that were not used to the light.

The forceful attack of the werewolves turned into a retreat as the flames grew brighter and the smell of burnt fur and flesh surrounded AZ, Tinker, and Monk as they squatted in the puddle of holy water.

"Is this going to be enough water to put the fire out?" AZ yelled.

"I think not!" Tinker screamed his response over the roar of the flames.

Smoke was now filling the cavern and making it harder to breathe.

"This way!" Monk pointed to the tunnel that was directly in front of them.

They each ran, dodging the deadly chain that maintained its undisturbed position. The sound of werewolf cries continued, but they were now the sounds of pain and anguish.

Monk saw that the wolves continued running from something with no interest in attacking them. Tinker, and AZ continued to trip and fall on the loose pebbles and rocks and put their goggles back on to see through the darkness. The wolves turned to the right. Monk noticed the light entering the tunnel to the left. It was coming from a hole that was too high in the ceiling of the cave for them to reach. "This way," he yelled.

Both Tinker and AZ saw the glow of light and removed their goggles.

"Do not lose them," Tinker demanded of AZ.

AZ respectfully held tight to the goggles as they continued running. Adrenaline kept them going as they cut left and right through the open tunnels. They were following Monk, but now found themselves back in darkness. They put the goggles back on and saw him turn left again. They followed. The tunnels seemed endless, and AZ began to wonder if Monk was sure of the way out. He was doing all that he could just to keep up and knew that questioning Monk would not help their situation. They turned left again and ran into the light of the rising sun. They had reached the mangled gate and pulled themselves over the bars. The light was blinding. Tinker and AZ pulled the goggles from their faces, and all three of them sprinted to the cave entrance and emerged into the cool morning air. They were soaked with blood, sweat, and holy water and panting in pain.

"So, how did that go for you?" A familiar voice came from behind them.

They turned and saw Vampire standing atop the entrance to the cave. The sun shone on him but didn't seem to bother him.

"See," Monk told AZ through his panting breaths. "Vampires can be in sunlight."

Monk stood upright and positioned himself in front of AZ and Tinker.

"Yeah, that's probably not a good thing," AZ whispered.

Vampire leapt down the twenty-foot vertical. As he made contact with the ground, he walked as if the drop was just any other step.

"That is impressive," Tinker admitted.

"Why thank you, Tinker." Vampire graciously accepted the compliment.

Tinker and AZ maintained their distance but were now confused and interested instead of scared. Silence lingered.

"So, from the sound of things, it does not appear that you got a stone," Vampire said, breaking through the silence and referring to the howls of the werewolves.

"No. We did not," Monk admitted with an immediately annoyed tone. "Why are you here?"

"I needed to talk to you," Vampire told him. "Privately."

AZ watched Monk's hands come into tight fists. "Monk's about to blow," he whispered to Tinker.

"I don't think that this exchange is meant for us," Tinker whispered back.

"Thank you, Tink," Vampire graciously replied.

Tinker looked at Monk who relaxed his grips and gave a nod that signaled for him to go. Tinker obliged.

"Those two have issues," AZ joked as they walked off into the morning light.

"Seems that way," Tinker replied with a giggle and a nod back.

"There is a lot that I have to tell you, Monk," Vampire admitted. "I'm not sure that you know who I am-"

"I've caught your scent before… Like a fireplace. It has always put a smile on my face."

"Good," Vampire said, returning the smile. "You and I have been connected over many lifetimes. Your lifetimes, of course. I am Immortal."

"Cez stones?"

"Sort of," Vampire replied and invited Monk to the top of the cave entrance.

The two sat in a comfortable silence as they gazed across the crater and the hilly entrances to the rest of the caves.

"Wait," Monk said, as he remembered his immediate needs. "If you were out here, who destroyed the gate?"

"Did you see anyone?"

"No. But I smelled orange and vanilla." Monk told him.

"Those gates are to keep everyone out, not to keep them in. Those creatures could never survive out here, not even at night. It is possible that whoever went in there before you was also looking for the Cez stone."

Monk stared quizzically into the sun. He squinted but did not shy away.

"But it's also possible that the gate was destroyed a while ago," Vampire added.

"True, but the smell was fresh. Something about it was new," Monk told him.

"Well, either way, you would need the boy to go back and find the stone."

"If it's still there," Monk said.

"If it was there to begin with," Vampire argued. "It's unlikely that someone would tell the location of a Cez stone as a gesture of good hope."

"True," Monk agreed. He turned to Vampire. "I'm not sure who exactly you are nor what your *quest* is, but I don't want my family to struggle anymore. Tinker and Seer have endured too much in this life. I want to make a better life for them."

"And you will," Vampire told him with a growing smile. "Always looking out for everyone else."

"My curse," Monk joked.

"Yes. I agree that we have to work together, but my quest is much greater than a single stone." Vampire sighed as he was going to have to be completely honest for Monk to believe what he was about to tell him. "There is a prophecy that calls for a beast to enter this world and destroy everything; everything that is, was, or will be. The effects of that will destroy every dimension that feeds off this one and every other one that has ever existed."

Monk listened without judgment.

"But there is a way to stop it," Vampire told him. "The prophecy states that certain individuals and certain weapons are required to destroy this beast and keep this from happening."

"Who are the players?" Monk asked.

"The Three of Legend and an Immortal. It takes an Immortal to destroy an Immortal."

"And the weapons?"

"A sword which I believe is the Sword of Sansit. A shield, but which one? I have not figured that out yet.. And Cez stones… Eight Cez stones."

"That's why the boy is important," Monk realized. "But eight stones. That's unheard of."

"Well, his family already has five. We were all hoping that you would find the sixth-"

"That didn't go so well," Monk admitted.

Vampire laughed along with him but then looked out in thought. "There's something else," he told him.

"Of course there is," Monk joked.

"You see, Monk. Eight stones fell for… *you*. It was centuries ago. It was the first time that our paths crossed." Monk listened with added curiosity. "I fell in love with you, and at the time of your death, I ripped a constellation from the Heavens to mark you. I needed to be able to find you upon your return to this dimension."

Monk said nothing.

Vampire continued. "I cannot help but think that these eight stones are the ones that fell for you. You must have something to do with this prophecy."

Monk began to nod his head. "Then, we are going to have to work together." He glanced at the sun and laughed. "This is about to get very interesting."

Vampire pulled him in and held his head to his own.

Monk looked at Vampire and then back at the sun. A slight sense of concern returned.

"Why were they so wet?" Vampire asked.

Monk laughed. "AZ spent a lot of time in the holy water," he said, through his laughter.

"It's completely shallow. Good thing he didn't jump," Vampire said with added laughter.

"No! He dove!"

Monk and Vampire laughed hysterically.

CHAPTER 8
City of Mortua, Palace of Mortua

Monk and Vampire found AZ and explained that they were going to the palace for an audience with the royal family. They made sure to include that the princess would also be present. He immediately agreed to join them.

The military escort set the quick pace through the minimalist-styled halls of the Palace of Mortua. Monk, Vampire, and AZ were being rushed by a unit of guards through the maze of corridors. AZ cautiously noted that Vampire did not produce a reflection on the polished floors.

A line of warm, white light shone down the walls of the corridors and turned on for ten feet ahead of them as they stepped forward and off ten feet behind them with every step. They turned left into a hall where twelve corridors converged. As teams of soldiers and servants moved past them with military precision, the entire area was illuminated. The guards ushered them forward. With every turn, the trio was handed off to another military guard who took them further into the palace.

"Rule number one," Vampire whispered to AZ.

"Know your way out? This place is more confusing than the caves. And there is light here." AZ's face showed a hint of distress. *We're fucked,* he thought.

The final guard led them to stop in front of a wall that was constructed with an assortment of precious metals sculpted into an elaborate display. The characters in the sculpture ranged from human to Immortal and included Mermaids. Beasts of all kinds, some extinct, were also reflected in the detailed work that made them appear as though they could just come to life from the wall. AZ, seeing it for the first time, was amazed at the detailing of each figure. He stood back and realized that it told the story of the King of Mortua and how he sacrificed himself to the Mermaids and saved humanity from extinction and gave the Mermaids the gift of mortality. AZ stopped his enchanted gaze when he realized that standing against the wall with guards blocking him was Sorcerer.

"About time." Sorcerer casually pushed the spears away, so that the guards closest to him uncrossed them and held them in a now vertical position.

"Who's this?" AZ asked, not recognizing him.

"Sorcerer is an old friend," Vampire replied. "You sort of met the other night."

"Ah, yeah," AZ remarked as he admired his cape. "At the tavern."

"Didn't know that you would be here," Monk added, from behind the collar that shielded his scar.

"Funny. I knew that you would be," Sorcerer shot back with sarcasm, while looking at Vampire. "I thought that we were doing this."

"Change of plans," Vampire told him.

A palace maid approached. She shook her head and shooed them aside.

Being pushed aside by a palace maid wounded Vampire's pride. He moved slower than the rest.

Vampire sought to regain his sense of authority and explained the current situation to Monk. "Sorcerer and I had originally planned this meeting to discuss the prophecy that I spoke of and a few other things. However, with the recent turn of events, I thought it wise to include you so that we can all work together."

The maid again shot them a look of disapproval. Vampire drew his fangs. The maid snickered and turned towards the wall.

"I disagree," Sorcerer said as he watched the maid prepare a potion. AZ was again enchanted by the sculpture. Monk stood quiet which made Vampire uncomfortable. The maid cleared her throat to get him to stop talking.

AZ let out a laugh but then tried to contain it.

"Yeah," AZ joked to Vampire. "This is not going well for you."

Vampire scowled at AZ and drew out his fangs again to scare him into being quiet. It worked.

The maid cleared her throat for a second time and gave Vampire a stare as if to say, *Quiet.* She approached a Mermaid figure within the sculpture. She gave Sorcerer a look of superiority and took a crystal vial from beneath a golden linen cover.

She uncorked the vial and poured a yellowish powder into her hand. The salty aroma that escaped drew Sorcerer's attention further. The maid gave him a half smile and nodded. He returned the gesture. The maid bowed to the Mermaid figurine and blew the powder as she repeated an incantation. She waved her right arm into the air. Sorcerer followed her movements with a sense of familiarity.

"This is a door," he said to the others.

"And so it is," stated the maid.

They watched as the Mermaid leapt off the metal rock on which she had been sitting. The other creatures in the sculpture also began to move in what seemed like a chaotic fashion. However, from further back, the order in their movements could be discerned. From a distance, the metal figures were unrecognizable and looked like links collapsing upon one another until they formed a door frame and left the grand opening exposed. The sound of metal smoothly gliding past itself seemed like music. The figures now resembled tiles, which twisted over and under each other until the metal wall was no more and the frame about the door marked the wide opening.

The maid gestured with her left arm to indicate that they were to enter without her company. Sorcerer bowed to her in respect. She followed suit.

"I will return when you come out, to guide you back," she told them with a smile and blew the powder at the center of the door. She then hurried off and disappeared around yet another turn.

"Thank you," Monk offered, but she was already gone.

"We are going to have to keep on topic here. If the princess does come to this meeting, things may go a bit off," Vampire said to the group and then faced AZ. "Keep your cool."

"What?" AZ screamed in panic.

Sorcerer showed the same worried expression.

"We lied to you. She most likely won't be in the meeting," Monk told AZ. "He's trying to get under your skin."

Monk quickly turned to Vampire. "Knock it off," he said to the now-giggling vampire. He walked through the metal opening.

"You're a dick!" AZ yelled, unaware of the loud volume of his voice. His nervous adrenaline was pushing hard through his veins.

"We all know that," Vampire spoke through his laughter.

"I do hope that that wasn't meant for us," Queen Sharon quickly put into the air.

With their focus on their own arguing, they did not realize that the Rulers of Mortua were seated on their thrones at the far end of the grand hall.

"Oh! Your majesty! No, no, no…" AZ spluttered and yelled an attempted apology, immediately dropping to his knee.

"Your parents would be proud," Vampire continued to kid.

"Enough," Monk demanded. He turned to see that Sorcerer was not entering. "You coming?"

"I think that I'll wait here."

"Probably for the best," Vampire agreed.

Vampire pulled AZ up from his apologetic position. They walked up the golden floor tiles that made their way to the elevated thrones. Vampire held AZ by the arm and gave him no choice but to stay with him.

The Queen sighed in annoyance and glanced at her brothers, King Charles, and King Jax, who shook their heads. AZ could not keep his eyes off the rulers. He was enchanted by the emerald crowns decorated with spikes in all directions.

As they had walked to the stairs that led up to the three rulers in their thrones, Vampire said into AZ's ear, "You owe them an apology." They bowed in front of the rulers. "Now," Vampire pushed AZ forward.

"Your majesties," AZ began with his face to the floor. "Please accept my most humble apology. My comment was to him, the… the…" AZ attempted to speak from his bowed position with his face towards the floor.

"Vampire. Yes. He is a dick," King Charles acknowledged.

"Your majesties," Vampire greeted and stood from his bow.

AZ looked up in astonishment at the king's jest. He was pulled up from his bent position and came to stand between Monk and Vampire.

"Really, boy. Do you have any social graces?" Vampire teased.

"What happened to—" King Jax began.

"The sorcerer?" Queen Sharon rushed to finish his question.

"He felt it best to wait outside… to avoid any complications that may arise from his presence," Monk apologized.

"I guess that was a wise choice," the queen reflected, with sorrow. "Many kingdoms still outlaw magic. Many worry that as it has turned dark, magic has the ability to alter the natural order of things. But what is still known of traditional magic is allowed in Mortua. When you see him, tell him that he and his magic are welcomed here."

"We will relay the message, your majesty," Vampire told her.

Queen Sharon turned her head to spy her daughter standing in the antechamber of the throne room. AZ noticed her interest and the queen's subtle smile when she nodded in greeting to her daughter. He deduced that it must be Princess.

The adrenaline began to rush through AZ again. Without the protection of alcohol, AZ was a blundering fool around Princess. Although with the protection of alcohol, AZ was a blundering fool around Princess. He had never been able to speak to her without making a complete fool of himself.

"We have yet to see Tinker," Queen Sharon said to Monk. "I was disappointed to hear that he was back in Mortua and has not come home."

"He lives here in the palace?" AZ asked.

"Tinker was raised here in the palace," Queen Sharon explained. "This will always be his home."

"It is my fault, your majesty," Monk confessed. "We have had urgent business that has kept him from coming to see you. I promise you that he will be here by the end of day."

Princess made a motion to come out from behind the curtain and join the conversation. Queen Sharon saw Princess' growing interest and shook her head as if to say, *No.* Princess held her hidden position. But the queen's actions confirmed for AZ that Princess had been present the whole time. His excitement grew.

"And finally, the reason that we are here." The queen rose and stepped down the stairs to approach and stand directly in front of AZ. She was taller than he'd realized. He had never been this close to her before — when he saw her in public, she was usually on a balcony, behind a railing or a podium.

"You have no idea what is happening. Do you boy?" she asked AZ.

His mind was spinning. *No idea about what?* he thought. The look on his face showed his confusion.

"AZ," Queen Sharon began, "in the past, Immortals have come into existence to destroy humanity. To cleanse this dimension. And many succeeded… temporarily. The Mermaids from whom my family descends were originally here with this purpose. However, Immortals do have free-will and at times, have chosen to help instead of destroying humanity. That was the case of the Mermaids, and my brothers and I sit upon these thrones as a result of our ancestor, who was a king of Mortua. He sacrificed his life to produce an heir with the Mermaid queen. He knew that he would die at the time of conception. The Mermaids saw his selflessness for his people as a reason to spare humanity and they chose another path. In choosing this new path, they improved humanity and were gifted with mortality."

"I know this story, your majesty," AZ told her in an attempt to present himself as scholarly.

"What you do not know is that the Vampire who stands beside you was also originally sent to destroy humanity," she told him. AZ looked at Vampire and gulped. "Like the Mermaids who preceded him, he too discovered a reason not to cleanse this dimension." The queen turned her attention to Monk. "Love."

AZ turned to Monk with confusion.

"Nine lifetimes and thousands of years ago, Vampire and Monk met for the first time."

"He was a slave who came into my employment," Vampire told him. Monk said nothing. "And yes," Vampire said with a smile and turned to Monk. "It was love at first sight. There was nothing in humanity that could be so bad that this love could not outshine."

AZ looked to the kings, who were well aware of the full story. He scanned the curtain to try and catch a glimpse of the princess.

Queen Sharon continued. "And they will need to work together to keep this prophecy from coming to be." She unrolled a parchment and read aloud.

All will come to light

But the end is not clear.

Fire will rain down

As the beast will appear.

The three of legend

Sword and shield

Must come into existence

For the beast to yield.

Stones of eight

Will lock their fate.

"Stones of eight," Monk repeated and faced AZ.

"This prophecy describes a new Immortal coming to destroy not just humanity, but all of time and space," Vampire added. "So that humanity will have never existed. All to punish me for not destroying humanity when I came into this existence. You see, AZ, the Mermaids were praised for their admiration of what they discovered with the king and his selflessness. I, on the other hand, am cursed for my selfishness. I refused to destroy humanity because I could not exist without him." He looked at Monk who stared back.

"And now, we are preparing to be able to battle and destroy what is being sent to destroy us," King Jax told him.

"And what is that?" AZ asked.

"We do not yet know. An Immortal beast of some sort," Vampire told him.

"But regardless of what it is, we need to be prepared. And to do that," Monk told AZ, "we need to find the eight Cez stones that fell when Vampire marked me with this." Monk pulled back his robes and exposed the markings on his side. "This is what happens when an Immortal marks a mortal to find them in the next life."

"And that is where you come in," Vampire said. "We need you to find the stones."

AZ shook his head repeatedly. "I can't find the stones. My brother, Saric, was able to find the stones," he added, backing away. AZ refused to believe what they were saying. He began to appear nauseous.

The princess walked to her mother with her emerald crown atop her head. Unlike the more elaborate crowns of the queen and kings, her crown had only a single spike that rose in the front.

"AZ?" Monk questioned and examined his eyes.

"First time meeting the girlfriend's family," Vampire added.

"Really?" AZ yelled. "She is not my *girlfriend!*"

As he yelled 'girlfriend', it echoed repeatedly throughout the stone and metal throne room.

"It's times like this that you hope for softer surfaces to absorb sound. A simple design flaw in modern throne rooms," Vampire whispered to him. "But no such luck. Girlfriend. Girlfriend. Girlfriend," he continued to whisper, mimicking an echo while moving his hands further apart as if pulsing.

AZ was not listening to him. His gaze was now locked on the princess, as hers was on him. He felt strong again.

"I'll do it," AZ told them with a proud posture.

Right on cue, Vampire thought, watching AZ's pride shine at the sight of the princess.

"Excellent," Queen Sharon stated. "Collectively, you will go forth under the guise of the Ambassadors of Mortua. The princess will accompany you and represent the crown. Her presence will give you access to most kingdoms and minimize any political barriers." The queen walked down the steps and stood directly in front of AZ. "The time has come for you to rise for a purpose."

AZ nodded in strong agreement.

Monk, Vampire, and AZ rejoined Sorcerer outside of the throne room. Guards escorted them out of the palace. From behind an ornate column came the sound of the clearing of a feminine throat. They all turned, as if choreographed.

"A word?" Princess asked.

AZ rushed forward with pride.

"No— Sorry, AZ, not you," she cautiously proceeded. "Him." She pointed to Sorcerer. "But I'll see you in Dellai." AZ nodded but hung his head in defeat.

"But AZ…" He looked up with wide eyes. "I was happy that you agreed to this." Princess smiled nervously.

"We'll be outside," Vampire said to Sorcerer and moved on with Monk, AZ, and the guards.

"Sorry, kid. Maybe next time," Monk comforted AZ.

But AZ had a grin on his face. "Are you kidding? She knows my name."

Monk glanced at Vampire and giggled.

"If this keeps up, he's going to be a bigger monster than I could only dream to be," Vampire kidded, as they followed the guards through the labyrinth of hallways.

Princess watched them go, and then turned to Sorcerer. "I'm sorry, sir," she began. "It's just that… I happened to be watching when you decided not to go into the throne room. The palace is full of secret passages and lookout points."

Sorcerer held himself in as casual a posture as he could. However, his heart was pounding so hard that he could swear it was audible.

"I am curious as to why you did not go in with the others," she continued.

"I'm sorry your highness. I don't understand why you want to talk to me."

"Are you my father?" she said, quickly.

Sorcerer's pounding heart stopped. His breath was pushed from his chest as if he'd just been punched in the gut. The silence lingered between them. "I'm sorry. It's just that your anticipated presence in this meeting threw my mother off her usual sense of control. And there just feels like a very comfortable air about you. Something familiar."

Sorcerer stood with his arms crossed, staring at the tiled floor. He said nothing. A breeze came through the corridor where they stood. The scent of orange and vanilla lingered and made both of them smile. The warm breeze seemed to increase as Princess became excited, but then rescinded as she grew calm.

Their silence filled the hallway again. A group of guards passed and marched towards the palace entrance. A group of maids walked the other way. They all did their part to appropriately acknowledge the princess while Sorcerer maintained his closed posture.

"I'm sorry," she began when they were alone again. "It's just—"

"It's complicated." Sorcerer attempted an explanation while keeping his gaze on her robin's egg- blue shoes. He giggled to himself and said, "Your mother's favorite."

"Yes, it is, but please understand it from my point of view."

“I’m sorry, your majesty.” He gave her a sorrowful look. “The answer to your question is too complicated for this moment.”

“Well, thank you for your time,” the princess said quickly and bowed as she turned to exit.

“It’s just—” he yelled out to her. “The time is wrong.” She stopped and peered over her shoulder. “You will have your answers. But when the time is right.”

Princess gave a subtle nod and rushed off.

“Damn it!” Sorcerer screamed and punched the silver-leafed column.

CHAPTER 9
City of Mortua

Vampire and Monk were in a whispered conversation when Sorcerer met up with them outside of the grand entrance to the palace.

"Everything all right?" Monk asked.

"Yeah. Seems so," Sorcerer answered, in a tone that made it clear that it was not.

"You know where to meet us," Vampire said to him.

"I do. I will get to Dellai before you to take care of my own business and meet Tinker. We will gather supplies," he replied and nodded as he moved on.

"They'll be there," Monk assured Vampire.

"Yes. I just hope his patience will hold out," Vampire said.

"He knows what he has to do. He understands the timing of things," Monk reassured him.

"Like you, right?" Vampire joked. "You are exactly where you are supposed to be. Divine timing. That's what you have been telling me forever."

"And look," Monk said, lightly. "I'm still right."

Vampire giggled.

Seer was quietly present on the palace grounds. He glanced at Monk as Monk threw his head back in laughter. Monk turned to adjust the saddle on a cinnamon-colored horse. AZ saw his jaw moving but was unable to understand what he was saying to Vampire. AZ walked up to Seer, who kept a watchful eye on Monk and Vampire. Seer's curiosity grew as he felt a push against his special gift. It was as if someone was keeping him from being able to 'see' into any part of the conversation or what it would bring about.

Vampire, he thought to himself. *Damn Immortals.*

Monk pulled himself atop the majestic horse as the sun reflected off the contracting muscles beneath the striking color of its hair. He held tight to the navy reigns and pulled at the stallion to start its trot. The others climbed onto the horses that had been provided for them and followed. Vampire rushed forward a bit so that he was riding next to Monk. Monk could not help but smile at the silly grin on Vampire's face. AZ and Seer kept a respectful distance.

"So, what is really going on there?" AZ asked Seer.

"Not sure, but there is definitely something."

"Is that a good thing or a bad thing?"

"Hoping for the former but fearful of the latter."

"Have you known him for long?" AZ asked, nodding at Monk. It was clear that Monk was fully enjoying the private conversation.

"Monk? Oh yes," Seer acknowledged. "For as long as I can remember."

"Neighbors? School?"

Seer turned and glared at AZ with a touch of rage. Seer quickly recovered himself, realizing how he had reacted to AZ's questions.

"No. I am sorry. Really AZ. I am very sorry."

"No problem," AZ said, deciding not to question him further.

They rode in silence through the streets of Mortua. A bridge had been cleared for them. Onlookers from the other bridges watched them with obvious curiosity.

"That's AZ!" yelled his friend, Harvey, with excitement. "AZ!" He waved.

"Hey, Harvey!" AZ yelled back. "Save me a seat at my favorite table."

Harvey gave him a salute.

The air was still salty but contained notes of the natural flora. Seer took a deep inhale and smiled. AZ wanted to ask about his smile but worried about making him angry again. Seer began talking as if he were bursting with the need to tell someone a long-held secret.

"It's just that our lives have been very, very different from yours." AZ listened without comment. "You see," Seer continued. "You have loving parents. Both Monk and I were brought to the monastery as orphans. Tinker, too; just much later. We were supposed to be educated in the ways of the brotherhood so that we could preserve the ancient knowledge and traditions."

"Seems as though that didn't work out. I mean no offense, but none of you seem very holy," AZ replied, unable to hold back his comment.

"I never completed my education," Seer spoke sadly. "I had only been there less than a year when the brotherhood discovered my abilities. I was cast out, just pushed out the door into the pouring rain with nothing. They stripped me of my robes and left me to live or die on my own."

"Not very brotherly of them."

"No. It wasn't."

"They suck!"

Seer stayed quiet as he privately recalled the pain of it all. AZ thought of several questions but stopped himself from asking anything further. He was being respectful of Seer's privacy and fearful of his anger.

Seer reopened the conversation as AZ listened to the story of a young boy with a special gift who had lost his parents and had taken revenge on their killer. And how he went from Tamsu to Mortua and ended up at the monastery with Monk being his only friend.

"Or at least, that's my side of the story," Seer admitted. "But Monk never left my side."

"How did he get away with that? I mean, the brothers must have come after him."

"There I was in the pouring rain. The other boys started to throw rocks at me to make me go. Monk did not. He refused. He ran out into the rain and stood in front of me to protect me. The monsignor came out after him. Monk took off his robes and covered me in them. He demanded that I run. He knew that they would kill me."

"And what about him?"

"He suffered for the aid that he gave me."

"The scar."

"He's a tough bastard."

"You have no idea," Seer told him. "The monsignor came at us. He held the end of his sword to my throat. Monk knew that he would have killed me. *Go,* he told me. I ran. I looked back to see the monsignor take his torturous metal glove with the three blades and slice it across Monk's face. Monk fell to the ground. He turned to me and yelled again for me to go."

AZ looked at Monk and saw him throw his head back in laughter at something Vampire had just said. He seemed so joyful. But AZ also remembered who he had met in the tavern. He understood more of Monk's character. He felt that Monk's commitment was unwavering. He could see Monk as the kind of rule breaker who had true purpose. And the kind of rule breaker who did not get caught. There was more to the story, but it was for Seer to tell and not for AZ to ask about.

"He never gave in," Seer continued. "He would study during the day and then sneak out and teach what he'd learned to me at night. He helped me to build a shelter. He brought me food. He taught me how to fight. He would get into the library when no one was there. One time," Seer laughed, "he even hid in a cart and grabbed the books from the lower shelves as the brother re-shelved the ones on the higher shelves."

AZ joined in the laughter. "I could see that happening."

"He searched for information to help me to understand my gifts."

"I guess that, maybe, I should start to see him differently."

"Maybe you should." Seer paused. "He has never forgotten my birthday, even when I do." They both laughed.

Seer went quiet. AZ thought that they were comfortable enough with one another for him to ask questions now. "Seer?"

Seer paused, then continued with the story of his life's journey. "But then a rift came between us."

"Why?"

"You see, AZ, like I said, we did not have a life like yours."

"Like mine? Well, good for you. I've always been considered second to my dead brother. Always considered a failure."

"Brother?"

"Yeah. He died when I was a baby. I don't remember him at all. My parents tell me about him, but I can't remember him. They say that is why we moved to Mortua. They had to get out of Telis. It reminded them too much of him."

"Funny. You do not have any trace of split energies."

"What is that?"

"I guess I could have said 'sibling' energies."

"Maybe because I don't remember him."

"No. The energy would still be there. But nothing."

Silence followed. AZ was a bit offended. But Seer continued searching for any sense of split energy.

"Well," AZ began. "It doesn't matter, anyway. He was born on the tenth of September. He was able to find Cez stones."

"And you?"

"Seven years later on the ninth of September. Came out too quick and have been reminded of it ever since."

"Your parents love you, AZ."

"I know. But their disappointment makes me question that. I'll never be able to find Cez stones. I'll never be able to match the riches that my brother led my family to."

Silence followed again. This time, Seer maintained a sorrowful face for his younger compatriot.

"Always remember, AZ, someone else had it worse than you." Seer pointed to himself.

"Well, you seem to be making the best of it."

"The best of what?" Seer asked, angrily.

"Are you two okay back there?" Monk asked.

"Yes. Yes. Sorry. Felt like my horse tripped," Seer lied, and Monk went back to his conversation with Vampire.

"Sorry," AZ apologized. "I didn't mean to—"

"No. It's not you. It's just that these memories are still wounds. I feel like when I talk about them, they are happening right now."

"Is that something that comes with your gifts?"

"Truth is, it is a choice to keep the wounds open. It's just that I have used that choice to enhance my gifts. It's a way to— well, supercharge my power."

"Pain?"

"Rage."

"But why now? Are your gifts active right now?"

"They are always present. I cannot shut them off. I can only focus them or attempt to distract myself from them."

"That must suck. It must feel like a song that you can't get out of your head."

"It's like a whole bunch of songs that play together, and you can't get them out of your head."

"Even ones that you don't like."

"Especially ones that you don't like."

They rode in silence for a bit. AZ was still hesitant to initiate conversation.

"Thank you, AZ," Seer said, as he turned to him with a smile.

"Umm, you're welcome."

"Conversation is a good distraction from what happens in my head."

"Oh, well, good. I can talk."

"Yes. Yes, you can." Seer agreed, making AZ laugh. "I don't…" Seer began shyly, "I don't make friends very easily. You see, I have a bad habit of focusing on myself in peoples' futures and not seeing myself there. It's lonely. And I've spent too much time being lonely."

"Oh, well, good then. I guess you see us as friends in each other's futures."

"No. I just keep myself from looking." AZ seemed disappointed. "It's just that most of the time, I end up feeling empty. I am enjoying your company and don't want to know whether or not you will be there in my future."

"Well, I guess that's fair. But for me, it's all about living in the moment. Tomorrow will take care of itself."

"Says the boy who has everything."

"Hey! That's not fair," AZ said, resentfully.

Seer did not apologize. The silence grew uncomfortable again. It was foreign to AZ not to be able to escape an uncomfortable situation. He rode on in silence but kicked his horse to trot a bit faster to avoid riding next to Seer.

Seer caught up to him but remained quiet. AZ pulled back on the reins to ride behind him. Seer followed his lead to again ride next to him.

"What?" AZ screamed.

"Horse tripped again?" Vampire joked.

"Sorry. Yeah," AZ said, sarcastically.

Vampire raised his eyebrows to intimidate AZ, who did not respond in the expected manner and rolled his eyes and shook his head. AZ was growing less interested in being part of this group.

"Sorry. It was my fault," Seer apologized. "I am being difficult."

"You can say that again," AZ whispered under his breath.

"I am being difficult," Seer repeated but in a lower volume.

"You heard that?"

"No. I saw this interaction between us happening and it was part of that. He…" Seer said, acknowledging Vampire, "was not part of it. Seers cannot 'see' Immortals. I didn't want this to go in a bad direction, so I decided to take action."

"So now you're looking into my future?"

"You opened me up to the idea," Seer said, with a hint of a smile.

"And what do you see now?" AZ asked, angrily.

"I'm not looking anymore. I'm waiting to see what happens *in the moment*. More like you. That might work better for me… with a new friend."

AZ smiled and extended his hand. "You people are really fucked up." AZ laughed but meant what he said. Seer, with his gloved hand, eagerly took AZ's hand and shook it so hard that AZ felt like he might fall off his horse.

"Well, now that we're talking again," AZ joked. "Can I ask you something?"

Seer hesitated. He rarely answered questions about himself. Someone could use what they knew against him. "Yes," he finally said. "But I reserve the right not to answer."

"I think that's fair."

Seer's posture visibly relaxed.

"So yes, you were kicked out of that awful place, but it might seem like Monk got the worst of it. I mean, look at that scar."

"That makes it even worse that he had to suffer on my behalf."

"But let me finish. If you ask me, he's stronger because of you. His commitment, his self-awareness, that kind of stuff grew in him because of this experience. You helped him become the crazy bastard that he is."

"I never really thought of it that way, but you may be right, AZ." Seer smiled as he looked at AZ. "Thank you. That perspective has been lost to me."

They continued on in a more comfortable silence.

"When you said that a rift came between you, you meant what? A girl? That's usually what happened with my friends."

"No AZ," Seer giggled. "Not a girl." He extended his hand to acknowledge Vampire and Monk. "He likes men."

"Obviously," AZ agreed. "But you never know who's interested in who." Seer hesitated. "Okay. Forget it," AZ said quickly.

"No, no, no. I'll tell you. You see, as I said, Monk would visit me at night. But during the day, I was left to my own devices. I practiced what he taught me and studied the books he brought me. And then they showed up."

"Who? The brothers? Military guards?"

"No. The most frightening darkness that has ever existed. The Dark Sisters."

They gave me no option. I either joined them or Monk would be eternally tortured."

"What?"

"They had rescued me when my parents were killed and taught me how to use my gifts for evil purposes. The darkness that came to me when I was alone began to show itself in everything I saw. They found me again in the woods and took me. He searched for me, but they made it so that he was unable to find me. Monk spent years searching for me and when he found me, the hate was strong within me. "

"Well, obviously he found you."

"The Dark Sisters went to destroy Ileana, the Queen of Witches. That was when he found me and we escaped," Seer reported. "I was beaten and weak. He found me in the Desert of Xedu."

Seer's expression turned sinister as his eyes tinged red. "I had learned evil from The Dark Sisters but now wanted to use the techniques for good. Every day is a challenge." Seer's tone slowly lightened and his eyes changed back to their original color.

"I could follow that logic. You need to be able to experience bad to know how to avoid it and how to deal with it when it shows up."

"And it will show up."

The two continued their easy stride, glancing ahead at Monk and Vampire's joyful interactions.

"It seems like they are on a first date."

"Actually, it's their ninth first date."

"What?"

"Nine lifetimes," Seer informed AZ.

"How do you know that's true? Can you see the past as well as the future?"

"It's not common for people like me, but I can, yes. I can't see Vampire or anything that is influenced by him. Immortals are immune to the gift of seeing. But I can see Monk in his previous lives. I can see him after these 'first dates'. The first ones are always good…"

"But?"

"His life always ends with death."

"Well, he is mortal after all."

"His deaths have all been caused by Vampire's pride."

"But wait a minute. If you can't see an Immortal, how can you see that?"

"I see his dead body. I see the fang marks. Once his spirit leaves the body, I can see through the spirit's visions."

"That's frighteningly incredible," AZ said, staring away thoughtfully. He turned back to Seer. "Did you tell him?"

"I have warned him."

"And?"

"He heard me. He knows that what I say is true. But he has to participate in this game to see what part Vampire has to play on this present journey. He feels that there is more at stake here than any one life."

AZ's concern was palpable. Seer reached out and held him by the shoulder.

"It will be OK, AZ. We will make sure of it. We can watch here in the moment," he pointed to AZ, "and keep our eye on the potential futures." He pointed back at himself. This gave AZ a sense of relief. "I thought that you didn't like him anyway," Seer added.

"I don't dislike him. But he's your friend, so..."

"You would do that for me?"

"I'm your friend, so yes. That's what friends do."

Seer felt a sense of fullness that he could not remember ever feeling before.

"Thank you, AZ."

"No problem," AZ replied, feeling strongly that he was doing the right thing.

The ride continued for a time in a comfortable silence.

Up ahead, Monk turned to Vampire. "Are you still thinking of this as a good thing?"

Vampire looked back and watched AZ and Seer laughing together.

"Can you ever recall Seer smiling?" Vampire asked.

Monk smiled as if pleased with Seer's obvious joy.

CHAPTER 10
Road to Dellai

The air had become hot and smelled of sulfur. The road had turned to a black surface. Up ahead were volcanoes with rivers of lava pouring down to burning orange lakes on either side of the narrowing road. Ash fell from the sky like snow.

"I know this place," AZ yelled. "It's dangerous."

"The middle of nowhere," Monk told him as he scanned around for any sign of life. "We are between kingdoms. This road is all that you'll find here. It is the only way from Mortua to Dellai."

"Don't you ever leave Mortua?" Seer questioned.

"Why would I?" AZ replied with an air of superiority. "Mortua is where everyone wants to be." AZ said the words but felt an emptiness with them.

Monk shook his head. "So much to learn." He whispered his thought so that Vampire was the only one who heard.

The road was spared from the lava.

"The Witches enchanted this path eons ago," Vampire told AZ, anticipating his question. "They used it for safe passage through this region and it has stood the test of time."

"So far," Monk said.

A sudden explosion caused them to throw their arms up to shield themselves. Vampire immediately pulled his horse closer to Monk's.

"What is that?" AZ asked, as he signaled his horse to trot faster.

"Not sure," Monk replied, squinting to protect his eyes from the oncoming wind. "It seems as though a volcano is erupting."

"Seems as though a volcano is always erupting," AZ said, glancing at the hot liquid beside the road.

"Then we had better move," Vampire said.

The wind was rapidly picking up speed. Monk faced Vampire, who stared back at him. Monk was unsure why, but he instinctively understood that Vampire's concern was his concern as well. He turned to Seer.

"Every possible path is towards it," Seer yelled, as the red glow in his eyes dissolved and he glanced at Monk.

"That makes sense, I guess," Monk said, nodding. "This is the only road."

"Never one to back down from a fight, huh?" Vampire asked.

"You tell me. You would know that better than I," Monk replied.

"True," Vampire said. "I'll rephrase it as a statement then."

"You can tell me all about it later," Monk told him. "Let's go," he said to Seer.

The road narrowed between the lakes of lava to allow the horses to pass in a single file. Seer followed Monk without question. AZ looked at Vampire.

"Choose your destiny, boy," Vampire said to the hesitant young man. "And get used to it. You're going to be leaving that laziness in your past." He kicked his horse and began trotting forward. "Or you simply will not have a future."

Vampire's horse picked up speed in line with his command. AZ sat. His horse seemed anxious. AZ was fearful, but he thought about Vampire's words. He was tired of being put down for not contributing. Yet, it was a challenge to break that routine. He finally felt a connection to something. *So, why hold back?* He pulled back on the reins, but his horse continued to pace as if straining to stay in place. AZ realized that he needed to go. He needed to follow the others into whatever danger lay before them. He needed to know that everything would work out. But he could not see that it would.

For AZ, not having control of a situation caused an unspoken fear. He had always been able to disguise this fear. He was more popular and richer than his peers. He was handsome and charming. Therefore, if he wasn't interested in something, it meant that it was not worth anyone having an interest in it. AZ's friends followed him down any superficial path because of his false status. But they, like he, were mostly superficial and not understanding the need for purpose. However, his disinterest came from a deep fear that he was a fraud. His charms would, someday, not get him past the velvet ropes of life, and he did not know what he would do then. Rather than figure it out, he chose to ignore it and go back to what he was used to.

AZ pulled back on the reins of his horse and turned her to trot back in the other direction. He was giving up on this insanity. He would go back to life as he knew it. He would get by. He would go back to being the one making the jokes, instead of being the one who the jokes were about.

AZ pulled hard, but the horse fought him. AZ was an excellent rider and was becoming frustrated with his inability to control this beast. He pulled one last time, but the horse reared onto its hind legs. AZ leaned forward to balance and held tightly to the reins. He squeezed his thighs tight against the horse's muscular torso.

Then he saw it.

Dragon, he realized.

The ferocious flying beast reflected the sunlight with each diamond scale of her external skeleton. She had been birthed from the closest volcano. She rose high into the sky and appeared to have either not seen him or thought him too insignificant to acknowledge. Either way, he was grateful. AZ looked to the road ahead but could not see the others.

Am I dreaming? Is it something in the air?

His shock caused him to loosen his hold on the reins just enough for the horse to regain control. She sped off after the others. AZ searched the sky for any sign of the dragon.

AZ searched over his shoulder for the dragon, just as his horse took off at top speed and knocked AZ from her back. The road was hard. His shoulder took the brunt of the contact. However, his head was not spared as it, too, hit hard. AZ saw a light tracing across the sky and then his own reflection in a stone next to him before he lost consciousness.

CHAPTER 11
City of Mortua — Perculfilus Estate

The ceiling seemed familiar. AZ tried to orient himself. Yes, he thought. I am home.

He attempted to sit up but immediately fell to his side and hit his face on the soft pillow.

"That was graceful," joked a vaguely familiar voice.

The rush of blood and pain added to AZ's confusion. *Vampire,* he realized.

"AZ?"

Another familiar voice. The sound was painful.

"Seer?"

"He'll be fine," Seer told Monk. "But…"

"But?" questioned the voice of Mrs. Perculfilus.

"But he'll be different. He has more paths ahead of him now."

"Will he still be able to-" Mrs. Perculfilus asked, as her husband grabbed hold of her arm.

"Will he keep you in your present style of living and social status?" Vampire spoke sarcastically to Mr. Perculfilus. "I thought his brother was the one who found the Cez stones."

"Well?"

"He will be making appropriate choices. Of that, I am sure, sir," Seer told him, attempting to be sensitive.

"Could you all please shut up and stop talking about me like I'm in a coma?" AZ screamed with frustration. "Just stop talking! My head is killing me!"

"You were," Vampire said, "in a coma. May I have just a touch more coffee, please?" he asked Mrs. Perculfilus.

She looked confused but clapped her hands to alert a servant. The clapping sound made AZ grab pillows to cover his ears from any noise. Mrs. Perculfilus immediately stopped and held her hands to her mouth. A young lady immediately entered the room.

"That's a bit dramatic," Monk said. "It wasn't a coma," he told AZ. "You were just unconscious for three days."

AZ appeared confused. He had no recollection of how much time had gone by.

"You have been breathing fine," Vampire added.

"The gentleman would like some more coffee," AZ's mother told the servant.

"Ummm. Hello?" AZ screamed.

"Shhh," Vampire told him. "Remember. Your head hurts."

"Why is *he* here?" AZ glared at Vampire.

"Really, Vampire. Enough," Monk said, putting a hand on his shoulder.

"I found him," Vampire argued. "And carried him here."

"How?" AZ asked. "By bouncing my head off rocks?"

"It was a thought, but no. I held you ever so safely in my arms," Vampire told AZ, motioning as if he were holding a newborn.

"I don't believe you."

"He did," Seer told him. "While you were out, he never left your side."

"But now that I'm awake, can he please leave?"

"Well, no," Vampire replied in a comical tone. "We need to get a move on."

Monk looked at AZ's parents, who gazed with concerned expressions at their son.

"We thought it best to bring you back here," Monk told AZ. "We figured, if nothing else, the familiarity of your home would offer some peace to your parents and to you when you came to. Like now." Monk leaned in to speak with AZ's parents. "I believe it is time to tell him the truth."

Mr. Perculfilus turned to his wife and escorted her out of the room without a word.

Seer walked over to AZ and broke the silence. "AZ. We found a Cez stone. You led us to it."

"It's not the only thing I found," he told them. He turned directly to stare at Vampire. "I saw a dragon."

"You saw a dragon?" Vampire asked, looking nervously at Monk and Seer.

Seer shook his head. "Dragons are Immortal. I can't—"

"You can't see Immortals. Yes. We know," Vampire said, finishing his thought.

"No one can see Immortals."

"Certainly helps to keep me off the radar," Vampire joked and then turned his attention back to AZ. "Tell us about the dragon."

"That dragon looked like it was armored in jewels," AZ told them.

Vampire gave him a worried glance. "Say that again," he instructed him. "And tell me everything you remember."

AZ's head hurt too much to argue. "I was trying to," he kept his gaze down, embarrassed. "Well, I was trying to turn my horse around to come back home. I did not want to go on with you. The horse fought me, and tried to knock me off, but I held strong. That was when I saw it. It rose from the volcano that was throwing all of the ash into the air. It flew straight into the sky. I was so…" AZ tried to find the right words. "I was so… I don't know what. I was frozen. My senses failed me, and I didn't even know that I fell off the horse. The last thing I saw was a light moving through the sky… and a mirrored stone that reflected the dragon."

Vampire was at the window, his back to the others. Monk sought to Seer for understanding. He shrugged his shoulders. AZ replayed the memory in his mind. He watched over and over again as the dragon flew past him until it disappeared.

"Vampire?" Monk asked, noting his obvious concern.

Vampire continued to stare out the window. "There is only one reason why that dragon is *here*."

"Like you said, to destroy things," AZ said.

"Not things," Vampire whispered, with the slightest shake of his head. "Everything. That dragon is meant to destroy all of time and space. This is part of the prophecy."

"So, we are too late," Seer said.

Monk looked at him but held tight to a glimmer of hope.

Vampire spoke on while staring at Monk. "She was sent for full destruction. Everyone. Everything. In every realm of existence. Past. Present. Future. On this plane and every other."

The room was silent.

"Vampire?" Monk walked across the room to him.

Vampire's concern was palpable. Monk tried to comfort him.

AZ's fear was stronger than the pounding in his head.

"And her first target is… you," Vampire said to Monk as he fixed his gaze deep into his eyes.

"Why me?" Monk questioned.

"Because it's a punishment for me. That is why she is *here*," Vampire told him. "I was sent to destroy humanity. But I didn't," Vampire said, recalling his own history. "That was because of…"

Seer and AZ glanced at one another as Monk crossed his arms.

"Love," Monk said as he looked into Vampire and smiled.

"Your love. Your love altered my path."

"It gave you a path," added Princess, who had entered the room as quietly as possible.

"Yes," Vampire admitted, looking surprised by her presence.

"The Jeweled Dragon has been sent to punish me by killing you and then, when I am at my weakest point, she will destroy all of time and space. I will be powerless to stop her. You will never have existed, and I will be left in a void with that beast."

"But for her to destroy everything, she must first destroy you," Princess said to Monk.

"Yes," Vampire agreed. "The constellation that I marked you with created the eight Cez stones that we must find."

"Well, then. We need a plan," Princess said triumphantly.

Vampire approached the handsome and rarely used desk that sat in front of a floor-to-ceiling window. He pulled a rolled parchment from within his jacket. "This is the prophecy," he began as the others gathered around.

All will come to light

But the end is not clear.

Fire will rain down

As the beast will appear.

"The dragon," AZ said.

The three of legend

Sword and shield

Must come into existence

For the beast to yield.

"We are collecting the Three of Legend," Vampire told them. "And I believe the sword to be the Sword of Sansit. But I do not know about the shield."

Stones of eight

Will lock their fate.

"And the eight Cez stones," Monk added with everyone focusing on AZ.

"That is what we will need to defeat the Jeweled Dragon, but it does not give instructions on how to destroy it," Princess said.

"We have to get moving," Vampire told them. "With the Jeweled Dragon being here, time is of the essence."

"Some of the stones are here. Or at least we hope that these are the necessary stones. But as for the rest and the sword and shield, we need to figure out the best plan to find them," Seer reported.

"We can only guess that the stones are all of the same constellation since they have not reacted negatively to one another," AZ told them.

"And the same with the Illusion stone," Monk added. "But until we have them all, we will not be able to test them against me."

"Okay. Time to go," Monk rushed his order to the group. "We are to meet with Tinker and Sorcerer and— maybe a few others in Dellai."

CHAPTER 12
City of Dellai

The loud ruckus of the mid-afternoon, local tavern bar fight was in full effect. Glasses and mugs were being thrown in all directions as wooden stools were being broken and used as weapons and shields.

"So, who the fuck are you?" the swordsman demanded as he held Sorcerer's throat with one hand and pointed his blade at his right eye with the other. The fighting continued around them.

A quick distraction came as one of the participants threw a bucket of water at the swordsman's head. He moved to avoid it. It was the split second that Sorcerer needed to reverse the situation. A knife came spinning through the air and Sorcerer ducked to avoid taking it in his forehead. And the table was turned again.

"I'm your father," Sorcerer admitted to the talented swordsman.

A second swordsman had arrived, ready to back up the first. "Can you *please* get on with it, already?" he asked.

The swordsmens' resemblance to one another showed their strong genetics.

"Aldrick," said the first. "Meet your dad."

"My dad?" Aldrick questioned.

"He said that he is my father."

"Hmmm," Aldrick remarked. "I expected him to be better looking. Axel, let's go." Axel took the blunt end of his sword's handle and hit Sorcerer hard on the back of the neck.

Sorcerer dropped to his knees.

Vampire and Monk entered through the broken door at the entrance to the bar. They stepped through the rowdy crowd and collectively ducked as a glass was thrown at the entrance. Monk spotted Sorcerer on his knees and leaned in towards Vampire to avoid another thrown glass, which shattered on the wall behind him.

"Should we step in?" Vampire asked Monk.

Monk took a goblet full of wine from a nearby table. He leaned back against the wall and sipped the surprisingly good-quality red.

"Nah. He deserves it."

"Aren't you a monk?" questioned a drunk who'd propped himself on the wall next to Monk.

"Sort of," Monk replied, laughing.

"I thought monks made wine," the man said, with confused anger.

"Yes," Monk told him. "To drink it," he said, taking another mouthful from the glass. He turned to Vampire.

The drunk closed his eyes and slid down the wall to land seated on the floor.

Tinker made his way through the chaos towards them. "Welcome," he said.

Monk pulled Tinker in for a hug as a glass shattered on the wall behind where Tinker had been standing.

"I see you're all caught up," he added as he extended his hand to point to Sorcerer, Aldrick, and Axel.

"The reunion doesn't look like it's going so well," Vampire said.

"Oh, I don't know. Their interaction sort of started this whole festivity," Tinker told them. "Sorcerer made the mistake of grabbing hold of his shoulder." He pointed to Axel. "He turned and punched him. As Sorcerer fell back, he hit that guy," he continued, pointing to an oversized man with braided hair. "He, of course, pushed him back and he hit into— ummm… that guy." Tinker pointed to a one-armed warrior wearing full armor. "He took offense and then… *voilà*," he concluded and gestured around the room to acknowledge the chaos.

"As we expected, yeah?" Vampire asked Monk.

"Definitely," Monk replied.

"So, you say that you're…" Axel began to question Sorcerer.

"I'm your father," Sorcerer repeated, making arduous attempts to catch his breath.

"How's that?"

"Well, you see, your mother and I—"

"Yeah, yeah, yeah. We know how to make babies," Axel told him.

"Are you fathers?" Sorcerer asked, with a hint of excitement.

"Not that we're aware of," Aldrick replied, and elbowed his brother.

"What if we don't believe you?" Axel asked and held his blade to Sorcerer's throat.

"I have proof," Sorcerer said, staring at the blade.

"Then you'd better show it," Aldrick told him.

Sorcerer slowly got himself to his feet. He pulled his sleeve up and exposed three tattoos, two of which matched those that the twins each had on their forearms. Sorcerer pointed to the marks which represented Earth and Fire. They were circular and about the size of a coin. They had a similar appearance, but with a simple alteration to make each one its own symbol. As Sorcerer touched the first, Fire, Aldrick felt a warmth spread through his body.

"You were first born."

Aldrick was at a loss for words.

Sorcerer moved further up to the second tattoo, the symbol of Earth, and did the same.

"And soon after, you. You never wanted to be too far from one another."

Axel felt a rush that gave him a feeling of strength and stability and then the same feeling of being overwhelmed.

Aldrick looked at Axel.

"You motherfucker!" Axel yelled as they collectively punched Sorcerer in the gut.

Seer, AZ, and Princess entered the brawl. AZ kept a protective posture over Princess. Glasses and metal goblets continued to be thrown in all directions. Swords and knives flew through the air.

"Ummm," AZ began. "How's it going?"

"Tinker!" Princess exclaimed and leaned in for a hug. She quickly punched a patron who came at them. The man was knocked to the floor. AZ gawked at her with complete surprise.

"Hello." Tinker returned the greeting with a smile and pulled her back in as a chair came towards them.

"Okay. Now's a good time," Monk told Vampire as he threw his wine goblet at another patron who was coming at them with his knife drawn. The man went down quickly after the forceful blow to the head.

"That's enough," Vampire demanded and pulled Axel and Aldrick back. They attempted to retaliate. Vampire held each by his throat and lifted them into the air. He squeezed and they lost their grips on their swords. They collectively tried to land blows that would force their release. But they were to no avail. Vampire's face showed that he was unaffected by their physical attacks.

"Vampire. Put them down," Monk demanded.

Vampire did not.

"Please," he added.

"Who's in control now?" Vampire asked with confidence.

"Vampire?" Monk asked again.

Aldrick and Axel's eyes widened.

"Yes. He's a vampire," AZ said. "I had the same reaction."

Vampire lowered them to the ground.

"He's a vampire?" Aldrick struggled to get out the words and coughed repeatedly. Axel observed him with curiosity, as if he knew him. Yet, he could not place him.

"I didn't expect much, but I did expect some level of comprehension," Vampire said to Sorcerer.

"Boys, meet your father. It's been a while," Monk told them.

Sorcerer made an attempt at a handshake. They did not comply.

"Really, Sorcerer. Your family dynamics need some serious work," Vampire said.

"Where the fuck have you been all these years?" Axel said, angrily.

"It's complicated," Sorcerer quickly shot back.

"As complicated as learning to fight and survive at the wills of slave traders, pirates, and mercenaries?"

"That does kinda suck," AZ said.

Sorcerer's expression was full of guilt and pity. He knew that what they said was true. And he knew that it was his fault.

"To be fair," Vampire interjected, "he would not have made a very good role model."

"You should stay quiet," Monk told Vampire.

"And that's your excuse?" Aldrick screamed at him.

"You would have been killed!" Sorcerer yelled back. "Your mother was the Queen of Witches. She was betrayed and destroyed by The Dark Sisters. Their followers would have killed you. I feared for your lives. I hid you for as long as I could, but they were catching up to us. I left you with no explanation and no direction because I feared that if I knew anything, I could betray you. Not on purpose, but they used magic, and they used seers to try to find out what I would not tell them. I went into hiding to protect you... To protect us all. I had made sure that I left no trace. I had nowhere to start. Rumors came up on occasion, but it was never you. The markings were all that I had to find you."

"Wouldn't those be a trace?" Aldrick asked.

"You were given those at birth by your mother. But she hid them, even from me. I didn't know that I had them, either. It wasn't until your eighteenth birthday that they appeared on my forearm."

"That's when they appeared on us," Axel said and looked at Aldrick with a surprised response. They turned and punched Sorcerer in the gut again. He fell to his knees.

"I feel better," Aldrick said.

"Me too," Axel replied, and they shook hands.

CHAPTER 13
City of Dellai

The Twins, Aldrick and Axel, led the Ambassadors through the stone streets of Dellai. Dellai was a city of wealth and although afternoon bar brawls were common in the outer neighborhoods by the city walls, the citizens were more refined at its center. As one traveled deeper into the city, the architectural design changed and became more elaborate and there were more details etched into the stones that made up the streets and sidewalks.

Unlike Mortua, which was ruled by the queen and kings, Dellai was ruled by the businessmen who made a religion out of trading their growing wealth. However, part of Mortua's prosperity came from its treaties to ensure the protection of Dellai. The members of the Royal Family of Mortua were celebrities in this kingdom. Princess would have to choose the right time to officially announce herself in the capital city. As her mother had stated, her status would give the Ambassadors access to whatever they might need.

Dellai had a more hierarchical lifestyle than Mortua. Access to restaurants and private clubs were based on financial portfolios and the day's business transactions. But today's position did not guarantee the same for tomorrow. A slight drop in finances could result in access denied.

The Twins tipped their hats at the eager ladies and gentlemen of Dellai. They had a reputation in Dellai as men both to avoid and to attract. They were known for their excellent swordsmanship. They were even better known for their physical prowess amongst the ladies who could afford their company. Their greatest cause, however, happened to be their own finances.

An occasional husband or jealous lover would stir up the courage to confront either or both of them. Often, they came with friends to encourage and assist them in regaining their pride. However, the Twins never lost a sword fight. Any man of Dellai had to accept that if his lover found favor with one of the Twins, he would have to move on or await her return. They also knew that the Twins were not interested in a long-term relationship. For them, it was just for fun.

Now, not every woman fell for their charms. There were several women, over the years, who found themselves immune to the enchanting Twins. However, they also found personal solace in the nunnery.

As the group casually talked and moved through the covered walkways and plazas filled with restaurants and shops, street entertainers, tourists, and businesspeople on their way to their midday meal, they were met with waves and giggles, smiling whispers, coy and seductive glances, and the scowl of the men accompanying those young ladies.

Sorcerer noted that more than one lady of privilege addressed the Twins with a subtle wave and nod as their husbands' backs were turned and their attention was to business.

"What?" Axel demanded. "We gotta eat. Right, 'Pops'?" he added, as he grabbed Sorcerer by the shoulder.

"Don't call me that," Sorcerer replied, with disgust.

"And these swords are not our only money makers," Aldrick added, holding his sword aloft with his left hand while groping his crotch with his right.

Tinker laughed as he turned to Princess. "They're funny," he told her. She shook her head and walked on. "What?" Tinker continued. "They are."

"So, what's your real name, anyway?" Aldrick asked Sorcerer.

"I don't go by a real name. None of us do," he replied and gestured to acknowledge the group of Ambassadors.

Tinker raised his hand as if to speak but then thought differently and put his hand down.

"It's for our own protection," Sorcerer said.

"Protection from. . ?" Axel began.

"Dark magic," said Vampire, as if the answer was obvious.

"So, then what do we call each of you?" Aldrick asked.

Sorcerer pointed at each member, beginning with himself. "I am Sorcerer…"

"Or Pops," joked Aldrick to Axel.

"No," Sorcerer reminded them. "Vampire, Monk, Seer, Princess, Tinker and…" Sorcerer stopped and cocked his head. "Well, I guess, we do use your name," he said, looking at AZ.

"Not my full name. AZ." AZ introduced himself and shook hands with the Twins.

"Well," Axel began, "you all know our names."

"So," continued his brother, "we think that it's only fitting that we know all of yours."

Princess seemed perplexed. She saw the prism of colors on the stones that made up the street. At first, she thought it was painted, but then realized that it moved slightly. She searched the sky for the source of its movement but found nothing. She walked a few steps from the group and then stopped in the middle of the street. She thought she saw something out of the corner of her eye.

The colors form where the light stops moving, she thought.

Immediately, she felt the air get ripped from her lungs. She looked towards the noon sun but again saw nothing. Her gaze went back to the pattern of stones that made up the street. The rainbow of colors was gone. She returned her gaze to the sky.

AZ saw her concern and came towards her. He stopped in his tracks. He heard it.

He heard it first. It was the same as the other day on the road. It sounded like a C-minor scale played on an out-of-tune piano; a bit rough but very striking.

She heard it now. "Dragon." She tried to scream it but was only able to form a whisper.

Princess felt the air as her hair blew about in the heated breeze. She felt her feet alternating in a progressively rapid fashion. Princess found herself running. AZ had her by the hand and was pulling her as they ran towards the others who were walking into the open center of the Plaza Formal.

"Dragon!" AZ screamed. "Dragon!"

The others watched in fear as he and Princess reached the center of the plaza. AZ pointed to the sky.

"I see nothing," said Axel.

"Nor I," added Seer.

"Then sharpen your eyesight. Dragon!" Vampire pointed towards the sun. The sky shimmered with a prism of color as the sunlight played on the Jeweled Dragon's scales. But in an instant, it was gone.

A second gust of wind came, hot, as if from the sun itself. But the blinding sun obscured their vision.

"Run!" screamed Vampire. His eyes, not affected by the blinding sun, saw the source of the hot wind. "Get underground!" he demanded of Monk. He had Monk by the wrist and was pulling him out of the dragon's line of sight.

She had seen them. And she was coming towards them. The dragon hid herself in the sunlight with her hard, diamond scales reflecting the sun's light.

Monk and Vampire knew that it was a lost cause. They knew that a battle would be over before it began.

"Shelter! Everyone to shelter!"

They all continued to run up to and through the gates that marked the different sections of the city. As Dellai was built on a solitary hill, many of the gates also opened to streets that ascended and descended and were partially covered by buildings as they ran to lower levels of the city.

"Dragon!" they yelled to the guardsmen who manned the Gate of Imperfections. The guards looked at one another with confusion, for although dragon drills were a part of their theoretical training, they'd never expected to actually have to use them.

"Ring the bloody alarm, you fools!" Vampire screamed and exposed his fangs.

Whether it was their fear of a dragon or of Vampire, the result was the same: they ran and rang the alarm. However, even as the alarm sounded, there was no urgency from the citizens of Dellai. It was clear that they assumed it was just a random drill.

"Damn fools!" Vampire said as they continued running through the labyrinthine streets of the walled city.

"Dragon! Dragon!" The guards continued to yell as they ran past the unconcerned townspeople.

"Enough," someone yelled back. Vampire and Monk stopped and looked back at the sun. Seer was keeping pace with them. The dragon had veered its course just enough so that it was able to be seen in the midday sky. Vampire stopped and pointed. "Dragon!" he screamed again. Monk stood near but under the covered walkway. Seer continued to run.

People stared to where he pointed in the sky. The expressions on their faces immediately changed from annoyed to disbelief to panic and fear. They started screaming and pushing past each other for shelter.

Vampire maintained his exposed position in the middle of the street and held his defensive stance.

Monk ran at him and grabbed his arm, pulling him out of the way as the dragon let loose the scent of comforting bergamot in her tinged gas. The gas was then followed by a scorching fire and destroyed everything in its path. Monk pulled Vampire beneath a covered walkway. The street and the walls were ablaze. The heat of the flames was blinding. Vampire pulled Monk further down the side street and pushed him tight against the wall as he covered him with his own body.

"Monk?"

"Sorry. It was a reaction."

"You could have been killed!"

"And you?"

Vampire kissed Monk deeply. "Thank you, Monk, but she cannot kill me with her fire. You, she can. And I can't have that. Do not do that again. Promise!"

"Yes. Yes."

"Promise!" He demanded.

"I promise."

Vampire pulled Monk in by the back of his head and held his forehead to his own. "I am not interested in waiting another lifetime."

The two men held their embrace until the heat of the flames grew unbearable. The side street was now aflame.

"Let's go!" Vampire cried and they ran further down the street full of panicked townspeople screaming for safety and for their lost loved ones.

Without missing a step, Vampire grabbed a solitary child who was crying with no parent to be found. He held him in his arm and pulled Monk from the wrist with his other hand, leading them through a maze of similar looking buildings.

"Who designed this place?" Vampire screamed in frustration.

"Luca!" screamed the child's mother from behind the now open door. "My child!"

She continued screaming as she ran out into the street to where they stood. Vampire handed her the crying boy.

A shadow came across where they stood. It moved slowly as if it were a cloud. Vampire and Monk glanced nervously at one another.

"Madam! You must get inside," Monk instructed.

"Underground," Vampire said.

Luca's mother was so distracted by holding her son that she did not hear them.

"Now!" Vampire demanded with a frightening volume and tone. "Go!"

She looked at him in fear as the shadow cleared and the sunlight came back to cross his eyes and show them twinkle. The woman was immediately mesmerized by the power of the vampire and did as instructed.

"Where are the others?" Monk questioned, quickly changing the subject back to the terror at hand.

"No idea. We have to find them. Come on."

They ran to the end of a covered walkway and looked out at the open street. The other side had stairs that led down.

"Probably a good idea."

They checked each other and searched in all directions.

The sunlight was shining on the street, no shadow. No dragon in sight. They ran out from a covered walkway and continued to survey the sky and up and down the street. They made their way to the stairs that led to a fountain in the center of the Plaza Canta and the grand entrance to the Opera House. Fire still raged further down the street. Café tables were overturned and on fire. Food stands were left unattended with products out of bags and crates. Wooden doorways were still burning with full interiors engulfed in unyielding flames. And the bodies. The horribly sweet smell of burning flesh, some still alive and screaming in pain and yelling for help. Others attempted to speak in just a whisper, as life faded from them.

"Vampire!" Monk yelled and pointed to a group of people hiding.

"Monk!" Vampire yelled back, seeing that the dragon was circling for another attack. Vampire knew Monk's intention and ignited the twinkle in his eye to stop him. It was too late. Monk was in the open with the dragon bearing down directly on him. "Monk!"

Dragon fire came down and upon reaching the stone street began to melt the rock into a liquid lava. Monk was in the center of the attack.

"Monk!" Vampire cried out in pain. He ran into the flame and although he felt the pain of the burn, he did not fear any form of destruction. He reached where Monk had been standing but saw nothing. The lava was flowing. He saw that some of it was flowing down into a hole in the ground. The hole was directly where Monk had been standing. Vampire jumped down through the opening in the ground and landed to the side of the melted rock. The solid bricks were burning hot to the touch.

Vampire's skin had been charred but was quickly recovering. His clothes were aflame. He quickly ripped the burning fabric from his body. He ran and followed the direction of the lava flow, avoiding the molten rock so that his skin could heal. He continued down the underground walkway and the lava stopped. He was back at sea level, near the city walls, when he heard voices.

Monk turned and saw him.

Vampire grabbed him in a tight embrace.

"Didn't we just have this conversation?"

"Yes. I know. There was no time and then…" Monk motioned to AZ, who had opened the trap door in the street causing Monk to drop out of the way of the dragon's flames. "AZ saved me."

"Well, I guess I owe you an apology," Vampire told AZ.

"I'm sure that there will be more of those in our future," AZ said and handed him a pair of pants from his backpack. "Always know the way out, huh?"

"AZ!" screamed Princess as she came running down the tunnel from the left with Sorcerer and Seer. The Twins met up with the group from the tunnel opening on the right.

Vampire felt a chill. Monk noted his discomfort.

"The dragon?" Monk asked quietly, not wanting to alarm the others.

"No. Something awkwardly familiar though."

Vampire peered into the darkness of the tunnel. A ghost appeared.

"Ghost?" questioned Vampire.

The Twins drew their swords.

"Those will do nothing," Ghost informed them. AZ pulled Princess behind him. "Nor will you," Ghost told him as he floated past. "Even less interesting," he said, passing Sorcerer. "Familiar," he said to Seer. "And then, there are you two," he concluded as he stopped in front of Monk and Vampire. "Always the same disturbance from the two of you."

"I know you," Vampire said, although he could not place how he knew him.

Ghost said nothing but maintained an eerie smile. "Total destruction," he announced. "The souls of this city are dwindling in number." Everyone was still in awe of the ghost's presence and his open communication with each of them. "See for yourselves," he instructed and motioned to the thin openings in the walls of the chamber that was protecting them. Each of them looked out the slivers of windows and saw that he spoke the truth.

Seer stood back with his eyes glowing.

"No," Ghost demanded. "Not safe. She will feed first. Stay here and rest. Your journey will be long and demanding. Once she is gone, you can get provisions, although I expect they will be limited, and then be off."

"There was no way to win this," Seer offered. "There was no other outcome for the people of this city."

The others knew that what Seer said was true.

"Did she follow us from Mortua?" Princess asked with remorse.

"No," Seer said. "I saw this earlier. This was going to happen."

"I thought that you were not able to 'see' Immortals," Princess said.

"What I saw were these people. Their pain. I was not able to see the cause, but I was able to see that this city would fall to flame," he argued in his own defense.

The Twins looked at one another skeptically.

"Ghost is right," Seer said. "We should wait here. Our journey will begin at nightfall."

Monk searched around and panicked. "Tink. Where's Tinker?"

They all looked to one another in silence. Monk faced Vampire with added fear.

"I'm sure that he's fine," Vampire said.

"I see him. Yes," Seer stated with certainty. "He is injured, but alive."

"Where?" Monk demanded, grabbing Seer by the arms.

"Monk?" Vampire attempted to calm him. "I will go find him."

The Twins had drawn their swords and were ready to rescue him.

"I cannot see the dragon, but I feel his fear," Seer whispered. "She must be near him."

"Seer. Where is he?" Vampire asked calmly.

A hard, smashing sound came from directly over their heads. Dirt and rocks loosened from the ceiling of the tunnel and fell directly where they stood. A second smash came and provided the same reaction.

Seer pointed directly up.

"Monk?" Vampire questioned.

Monk was already running. The Twins were beside him. Vampire ran after them and soon surpassed their pace. AZ pulled Princess to the side of the tunnel. He looked up and saw that no dirt or rocks were falling. "Stay here," AZ demanded of Princess. He turned and ran after them.

Princess attempted to follow them but was held back by Sorcerer.

"No. She will smell you and attack," he told her. "Seer, let's go!"

Sorcerer and Seer ran after them leaving Ghost and Princess alone in the tunnel.

"He is right, your majesty. She will smell you," Ghost said, in his stoic tone. "It is possible that she is sniffing you out as we speak."

"What do you mean?"

"Monk. No," Vampire demanded. "Monk. Look at me."

Monk refused.

The dragon was sniffing around and feasting on the charred carcasses that lay dead and dying in the city's main square, the Plaza Salamanca. She was unaware of Monk, Vampire, and the Twins.

"Are you planning on just running up to each body to see if it is Tinker?" Vampire asked.

Monk feverishly scanned the square. The Twins were right behind him. Aldrick smacked Monk and Axel and pointed. They spied AZ on the third-floor catwalk that wrapped around the plaza.

"What is he thinking?" Vampire questioned. "That fool."

Monk was back to searching for Tinker when Sorcerer and Seer ran up to them.

"There," he ordered and pointed directly below where AZ was on the exposed walkway.

"What is he doing?" Vampire asked in an increasingly annoyed tone of voice.

Axel signaled AZ as the dragon was feasting with her back to them. AZ signaled back. Axel pointed to where Seer said Tinker was. AZ came to notice that the dragon was preoccupied and peered over the rail. He saw Tinker's motionless body and gave them a 'thumbs-up'.

The dragon raised her head to the sky and sniffed deeply. Something in the air had caught her attention. She moved around feverishly and sniffed up and down. She sniffed the bodies and then the air.

AZ was down behind the rail. The others had all pushed themselves out of sight of the dragon.

"No," Sorcerer whispered. He made an attempt to look out but was pushed back by Vampire. With panic in his eyes, he turned to Vampire, who immediately knew what he feared. Vampire shook his head in silence and pushed him back.

The dragon began to stagger and crush the bodies that lay in the square. She was frantically searching for something. The beast had become obsessed with whatever it was that she had smelled.

"Is it us?" Aldrick asked. "Fresh meat?"

"It is not us," Sorcerer told them. "It is—" He hesitated. "It is the princess."

Princess exposed herself to the dragon. Ghost was flying around the square, whipping the scent of the royal beauty so as to confuse the dragon. AZ peered over the balcony and saw Ghost. He again hid himself as the dragon's attention was drawn in his direction. He then heard Princess rush to the far side of the square and saw the others all preparing to move.

Axel caught his eye and pointed to Princess.

AZ cautiously looked over again and saw her. He rose to his feet. "No!" he screamed.

His scream immediately drew the dragon's attention. She turned to him and let out a prehistoric scream that shook the foundation of the buildings around the plaza. Windows shattered.

Ghost continued circling the square and came closer to the dragon. The dragon began turning in circles. She was hysterical now.

Using the distraction, Vampire ran out to grab the lifeless Tinker. Before he could get there, the dragon caught sight of Princess and focused on her prize. Vampire stopped running and turned his attention to Princess and her safety.

"No!" AZ yelled again.

The dragon shot him an angry stare. The smell of bergamot was in the air. AZ was frozen in place.

"AZ!" Vampire yelled, drawing the dragon's attention. "Run!"

The dragon aimed her mouth at where AZ stood and inhaled. He began to run as fast as he could.

As she was about to release her fiery breath, Tinker turned from his face down position and unleashed a sonic boom from a handheld device that pushed the dragon off her feet and into the walls of the buildings that made up the eastern side of the square. AZ had made it down the stairs and grabbed hold of Princess. They ran back to where the others held their position. Vampire had made his way to Tinker who was already on his feet. The Twins held Monk back.

The dragon had been knocked off her feet and seemed stunned but was very much alive.

"I think that's all that I have," Tinker told Vampire.

"Then we should go," he told him. They cautiously jogged back to the others.

They all made their way back to the unoccupied tunnel.

The dust had settled in the tunnel where they had previously and were again protected. Monk took a non-verbal head count. This time, he started with Tinker.

"So, does someone want to tell me what just happened?" Vampire demanded.

"You," Vampire demanded of Tinker. "What happened to you?"

"Well…" Tinker cautiously began. "I knew that I would be able to use my *Dazer* to stun the dragon…"

"As we all just saw," added Seer.

"But?" Vampire continued looking for more of an explanation.

"Well, I had to go and get it, and then I sort of got caught in the terror and destruction of it all."

"And almost killed," Vampire reminded him.

"And you," Vampire directed his anger at AZ. "What was your plan?"

"I— I didn't really have one. I thought that maybe I could distract the dragon and—"

"And almost get *yourself* killed," Vampire said. "And then there's you," he yelled at Princess. "Please explain."

"There was no way that I was going to be just sitting here while my best friend's life was in such danger. And then Ghost told me about dragons having the greatest appetite for Mermaids so we…"

"You mean—" Vampire stopped himself, which forced the adrenaline from his system. "All that I am saying is that lack of planning could have gotten you all killed. From now on, there will be no more rash responses. We are all in this together, but you are not to prioritize him. And you are not to prioritize her. We have to function as a single unit. That is the best chance we have for success. We cannot beat the dragon until we have all the weapons. All we can do is protect ourselves and each other by thinking clearly. Understood?"

The group nodded in agreement.

"We agree," Sorcerer spoke for the others.

"I mean, it was a shit plan…" offered Axel.

"It was no plan at all," Vampire reminded him.

"But it worked," concluded Aldrick.

They looked at Tinker and gave him a wink. He smiled. Princess hugged him from the side and joined in the laughter. AZ laughed, too, but then met Vampire's gaze and turned his expression serious. But soon he laughed again, and this time avoided Vampire's stare. Vampire focused on Monk and saw that he, too, was smiling. Monk walked over to Vampire and hugged him.

"They're right," he whispered. "It worked."

"Monk?" Vampire whispered and pulled him to the side.

"I know," he said and pulled him in again. "But realize that your demands go for you, too."

"What do you mean?"

"You cannot prioritize me. This has to play out for the betterment of all. None of us can behave selfishly."

Vampire nodded.

"That doesn't mean 'yes'," Monk told him.

"Sure, it does."

"Neither does that," Monk said with a laugh. "Just say the word 'yes'."

"Yes."

Sorcerer pulled the Twins to the side to speak to them in confidence. "Quentin Sinclair," he told them.

"Who is *Quentin Sinclair?*" they asked in unison.

"He is," Princess told them. "Brae Salingalees," she added, telling them her own name.

"Are you kidding me?" Vampire demanded. "There's a dragon who is possibly continuing to piss fire on this city and I am trying to figure a way to swoosh her away, so if you don't mind—"

"Thaddeus," Monk said, pointing to Vampire. "Phineas," he added, pointing to himself.

"Kindron Smug," Seer said, with a wave.

Vampire threw his hands into the air and paced.

"Azurus Perculfilus," AZ added, with a handshake. "I go by AZ."

"We understand why," Aldrick said, in jest.

The Twins looked to Tinker. Tinker glanced away and immediately to Monk who shrugged his shoulders.

"Tinker," he said, with humility. "My name is Tinker."

Princess smiled and again pulled him in for a hug.

"I named him," Monk admitted. They looked at him with uncertainty. "What? He was always tinkering about. I had to call him something. I mean, the other option would have gotten him beat up every single day of his life."

"No," Tinker demanded.

"Squirrel," Monk said, plainly. "He moved about with such nervousness," Monk stared at Tinker and laughed. Tinker shook his head. "And he followed me everywhere," Monk added, playfully ruffling Tinker's hair.

“Still does,” Seer added.

“To Hell and back,” Tinker said, nodding with strong conviction.

“To Hell and back,” Monk repeated.

Monk turned to see the Twins’ continued disbelief. “What? I named a dog ‘Dog’ once, too. It just made things easier,” he said, with a shake of the head as he walked out into the now demolished plaza. Immediately, the mood turned serious.

“She’s gone,” Ghost told them as he hovered nearby. He led them out of the tunnel and back to the streets.

“So much destruction,” Princess said, tearing up. “Is there anyone left alive?” she asked Ghost.

“Very few,” he replied.

Princess turned to Sorcerer. “We need to get word back to Mortua for aid.”

“We need to get the living to Mortua,” Seer said.

Sorcerer nodded and turned to put forth an incantation that attracted a white dove.

“Tink?” Princess asked.

He handed her a pencil and paper. She wrote a message to her mother to call for assistance for the people of Dellai. She handed the note to Sorcerer, who placed it in the clawed foot of the dove. The dove took to the air.

Vampire and Monk were in the center of the plaza, as was Tinker. Tinker had pulled a copper box from his inner jacket pocket.

"What is that?" AZ asked.

"It is a *Jewel Indicator*," Tinker told him, as he hit the button on the side. "You are sure that she is gone?" he asked Ghost. "And not coming back?"

Ghost nodded.

He looked to Seer. Seer's eyes were aglow. The red brilliance went out.

"I do not see pain in our near future," he told him.

"That confirms that she is gone," Monk stated. "But what are you looking for?"

"A possible weakness," Tinker replied.

Vampire attempted to argue.

"I know," Tinker rushed. "But we still need to defend ourselves, and if she lost a scale or a claw, we may be able to find some weakness that she possesses."

"He's not wrong," Monk told Vampire.

Tinker made a condescending sound. "No surprise there."

The top of the box began to glow. Tinker lowered it to the ground and stepped back. A beam of light shot out from the top. The beam pulled itself back and then the sides of the box began to light up and produce beams in an alternating fashion. The light beams began to move faster and faster until all four sides of the box were producing light. The entire ground of the plaza was now aglow. The beams of light began to move upward in unison, illuminating what was left of the walls that surrounded the plaza. As the light moved, it left glowing remnants behind.

Seer walked over to one of them and picked up a ruby ring. He held it aloft.

The Twins looked to one another with excitement. "Any way we can have that?" they asked Tinker.

"No," Vampire replied.

They held their arms up in surrender and stepped backwards.

"There!" Tinker exclaimed as he pointed up to an area of the third-floor walkway that was now inaccessible.

Monk faced Vampire and nodded. Vampire growled in frustration and squatted. He took a leap that seemed effortless and landed on the edge of what was left of the flooring. He reached out and pulled the glowing gem from where it had embedded in the wall. He examined it as the glow receded. It was the largest diamond that any of them had ever seen. Vampire turned and dropped to land and stepped in time, as if he had just been walking.

"Will this be big enough?" he joked to Monk.

"Not exactly the cut that I was hoping for, but…" Monk joked back with a wink.

Ghost blew through Vampire, and Vampire followed him away from the others. "There is something that you must know."

"What is it?"

"Mavi has been looking for you," he told him. "She sent me to find you six years ago."

"What does she want?" Vampire asked, knowing that Mavi, the controller of Gokyuzu, the cloud city that sits between dimensions, may have an understanding of what was happening.

"She did not say. Only to find you and bring you to her," Ghost confessed.

Vampire was quiet as he thought. "We will need a way up there," he told him. "And I am not letting Monk out of my sight." He watched as Monk and the others searched for survivors. "Sorcerer cannot create a portal without it being on someone's radar. We need another way." He looked up at the sky. "A rainbow can get us there." He walked back to the group. "We are heading to Dremora," he told them. "There is someone there who can help us."

CHAPTER 14
City of Dremora

"So, this is what Hell looks like," AZ said, cautiously.

"Parts of it," Vampire replied.

Seer's eyes were aglow. "Down there," he told them and pointed to the narrow pedestrian walkway to the left.

The dark streets were poorly lit and the slippery ground that made up the uneven paths were as black and slimy as the building exteriors. The wet stones reflected light from the dim streetlamps and the moon when the clouds moved enough to uncover its glow. The cracked moon glowed white. The time of the Blood Moon had ended, and thoughts of celebration were over.

Even in the daylight, Dremora was a dark place. It was originally built in the shadows of Mount Condamner to protect it from assault and had been a peaceful place. However, as The Dark Sisters rose to power and magic became tainted, attacks from neighboring kingdoms became more common. Dremora had become a city of ruin and dark magic. It was now best known for its trading of illegal market goods and services.

Seer held his arm out to stop Vampire from going forward.

"She is not to be trusted," he told him with conviction.

"She's a Leprechaun. They are never to be trusted," Vampire assured him.

The air was humid and thick. The poor lighting and the fog limited how far one could see. As they turned a corner, the street became completely dark. The fog kept the moonlight from reaching the wet stones.

Sorcerer said an enchantment that lit random street torches. But the wind blew most of them out.

"Tink?" Monk said.

"Already on it," Tinker replied.

Tinker had left his horse and cart outside of the city. He knew that had he brought it in, it would be ransacked, and all his work would be lost. However, he did anticipate a few needs.

He put a visor with a light source on his head. Unlike Sorcerer's more subtle approach, Tinker's light was bright. The shocking intensity forced the previously unseen alley squatters to dodge out of sight through open windows, broken doors, and sewers. The vermin that crept across the walls and slid across the ground also scattered in fear of the light. The path was now clear except for the occasional creature that ran through and out of sight on the other side of the street.

Tinker's light initially followed the creatures as they ran. Each of them disappeared into the walls. As they walked closer, Aldrick felt along a wall but noted that it was solid. *Where did they go?* he thought.

A sewer plate in the middle of the street began to open as bony fingers pushed it up and slid it over the stones with a screeching sound. Tinker quickly shone his light and saw the fingers begin to burn and pull back into the hole in the street.

Very dim candlelight came from what seemed to be a pub. As they walked past, they were able to make out the glowing silver eyes of some of those inside.

"You should feel right at home," Princess joked to AZ, with a quiver of fear in her voice.

He cracked a smile but only to be polite. "Just like the Taverne Ayer."

Fear was sitting heavy in their minds. They huddled closer together.

Vampire was quiet. Monk watched him for any reaction. Sorcerer squinted as he surveyed their surroundings. Seer was again using his gifts to guide them all towards their destination.

"She's in there," he said, and pointed to a wall at the far right of the alley.

"Ummm, that's a wall," Axel announced.

"Only if you see a wall," Sorcerer told him. He felt around his belt and closed his eyes to sense the contents of each of the vials. His hand moved slowly around his side and then began to increase in speed and accuracy as he stopped for various seconds of time over three different small bottles.

"Three parts, one part, three parts," he said, as he took the vials from his belt. "Do you mind?" he asked Vampire, who was standing closest to him.

Vampire extended his hands. Sorcerer placed a small iron bowl in his palm.

"Three parts," he began, as he poured out the glowing solid particles of the first vial. "One part," he continued, adding a greenish powder from the second. "And this is the tricky part," he said, looking at Vampire and taking out another iron bowl, holding it upside down. "Three parts," he concluded as he caught the chartreuse vapor in the upside-down bowl. "Thank you," he said, bringing the two bowls together and speaking an enchantment with his eyes closed. He swirled the bowls slowly in a counterclockwise direction, being sure to keep the rims in perfect contact to not allow any of the potion to escape. After the third swirl, he lifted the far side higher than the near side and blew with force. The potion spread through the air and onto the wall. The potion covered and illuminated the wall and then started to drip down. The wall was the same, with the simple exception of an open doorway.

"That was impressive," Axel told Sorcerer.

"Thank you," he replied. "But do not enter that door. You must enter the wall."

The Twins glanced at one another with curiosity. AZ and Princess stepped up to examine the wall but did not proceed further.

"It's a wall," AZ told them.

Immediately, a hand came out of the wall and grabbed Princess by the throat. AZ attempted to pull her back, but she had already been pulled through the wall. AZ ran into the wall which was now solid.

"Damn it," Sorcerer yelled. "The door!"

Vampire and Monk were already in. The others followed with Tinker maintaining his light source. Even with the light, there was only blackness. The light was on and intensely bright, yet it showed nothing.

"What's going on?" AZ asked, panicking. "Where is she?"

"She's on the other side of this void," Vampire told him. "We are in that place where light stops moving."

"At the end of the rainbow," Monk added.

"Rainbows are full of colors," AZ argued.

"Rainbows reflect colors," Monk told him. "Dremora is a point on every rainbow. Void of light and color. We need to get to the other end of this rainbow."

"And it's a good thing that we have this," Tinker added, as he pulled out the diamond scale of the Jeweled Dragon and held it aloft.

"Everyone must touch and maintain contact with it, or you will be left here," he told them as he kept his light source facing down and away from the dragon scale. "Everybody touching?"

A synchronized 'yes' was heard and then he looked up to shine the light on the scale. The prism of colors was magnificent. Thousands of shades of each color danced around the void. The blackness began to absorb the varied hues until it faded and the world behind it was visible.

"Do not let go," Tinker told them. "Not yet. I will tell you when."

As the world behind the blackness came into view, shapes started to form. It was a field of tulips. Princess was standing next to a tall, red-haired beauty. She did not seem to be in any sign of distress.

"Okay. You can let go," Tinker told them.

Vampire, Monk, Sorcerer, and Seer were already walking over to the two women.

AZ was hesitant to let go, but then attempted to rush past them.

"Slow down, boy." Vampire held him back with his arm across his chest. "Cadet Le Bougier is not to be trusted."

"Oh, please," Cadet said, through her laughter. "You're one to talk."

"You can let go, now," Tinker told the Twins, who were still holding the scale as they continued to piece together what had just happened and hoped that they would be able to keep it.

"Where are we?" Aldrick asked.

"Dremora!" Cadet yelled out. "Or rather, what exists in the shadows of Dremora."

"It's beautiful," Seer said, as he observed around the open field and smelled the fresh and fragrant air.

"We keep it hidden to keep the tourists away," Cadet joked. "Hello, Phineas," the striking Leprechaun said to Monk. "Nine lives later, I would have hoped that you learned to avoid him, but nope!"

Monk could not remember ever meeting Cadet Le Bougier. He had only heard rumors of her trickery. Her fiery hair, graceful silhouette, charm, and lightness were things that he would not have forgotten.

"She has known of you, but you have never met her," Vampire whispered.

"And who's fault is that?" she asked and walked over to them.

AZ quickly ran to Princess. "Are you okay?"

"Yes. Fine." She gently pushed him away.

"He's all 'damsel-in-distress' about her, isn't he?" Cadet asked the group regarding AZ. "She definitely does not need your protection, kid. But you would be wise to get under her umbrella," she joked. "Speaking of umbrellas," she continued as she stopped in front of Vampire and looked him in the eyes. "How's the perfume business?"

"I've discovered other purposes lately," Vampire told her.

"Same purpose," she said, and turned to Monk. "You know about the umbrella symbol? No?" She peeked back at Vampire. "We got rich off you," she told Monk. "Your scent. But he never thought that it was right, so he discontinued it. The money dried up and here we are."

"What is she talking about?" Monk asked Vampire.

Cadet skipped over to a granite boulder in the middle of the tulip field and leapt up, landing in a reclined position.

"Bring it here," she demanded of Tinker. "Let me see it." She pointed to the dragon scale. Tinker walked over to her, and she leapt back down to the ground. "I do like a man who does what he's told," she said, flirtatiously.

Tinker's face turned red with embarrassment.

"What do you want for it?" she asked.

"We need—" Vampire began.

"I didn't ask you," she interrupted. "I asked him." She faced Tinker and winked.

Tinker attempted to speak, but his nerves kept him from saying anything.

Cadet giggled. "Relax kid. You're not my type. I just like to play."

Tinker's voice cracked as he said, "We need to know how to get to Gokyuzu."

"Mavi is looking for me," Vampire told her.

"Why?"

"Not sure yet, but probably to do with the beast from which this scale came," Vampire replied and pointed at the dragon scale.

"You think it's that serious?" she asked.

"Yes," Vampire replied. "The Jeweled Dragon has already attacked and destroyed Dellai. Who knows her next move."

Cadet's playfulness came to an end. She became quiet and introspective.

"Well then, who's coming?" she asked with a renewed sense of purpose and bravery. "One rainbow won't be able to take all of you," Cadet began explaining to mostly blank and confused faces. "It can only attach to so many energies at once. And you need a Leprechaun to give you access to the Rainbow Network." She motioned towards

Tinker. "Unless, you know what this guy knows. Using that giant diamond was genius."

She was met with confused stares. Cadet gave Monk a cautious glare.

"At the end of each rainbow is—" Cadet began.

"A pot of gold," Axel interjected.

"No. That's what we tell people, so they ignore the glowing, colored stone they see and think it worthless." Cadet walked over and sized up Axel. "There is a Cez stone at the end of each and every rainbow. A Cez stone is created when a star is pulled from the skies. It could be in this world or another. They are the most precious form of energy, and their value is greater than anything else in any realm, any dimension. But they are visible only as long as the rainbow is present. If the stone is not harvested, it will go dormant and then only a tracker can see its true radiance." She turned back to AZ. "You must be the boy from Mortua." She looked at Vampire. "How many has he found?"

"You can't be trusted," Vampire told her.

"What is that supposed to mean?" she asked. "I'm really starting to take offense to the anti-Leprechaun agenda that you're promoting," Cadet said, with her hands on her hips.

"Get over yourself," Vampire said. "You are untrustworthy, and at this point, it has nothing to do with you being a Leprechaun."

Cadet stood with her arms crossed and refused to help.

"Six," Vampire told her to keep her interest. "But that is not why we are here."

"Gokyuzu. Right!" she remembered but kept that information for later.

Cadet reached into a pouch that she kept around her waist. She pulled out flecks of silver and gold and shook them in her hands. She whispered *Gokyuzu* and then knelt down to place them on the ground. Immediately, colors began to combine and come apart as they climbed into the air.

They all watched as the colors created a rainbow and lit the darkness above Dremora.

"Come on," Vampire said to Monk. "Ghost," he ordered. "You too will be joining us." He then looked at Sorcerer. "We will meet you in the caves below the city. Keep them all together."

Sorcerer nodded and the others gave them assurance that they would wait.

Chapter 15
Gokyuzu, the Cloud City

Traveling via rainbow stimulates the senses to their fullest. The traveler appears as part of a glistening gem that has been cut to perfection to catch the light and draw full attention. The sound is like a perfectly pitched, high C on a violin; similar to the one the Jeweled Dragon emits before striking. The aroma varies with the color, but the fragrant scents are all intoxicating. The moisture adds to a taste that charms its way into the mouth like an infused drink that quenches a thirst that had not been recognized. And lastly, the feeling of such travel is its most alluring trait. The tingling sensation is comfortable enough to not feel like tickling, but more like a gentle stimulation that is almost sensual.

It was a very rare encounter to have met someone who has ever traveled by way of the Rainbow Network, but the experience is unforgettable.

The path of the rainbow met the lavender cloud at a point just before its apex. Cadet, Vampire, and Monk all stepped forward as they felt the solid surface under their feet.

"Monk," Cadet began. "I'm impressed. I did not realize you had traveled by rainbow before."

"First time," he told her.

She was taken aback. "You seemed to know how to do it without me saying anything."

"I just did what he did." He glanced at Vampire and smiled.

"Cute," she said, rolling her eyes. "But I doubt very much that this is going to be a honeymoon. So, I suggest that you wipe those smiles off your faces and get back to business."

They stood in a field full of glistening, white flowers. The sky seemed endless. It had a sense of a greenish golden light. The air had a fresh aroma to it; unfamiliar but welcomed. They could not see anything other than the field and the open sky. The field sloped up, limiting any view of the world below. No one was in sight. Monk and Cadet walked towards the edge of the field.

"I wouldn't do that," Vampire told them. "The closer you get, the more holes you find. The more holes you find, the more likely you will fall through one and then…"

"First step is a doozy," Ghost joked but grew serious as he appeared directly in front of Monk, as if to scare him into stepping back and towards the edge.

Monk stared him down but heeded the warning. He walked through Ghost and controlled the eerie sensation of the chill.

"Why is Mavi looking for you?" Cadet asked.

"We do not yet know," Vampire told her. "Ask Ghost."

"You're about to find out," Ghost told them and vanished.

"Hullo," came a greeting in an alluring feminine voice.

A woman was standing in the field as if she had been there the whole time and they'd somehow overlooked her. Cadet appeared confused as she tried to figure it out.

"She came out of nowhere," she said.

"Mavi," Monk said, with a smile.

"And you brought me a gift," Mavi added, extending her hand for Vampire to kiss. "Two, actually," she said in jest, extending her other hand to Cadet. "Thaddeus, time continues to be exceptionally kind to you."

"And to you," he replied with an air of flirtation as he kissed her bejeweled hand.

"You must be the Leprechaun," she said to Cadet, who curtsied and bowed her head.

"At your service," she said.

"Oh," Mavi laughed. "I hope that to be true. Getting here is no simple feat. You obviously have a very particular skill set; one I would like to tap into." Mavi gently drew her long plum-colored fingernails across Cadet's neck and down her chest.

Mavi was a woman of true distinction. She was the controller of Gokyuzu, the Cloud City. Mavi's roots were Amazonian. She was a queen and the fiercest warrior. She fought alongside the Immortal warrior, Gnim, and had at one time been gifted Gnim's ruby shield. However, Two throusand years ago, she found herself in battle against another Immortal warrior, Sansit. His rage towards her grew at the sight of Gnim's shield. He fought without remorse and almost destroyed Mavi. That was when the shield was broken into two parts, the outer gold metal ring and the ruby face.

At the time of Mavi's near death, the Heavens opened up to her and offered her life. It came with the price of running Gokyuzu and a sense of immortality. Mavi's ego could not decline the offer, and for two thousand of years, she has run Gokyuzu like a business; watching it prosper and grow in importance to all of the dimensions.

Although Gokyuzu always functioned as a point of transfer between dimensions, it has never been bound to any of them. This allowed it to float freely. However, travel between dimensions came with a cost.

Angels and demons have long traveled through Gokyuzu to entertain themselves with mortals. The price for their entrance and exit was a piece of their wings, white for angels and black for demons. Mavi, although not Immortal, used the feathers to stay alive and to prosper.

Mavi realized that Cadet was in awe of Gokyuzu.

"Why would I want to leave this?" Mavi asked her. "I see what happens on the other sides. I'm not interested. I enjoy being celebrated; being…" she paused for dramatic effect, "worshiped for what I supply to the cosmos."

"As you should," Cadet agreed.

"And you can judge me all you like!" she yelled out.

Monk and Vampire traded glances and shook their heads.

"But I know your secrets too, Ghost," she said.

Ghost appeared over her shoulder.

"You are trapped, just like I am," he told her.

"A matter of perspective, my dear," she said. "Just like the sins that these angels and demons find themselves fighting and bonding over." She motioned for them to follow her through the open field. "It's true. I am trapped by my pride and greed, whereas you are trapped by your envy and anger. You *finally* completed your assignment."

An elaborate tent appeared in the field. Mavi guided them towards it.

There was a line of bodies in front of it. Their skin was tinged with various shades of green. As Mavi approached, the angels and demons standing in that line attempted to gain her favor. Their colors began to change.

"Welcome to the show," she told them, as a muscular demon pulled back the curtained entrance to the tent and exposed the action inside.

An orgy was in full effect. They saw acts of lust, gluttony, and greed. Pride showed itself through Mavi and the demon allowing the others through the curtain, and there was envy in those not chosen. Sloth was represented by the ones elevated above the crowd and not participating and lastly, there were acts of wrath. Angels strangling demons. Demons beating angels. All of these acts ended with a kiss.

"Everyone wins here," Mavi told them. "Perspective. We were all born with sin, and we all use it to our advantage. That could be through creating acts that benefit others but also by ignoring them and benefitting only ourselves." She looked back at Ghost. He faded from view.

They walked through the crowd that now seemed wholly focused on a particular sin: Lust.

Vampire gazed at Monk. Monk pulled him in for a sensual kiss.

"Go ahead, my dear," Mavi told Cadet. "I'm sure that you can find pleasure in any of these options."

Cadet smiled as she bit into her lower lip. She turned and was pulled down by two demons and an angel. She did not resist the hands that pulled her in.

Mavi smiled with a proud grin and walked through the crowd.

"She is gone," a barely visible Ghost said.

Monk and Vampire slowly pulled away from each other, although they maintained their increased sexual energies. They were here for a reason, and they needed to find out what that reason was.

"She blackmails these creatures and steals a bit of their Immortality," Monk said, reviewing what they knew. "For herself, to remain alive."

"Seems harmless enough," Ghost interjected.

"Yeah," Vampire thought aloud. "That's what's wrong with it." He watched Mavi disappear behind a curtain. "Let's go," Vampire said.

"What about Cadet?" Monk asked.

"I'd rather do this without her," Vampire replied.

"Agreed," Monk said.

Ghost disappeared.

CHAPTER 16
Gokyuzu, the Cloud City

Behind the curtain was the entrance to the true city in the clouds. The angels and demons did not enter the true city; they stayed on the outskirts, in the fields. That was the bridge between dimensions, their sinful playground. The city was a place of business. The transactions that kept the bridge open between dimensions were financed and calculated behind the curtain.

The city itself was made of towering skyscrapers, the overall design feeling utilitarian. The pristine streets looked as though they had never been stepped upon. The buildings were spaced with enough distance between them to allow the golden light from all dimensions to fall onto the streets. A slight snowfall was in the air.

The city contained a very different energy than the tent. This was the business side of Gokyuzu. The creatures that hustled through them were of various species. Monk noted that some were animals from his world. However, they were walking upright with top hats and satchels. He saw humans walking in conversation with others made of fire or water. A rock creature was sipping tea, served by a fairy the size of a bird, as he was reading a newspaper.

Vampire snapped his fingers to draw Monk's attention. "I get it, but we are here for her." He nodded towards Mavi, who walked ahead of them.

Mavi was walking half a block ahead and strutting down the middle of the street. Creatures repeatedly approached her and asked her to sign papers.

"And I'm the proud one?" Vampire joked.

"Some of that is business, I would guess," Monk said.

"And most of it is ego. Those creatures are fans. She cannot live without the spotlight," he went on.

"You're sounding a bit jealous," Monk said.

"No," Vampire assured him. "This was offered to me. I refused it."

Monk was taken aback. "What do you mean, 'offered'?"

"When I chose not to destroy humanity, I was offered Gokyuzu by the Enlightenment. I could have ruled here and controlled the gateway."

"Ah," Monk said, as he understood. "Well, all the better for me."

"And me," Vampire replied with a wink. "Now, let's go. She went down there."

Vampire pointed ahead to what looked like the entrance to an underground station. He scanned around to make sure that no one was following them. He and Monk descended the stairs. At the bottom of the staircase was a train platform. A bistro table had been set with floating fairy lights. Mavi was seated and sipping from a champagne flute.

"Come, boys," she invited them. "It's just us."

They walked forward with full bravado.

"I do like that look on you, Monk," she said, with a flirtatious smile as she acknowledged Monk's strong posture. "I'm used to it on him," she added with a wrinkle of her nose as she glared at Vampire.

"Why are we here?" Monk asked.

"I have been looking for you for years," she told Vampire. "I had sent Ghost to find you and to bring you here when he came through, but he failed to do so in a timely manner."

"Yet, here we are," Vampire teased back.

"A little too late," Mavi argued. "The Jeweled Dragon has already been sent."

Monk could not hide the worry on his face.

"Yes. Of course, I know about her," she told them, as if insulted. "The paperwork all had to be filed through here before she was birthed from that volcano." She looked at Vampire. "I don't blame you for not taking this position. It has its perks, but also its headaches. You cannot imagine how many things go wrong every day in every dimension and every world in every time. And if that was not enough, I'm supposed to keep the 'fallen ones' entertained out in the tent to keep them from screwing anything else up before their trials."

Monk seemed confused.

"Think of it as a happy prison. They don't even know that they are awaiting a trial for their 'fallen' actions. They all think that it's a reward or that they are getting away with something. Seriously — mortal, Immortal, human, beast; it doesn't matter. Ego is the same, no matter what." Mavi shook her head with disappointment as she finished her last sip of bubbly. The glass refilled itself as if from the air.

"So, any idea what you may have that can help us destroy the dragon?" Vampire asked.

"How about a mountain of paperwork?" she joked. "Kidding." They did not laugh. Mavi thought for a minute. "Look," she began with all seriousness. "I know that you don't trust me. Hell — I don't trust me."

"But I also know that if that beast wins, I too lose everything. Everything."

She stood up and began to pace. "This place. This is me."

Mavi marched up and stood in front of Monk. "I do not know for sure if this is what you need to hear, but I have information that might help."

"Go ahead then," Monk said, staring back into her eyes. "Tell us what you know."

Mavi started pacing again, while she collected her thoughts. "All right!" she yelled as she broke the silence. "First off, the seers. You cannot trust them."

"We'll add them to the list," Monk told her, but awaited more information.

She threw her hand up and shook her head as she continued. "I know. I know. You have one. And you've known him for most of this life. But think about it, Monk. There was a time when he was dark. You know it to be true." Monk did not argue. "This whole quest that you have ventured out upon," she continued, to the surprise of both Vampire and Monk. "What? You think that my knowledge of things stops at the edge of this cloud? No, no, my friends... Mavi's arms extend far and wide. They have to, for me to make sure I am doing what I need to in order to preserve what is mine."

Vampire nodded at Monk as Mavi continued. "This all started with a prophecy. That prophecy was put forth by seers. But the prophecy only tells part of the story. It does not tell the end."

"That prophecy was in place before your quest, my darling," Mavi said to Vampire. "It's the reason that I called for you." She screamed out in frustration. "I'm trying to help you, damn it!"

Monk realized that she was right.

"The Enlightenment dare not allow knowledge of how this will end. Truth is, they do not yet know. But you must know this. They are manipulating this whole thing and fighting each other for control. As of yet, they cannot pick a side. But they will come together. They will act as one and rage against anyone in their way."

Monk heard her and fought the feeling that she was right. "That's what you know?" he asked her. "That's why we are here?"

"No," she said. "That was just free advice."

"Mavi," Vampire said. "We do not have much time."

"That is true," she agreed. "The Cez stones. You have them all now, yes?" They looked at one another, not sure whether to divulge that they did not yet have all of them in their possession. "That means 'yes'," Mavi said, shaking her head and walking up to Monk. "It's you."

"What's me?" he asked.

"The Cez stones," she answered.

"I don't understand," he told her.

"I do," Vampire said.

Mavi smiled as she continued to stare into Monk's eyes. "Tell him," she demanded. "Tell him," she repeated, moving to stand in front of Vampire.

Vampire walked over to Monk. "The marks on your side, Monk."

"The Dracu constellation?"

"The dragon constellation, yes. When I took it from the Heavens and the stars fell, they became Cez stones: the exact ones that we seek."

"They are connected to you," Mavi said. "She is here for you. She is looking to destroy you and then all of time and space."

"We already knew that!" Vampire yelled.

"But you didn't know that you have power over her with those stones. You know that you need those stones, but not how to use them," Mavi said. "You can turn this tide. You can win this. But you will need to get those stones aligned. And you need to find the Book of Spells. Ileana, the fallen Queen of Witches, made a copy of all of the Witches' spells. The spell that tells you how to use the stones is in that book."

Vampire walked over to her. "Mavi," he said as she collected herself and calmed down. "We know about the Three of Legend and the stones, and have figured out that the sword is the Sword of Sansit.

But we do not know about the shield. What shield is it and where can we find it?"

Mavi cracked a smile. "My shield, the one that Gnim gave me. Last I knew, it… or at least part of it…was in the city of Istanbul."

"And the rest of it?" Vampire asked.

Mavi chuckled. "Add that to your list of things to do. It was lost. Even I don't know where it is."

Vampire and Monk stared at each other in silence. A loud eruption occurred.

"What was that?" Monk asked, as the explosion shook the floor.

"I don't know, but we had better find out," Vampire answered, leading them towards the stairs.

"There will be Hell to pay!" Mavi yelled out as they reached the street. "After all, things like this are usually Hell's fault."

They saw nothing unusual. Night had fallen. The night sky glowed orange, as if it were about to snow. That was the natural night sky in Gokyuzu. The skies from the different dimensions gave it that color.

Those walking on the street seemed cautious but continued with their regular business.

"Thaddeus!" yelled Cadet as she and Ghost came running and floating up to them. "It's bad," she insisted.

"What's bad?" Mavi demanded.

"The Jeweled Dragon," Cadet told them.

All eyes widened.

"What? Where?" Monk questioned.

"She attacked the tent," Cadet told them. "So many were destroyed," she explained, sadly.

Mavi also reacted with a strong sense of loss.

"Where is she now?" Vampire asked.

Cadet looked at Ghost.

"Feeding," Ghost said.

Mavi again let out a pained sigh.

"Mavi," Monk said.

"No," she said.

"Mavi, please," he begged.

She shook her head. "This is where I belong," she said, as she began to cry. "This is what I have done and what I will be judged and remembered for."

"Mavi!" Vampire yelled at her. "You and this city will be destroyed."

Mavi collected her emotions and spoke with clarity. "And that is why you must go." She grabbed Monk's hands. "You must find that book. I cannot help you with that."

Monk nodded that he understood.

A line of fire shot across the sky and into the tallest skyscraper. The building was sliced in half and the upper part slid off and fell to the ground. Its impact came with more shaking and screams. The dust that followed blinded everyone.

"Ghost!" Vampire yelled. "Lead us to safety."

"You have to go!" Mavi yelled.

"We have to get out of here!" Cadet yelled. "But a rainbow will surely draw her attention."

"I can help with that," Mavi told them. "Follow me!"

They ran through the panicked streets and followed Mavi into an alleyway. Mavi pulled a remote control from her pocket and hit a series of buttons. The wall at the end of the alleyway began to separate. Light illuminated the alley as two sets of wings floated and softly flapped. One was white and the other black.

"It's not what you were expecting, I'm sure. But it will get you to safety," Mavi told them as she handed the white wings to Monk. "You will have to hold Cadet."

Monk nodded but struggled with how to put the wings on.

"Just turn around," she told him. "They will do what they need to do."

Vampire grabbed the black wings and Cadet took them from him to hold them to his back. Both Monk and Vampire felt the wings push into their backs. Monk felt the tattoo on his back tingle.

"Just think about what you need them to do, and they will do the rest. It is totally safe, I promise," Mavi said.

"This time, I do trust you," Monk told her and gave her a tight hug. "Come with us," he pleaded again.

Mavi ignored his request. "And Thaddeus," she called with a softness in her eyes. "Good luck."

Vampire thanked Mavi as he stared into her eyes.

"You can't enchant me, fool," she reminded him as she saw the twinkle in his eyes. "Now go," she told him with a smile. "I am where I am supposed to be."

Monk understood and shook his head. Vampire made a last-ditch effort to convince her to join them.

"Take this," she said to him as she removed a bracelet and put it on his wrist. "This way, you will always remember me for who I truly was." Vampire did not look at the bracelet but rather into her eyes.

"I already told you, your glam won't work on me," she told him. "Go. Go now."

"Ghost!" Vampire yelled.

"I have a route," he told him.

"Just see yourself flying and the wings will do as you need," Mavi reminded them.

Monk was hovering with his white wings flapping in a slow and relaxed fashion. "Cadet," he said and extended his hand.

She grabbed it and he pulled her tight against himself.

"I have you," he told her.

"I know," she said.

Vampire was now aloft, too. His black wings moved with the same control as Monk's.

"Thank the angels and the demons for us," he told Mavi with a wink.

She nodded.

"We need to go," Ghost told them and floated off.

Vampire followed. Monk's larger wing movement seemed more relaxed but still kept up with Vampire's. Cadet felt the cool air as she looked back, over Monk's shoulder, to Mavi. Mavi's expression continued to be content. She had decided her own path and was at peace with where it would lead.

As they rose higher above the fiery inferno and toppled buildings below, they had a different understanding of the interactions between dimensions. They saw angels and demons fighting together. They saw creatures of all sorts working to get each other to safety. The efforts were futile, but they were efforts, nonetheless.

The Jeweled Dragon continued her assault on the Cloud City. It was engulfed in flames. She circled above as her fire continued to rain down upon it.

Ghost led them around the city, opposite the dragon and underneath the cloud before descending to the ground below. The Jeweled Dragon did not spot them. Cadet watched in horror as Gokyuzu began to crack and then fall. She noted the sky was changing, as well. The city was splitting in half and the opening between the dimensions was about to close.

"Monk!" she screamed as a large part of the city fell towards them.

Monk innately knew to fly out of the way by her tone of voice. The solid piece caught fire and was the first of many pieces to fall to the ground like a meteor. Explosions and fires followed. Craters were pushed deep into the land. Gokyuzu was no more.

Mavi, too, was no more.

CHAPTER 17
City of Dremora

As Gokyuzu was breaking apart and its pieces were falling into different dimensions, the Twins found a cave along the river where the group could hide and stay safe from the detritus that dropped to the ground and created craters upon impact.

The destruction continued. Tinker was looking out of the cave opening through yet another peculiar spyglass. He kept repositioning the lenses in and out to offer different focuses as he observed the night sky in the direction of the dragon. She continued to fly around the last remnants of the cloud city and fan the flames with her powerful wing movements. The reign of fire was also dispensed through the cloud and pushed downward by the fanning of the dragon's wings.

Tinker pulled the spyglass to his forehead and feverishly turned pages in old books, some with precious metal binders, before he went back to tracking the dragon's movements in the sky. He made notes in his illegible penmanship and rummaged through the drawers of his cart for various measuring devices, which he used to make calculations. Tinker sketched with colored pencils in notebooks already containing drawings of fantastic creatures, mostly those of legend, but some of truth. Included in these drawings was one of a gryphon and her chicks and another that looked like a winged man. Tinker's page-turning was feverish and the rest of the group knew not to ask questions.

Princess comforted AZ, who appeared shaken with concern for Monk, Vampire, Cadet, and Ghost. The Twins sat quietly with their eyes closed and their hands on their swords. Seer searched what was left of the city above for life but found none. Sorcerer, like Tinker, was active during this quiet time. He mixed combinations of herbs and liquids into tubes of various lengths and smaller, bulbous glass containers with cork stoppers. He spoke the words of ancient spells as he continued with his task. He went off into one of the tunnels and returned with a tattered cloth. He ripped the cloth into pieces and doused each of them in some of the liquid solutions he was preparing.

"Give me your swords," he demanded of the Twins, and then of AZ. He rubbed the soaked fabric onto the swords, spreading the potion that temporarily changed the color of the blades. The color change was different for each sword.

"Why is it different?" questioned Princess.

"The color comes not from the potion, but rather from the soul and purpose of the swordsman."

"Or Swordswoman." She pulled a sword from under her coat and then smaller weapons from her leg harnesses and small circular blades from her belt loop.

"Or Swordswoman," Sorcerer agreed and rubbed the potion onto her sword and her other assorted weapons.

Once she'd hidden those blades again, she surprised them all by pulling out a second sword. Sorcerer chuckled as he added the potion to this blade, as well.

"Where has she been keeping those?" asked Aldrick

"Up my sleeve, so to speak," she replied.

"And I expect a few other tricks," followed Axel.

"No. Much more than a few," she said.

"Regardless," Sorcerer spoke through his laughter. "This potion hardens the blades and makes the strength that of the bearer's intent and honor in his or her purpose."

"As long as the purpose is pure," Princess added.

"Correct. We do not know what other mystical creatures we will continue to encounter on this quest." He nodded at Tinker's sketches. "So, we need to be prepared. We need to protect ourselves with more than just luck."

"Maybe the need for magic is more necessary than we think," said AZ.

"Oh, my boy, that is a definite," Sorcerer told him.

"That, too," Tinker added as he returned to survey through his spyglass and writing and drawing, "is truth at its best."

"How long are we supposed to wait to see what happened to—" Aldrick began to ask.

"You may want to shut up and pay attention if you want any chance of beating the dragon," Tinker shot back, not letting him finish his question about the fate of Monk and the others.

The Twins stared in astonishment.

"Good on ya, Tink," Axel said, as they sat down near the front of the group.

"Sorry, Tink," Aldrick apologized. "I didn't mean anything by it. I'm sure they are fine."

"No," Tinker also apologized. "I know that they are fine. I would feel it if Monk wasn't. It's just that I can't let go of the feeling of uncertainty."

Princess came over and hugged him. She looked over his shoulder and watched Seer continue to search through his visions.

Tinker went back to his illustrations and explained the process of how dragons produce fire from their breath and in particular, how the Jeweled Dragon produces fire.

"It's not a complicated system. But it is highly specific to the type of dragon. We are dealing with the most vicious type."

"Of course, we are," AZ said.

"God forbid it be an easy type or a trainable one," offered Seer, with his usual sense of doom. He shook his head at Sorcerer as if saying 'no' to an unspoken question.

The Twins shot an angry stare at Seer. He lowered his head.

"As I was saying," Tinker continued, "it's not complicated. We all saw this dragon appear and disappear in the sky. Its scales are made of diamonds that absorb and reflect light. She can use sunlight to produce rainbow-like prisms that can add to her distractions, or she can use it to hide. Yet, she still produces a shadow. Her destructive power comes from the gemstones that make up her inner anatomy. This type of dragon has two chambers that connect into her lungs. She, like most dragons, has the ability to produce fire in her breath. One of those two chambers is lined with rubies and the other emeralds. Rubies are formed in holes in magma made of gas bubbles in volcanic rock. That gas is housed in the ruby-lined chamber. And when a flame is produced, it ignites the sulfur cilia that line the dragon's esophagus and, therefore, creates fire in the breath. The flame source is triggered from that high-pitched scream that the dragon emits, and the cough of gas that smells like bergamot."

"I do like that smell," Axel said.

"Most do. That's what makes it even more dangerous. The scent attracts you and clouds your judgment so that you won't run."

"Easier targets," Aldrick added.

"Yup."

"And the emeralds?" Princess asked.

"The emeralds shut it off. Emeralds require a hydrothermal process to form. The solutions involve rainwater or water derived from cooling magma bodies. They crystallize when the water encounters open spaces, such as cracks. As a result, 'veins' of minerals fill pre-existing cracks. The water element acts to control the fire element."

"The ruby chamber turns the fire on. The emerald chamber turns it off. Seems simple enough," AZ summarized.

"Okay, but so what? It's not like we can turn the emerald chamber on to stop the fire," Seer said.

"And now that we know that, how does it help us to stop the dragon from killing us? Would we benefit from diamond shields?" Sorcerer asked.

"That's actually not a bad idea. But not very realistic," Tinker told them. "So, at this point, what I suggest is—"

"To avoid her altogether," Axel concluded.

Tinker nodded his agreement. "We can't do anything without the weapons listed in the prophecy."

Hours later, they had all fallen into some degree of sleep. AZ heard it first: the sound was frighteningly familiar. It forced him to stand to attention with his hand on his sword. But then came the second screech. They all heard it and were on their feet. She was close.

That high note was clearer this time. The first was a warning cry. This one was intentional. It was meant to be heard.

"Stay hidden," Tinker told them.

"We have to figure a way to work around her," Sorcerer began to formulate a plan.

"And to not attract her," added Seer.

"We need to complete this quest. That will defeat her," AZ reminded them.

"Yup. That sums things neatly," said Tinker.

There it was again. The high-pitched sound that came just before fire and destruction. Axel and AZ ran to the entrance of the cave and stood to either side of the opening. They looked at the sky and then off into the darkness along the river.

"I don't see her," AZ whispered.

"Me neither," added Axel. He made a step to exit the cave but was pulled back by Sorcerer. The shock of the physical force caught him off guard and he turned but did not resist. Sorcerer shook his head, and Axel agreed not to move. A gentle breeze blew on the back of Axel's neck, causing his hairs to stand up. He felt the chill of Ghost moving past him and out into the dark night. He was more transparent than usual, as if he had taken to a self-imposed 'dimming' of his essence.

"Ghost camouflage," Princess whispered as she and Aldrick joined them.

"They are safe," Ghost told them when he returned.

"Tell us everything," Seer demanded.

"Shhh," Tinker ordered. He hid his relief but felt truly appreciative of the news. He had his back to the others as he fought back tears of joy behind his tightly closed eyes. An experiment needed to be performed.

Tinker was one step away from the cave opening. He was again wearing that peculiar spyglass, but this time he'd placed a different filter over the lens. He cautiously stepped one foot forward. The sound of the river rocks as he stepped upon them made it impossible to hide his presence. He was sure to scan the entire area of the sky visible through the opening and increased his scanning distance with each step.

"Tink?" asked Princess.

He did not answer.

No one questioned Tinker further. His silence meant that he was too consumed by the noise in his head to hear anything else. Nothing short of physically shaking him could bring him back to his senses.

The others kept to the sides of the cave entrance. Tinker held out his right hand. Sorcerer placed a vial into his hand. Tinker continued his slow and cautious stepping out of the cave as he concentrated on scanning the night sky. He stopped as soon as he was three steps outside of the cave entrance.

Tinker uncorked the vial and they all smelled bergamot. They looked at each other with concern. The scent changed and became an increasingly sour aroma. They heard another high pitch but did not see any fire.

Tinker turned to the group and took off the spyglass. "Sorcerer? I think it worked," he announced, excitedly.

And, immediately, the dragon rushed past the entrance to the cave with such speed and force that Tinker was thrown ten feet in. All the others felt the rumbling of the rock around them and the cracking and smashing of the trees that came down to partially block the entrance of the cave.

"Oh shit!" Axel exclaimed.

Tinker was laughing hysterically. He was face down on the cave floor and laughing uncontrollably. Aldrick and Princess went to his aid and turned him over.

"He's officially lost it," Aldrick stated.

"Tink? Tink," Princess said, attempting to bring him back to the present. "Tink!" she exclaimed and slapped him.

"What? What. . ?" he asked, as he continued laughing.

"Tink — have you lost your mind?" she asked, with true concern. "You could have been killed!"

"No. No. It worked," he told her.

"What worked?" she asked.

"The potion."

"With Tinker's understanding of the dragon, we were able to concoct a potion that helps to camouflage us," Sorcerer explained.

"That's why she's so pissed. We basically disappeared and she is not able to track us," Tinker said.

"That is, until the potion wears off," Ghost added.

"So, are we going to be bathing in that stench?" AZ asked.

"No. But we will have to stay very close for all of us to be concealed. If we each have it and are separated, she starts to see multiple empty spots and realizes that she needs to fill them in," Tinker told them.

"And she'll fill them in with fire," Aldrick added, as he understood more.

"However, if we stay close," Tinker continued, "her own senses will not accept that there is a singular blank spot and will fill in the empty spot with the surroundings."

"Therefore, camouflaging us," Aldrick continued.

Tinker got up from the dirt and began walking deeper into the cave.

"Where are you going?" Axel yelled.

"To bed. That was exhausting."

They all swapped glances.

"I suggest you do the same," Tinker told them. "Tomorrow is not going to be an easy journey."

They all followed suit and moved deeper into the cave.

"Where did Ghost go, anyway?" Seer asked.

"Not sure," answered Sorcerer as he scanned out over the fallen trees that partially blocked the cave entrance.

CHAPTER 18
City of Dremora

The following morning, they had still not rendezvoused with Monk, Vampire, and Cadet. Ghost had not come when called, and therefore, the rest of the Ambassadors agreed that it was best to go back to the city center. Their return to the main part of the city had created an interest. A mob had gathered and had blocked all the streets.

"Swords, spells, what? How do you suggest we get past this mob?" Seer asked, clearly frustrated.

"By avoiding them," Princess said.

AZ was quick to follow Princess' thought. "This way," he said and showed them an empty side street with an opening at the other end.

The next turn revealed what they had been waiting for.

"Monk!" Tinker shouted and slapped Seer on the shoulder. They ran up to him and hugged him so tightly that he started to laugh from embarrassment.

"You're okay," Tinker said through his tears.

"Yes," Monk assured him. "And you?"

"We watched the dragon destroy Gokyuzu," Seer told him. "It was terrifying. I could not get anything about you because of—"

"Because of me," Vampire concluded.

"And the dragon," Seer told him, in a sorrowful voice. "We were all very happy when Ghost told us you were all safe."

Vampire nodded in gratitude.

Cadet had been cheerfully greeted by the Twins.

"What happened here?"she asked them, hearing the mob that had gathered nearby.

"Oh, just your regular day," Aldrick joked.

"But last night, we sort of had a dragon attack," Axel continued.

"Tinker almost getting himself killed," Aldrick finished.

"So — like any other day with this lot," Cadet joked.

Sorcerer came up to Vampire and hugged him.

"Mavi is dead," Vampire whispered.

"Very sorry to hear that," Sorcerer said. "She was something else, huh?"

They each smiled in her honor.

Princess and AZ had joined Sorcerer in expressing their joy at Vampire's return.

"How did you get back to the ground?" Tinker asked. "I was searching the night sky for a rainbow but could not see one."

"The dragon would have seen it. We took to flight," Monk told him, piquing his interest.

"So, you jumped?" AZ asked. "Fell?"

"Were pushed?" Axel kidded.

"We were given wings that had been constructed from the feathers of angels and demons," Vampire explained. "They allowed us to descend back to the ground safely."

"Where are they now?" Tinker asked, with an intense interest.

"Sorry, kid," Cadet told him. "They just fell away and blew off with the wind as soon as we hit the ground."

"What?" Tinker yelled with utter disappointment.

"Hey," Vampire said. "We need to get our heads back on track." He focused ahead. "We need to go back to Mortua to get the stones."

"Kid? What are the colors of the stones that your parents have?" Cadet asked.

"I don't know," he told her.

"What?"

"I've never seen them."

"Seer," Vampire, Monk, Sorcerer, and Cadet all said in unison.

Seer closed his eyes, and the red light ignited like a furnace behind his eyelids.

"He's looking into it for us," Cadet reassured AZ.

"They do not have them all in their possession. They've gifted some to maintain their secret." Seer opened his eyes as they returned back to their normal state.

"They do have a light blue one, which is the smallest," Seer said, looking at AZ. "Another blue, much larger." He turned to Monk. "Purple, which is mid-sized," he continued and cautiously glanced at Vampire. "Those are in their possession."

"And the others? Where are they?" Monk asked.

"Orange is in Caarfu," he said. "Red…" he hesitated. "That one is in Bacaa. Orange is smaller than purple but red is larger."

"Those must be with my uncles," AZ told them.

Cadet was counting on her fingers and matching colors to numbers. "We're missing green," she said. "And yellow. But you have an Illusion stone. That is an eight-stone constellation. That is power."

"It appears that we will be splitting up to get the orange and red ones before going back to get the others," Sorcerer said.

They all waited, wondering who would be going to Caarfu and who would be going to Bacaa.

"Not a good idea," Monk said.

"I agree," Tinker seconded Monk's caution.

"Of course, you do," Seer said, blankly.

Tinker looked at Monk.

"How do we communicate if we are split up like that?" Monk asked.

Arguments broke out. Everyone talked at the same time, but no one had a solution. Princess was quiet and withdrawn. Monk, too, held his tongue.

"I do know that those stones are dangerous. We had a servant who thought that she would be able to gain my mother's admiration by attending to the stones. She grabbed hold of one and…" AZ was lost in the horror of his memory.

"All of the energy was pulled from her until she was nothing but a skeleton," Cadet finished for him.

"When we attempted to move her, her bones crumpled into dust," AZ said.

"There are only three types of people who can touch them with their bare skin," Sorcerer remarked. "The one for which they fell," he said, facing Monk. "A tracker," he added, looking at AZ. "Or… a Witch," he concluded and avoided making eye contact with anyone.

A cold breeze chilled each of them as Ghost floated through them one by one.

"No," said Vampire as Ghost's shadowed form became visible directly in front of him.

"You saw me?"

"As can she," Vampire told the specter, nodding at Cadet.

Cadet gave him a flirtatious wave. "You can't hide yourself from my kind," she said.

"This conversation is pointless. It is settled," Vampire announced. "We will break into two groups and then meet up on the road to Mortua."

"It is rumored that a green Cez stone and the Sword of Sansit are in the Palace of Tebbs," Cadet told them. "Maybe it's the stone that we need."

Princess looked at Vampire.

"Not just rumored," Vampire told Cadet. "It is there."

No one spoke.

"The stones in Mortua are safe," he added. "We will retrieve them after we obtain the other three. "AZ will be our 'in' to Caarfu and Princess the 'entry' to Bacaa. Your uncle will welcome you," he said to AZ, "and his other uncle will not be able to refuse you," he said to Princess. "Now as for the rest of us. Monk, Seer, Cadet and I will go with AZ, and Sorcerer will go with Princess and babysit the other children—"

"Including his own," Seer joked.

Sorcerer giggled and fist-bumped Aldrick and Axel.

"And Ghost," Vampire yelled as the specter appeared again. "You're with us."

"AZ and I should go to Caarfu alone," Cadet said. "I feel as though-"

"No way," Monk said.

"You can't be trusted," Vampire told her.

"What is that supposed to mean?" she asked.

"Oh please." AZ laughed. "They think that you will kidnap me to make you rich."

"Yes," Vampire agreed.

"I'm really starting to take offense to the anti-Leprechaun agenda that you're promoting," Cadet said, with her hands on her hips.

"Get over yourself," Vampire said. "You are untrustworthy, and it has nothing to do with you being a Leprechaun."

Cadet shrugged her shoulders as if she no longer cared to argue.

"Regardless, getting to either city by magic is not an option," Tinker reminded everyone. "It's outlawed in both places."

"So it is," Vampire agreed. "I hope that everyone is wearing comfortable shoes."

"Three days," Monk said. "That should give us enough time to get the stones and to meet on the road."

"Just in case," Sorcerer added, "we can communicate with each other through the birds."

"And we can send Ghost," Vampire said, looking Ghost straight in his dark eyes.

Ghost did not argue. He was, however, not comfortable with being a messenger.

"Then, instead of heading back to Mortua, we will meet in three days on the road to *Tebbs*," Monk said. "We need to get that green stone and the sword."

They all said their goodbyes and well wishes and walked in opposite directions.

As they exited Dremora, Tinker found his horse and cart in the field. He held up samples of birch bark to his horse's nose. He was giving the horse instructions to meet them on the road to the Palace of Tebbs. His horse responded as if he understood and turned himself and the cart off in a different direction.

"Amazing," Vampire whispered.

Princess turned around to glance at AZ. She was embarrassed to find that he was doing the same. He gave her a nod, a wink, and a thumb's up. She blew him a kiss and turned back to her group.

"I hope that he's worth it," Aldrick said to her.

"Not yet, he's not," Princess said and glanced back again. "But he will be."

"And if he's not," Axel added, "we have no problem kicking his ass." She laughed. "We won't even charge you," Axel told her.

"Thanks, but I can take care of myself."

"And Tink will help, too," Axel said, and gave him a playful push.

Tinker flexed and smiled.

They all laughed. Sorcerer felt joyful as they made their way to where the road split.

"Tink?" Monk said, as he grabbed him back by his shoulder.

Tinker turned and looked. Monk pulled black and white feathers from his pocket. Tinker's eyes widened in excitement.

"Don't get sidetracked," Monk told him. "There will be time for that later. I promise."

Tinker took the feathers and put them into a bag. He pulled out a notebook and cataloged his new treasures.

CHAPTER 19
City of Caarfu

AZ was running his mouth. Cadet held her annoyance in her ruffled brow. Seer kept coming in and out of his visions, looking for success. Vampire kept himself distracted from AZ's ranting by catching glimpses of Monk from the side and accidentally brushing his hand against Monk's while they walked along the open road in the late afternoon sun. Monk did not pull away from any of the casual contact.

As they were near Caarfu, Monk stared out to the open sea and held a slight smile. He was thinking of some of his better dreams. He felt joy and peace with what Vampire explained to him were the reveries of past lives. He felt the energy of Vampire's love as they were kissing in front of a fireplace in a snowy mountain cabin, laughing over drinks in a city that he did not recognize, and a handshake in a church.

He was brought back by another brush of Vampire's hand. This time, Monk took it into his own and held it as they walked. Vampire smiled.

"This should not be a challenge," Seer said to AZ. "Your uncle is just going to take some minor convincing."

"It's funny," AZ said. "I was named after him. It seems that he was the richest in my mother's family."

"And they wanted to gain good graces," Cadet said, laughing.

Silence followed as they continued to make their way along the packed sand that made up the road that led south to Caarfu. The yellowish road wound along the coast and swerved through the tall grasses.

"When were you last here, AZ?" asked Seer.

"I don't recall ever being here," he said, sounding surprised at himself. "The family always traveled to Mortua for celebrations. We have the biggest estate and are able to host the whole family."

"Security risks that come with being a rich brat?" Cadet snickered. "You run around dive bars in Mortua with a guard?"

"No," AZ said proudly.

"Then, why couldn't you go to see your uncle in Caarfu?" Cadet asked. "And what about the one in Bacaa? Same security issues? Scared of getting kidnapped?"

"I don't know! All right?" AZ yelled out in frustration.

"Think about it, AZ," Monk added. "I'm sure your uncle loves you and will be overjoyed to see you." He glanced at Vampire. "But we are asking for him to give us his Cez stone. He might not want to help us if he knows he is not going to get it back."

AZ nodded his understanding, but he was still angry. They continued along the road, mostly in silence. Hours passed. The dirt and sand that made up the road gradually changed to white.

"This is how you know that you have entered the territory of Caarfu," Monk said.

"Good," Cadet told him. "I'm a bit tired."

"You get lazy traveling on rainbows, huh?" Vampire joked.

AZ smiled, calm now that they no longer questioned him. Yet, he did not say anything. They continued in silence.

AZ turned to Seer. "What do you think?" he asked.

"About?"

"Have I been lied to my whole life?" he asked, with a hint of sadness.

"You already know that answer, AZ," Seer told him and placed his hand on his shoulder.

AZ nodded. "Yeah," he admitted. "I think that I have always known, but it felt nice to have a brother. And then I just got used to being, well... useless. No one expected anything from me. I guess that I just got used to doing whatever I wanted with no regard for anything."

"AZ," Monk said. "I know it's not easy to find out that there is an entire other story about your life."

"Or all of your lives," AZ joked.

"Exactly." Monk laughed and watched Vampire shake his head. "It is fair to say that you will need time to understand and accept that you have been lied to your whole life."

"Well," AZ said to Monk. "You seem to be doing all right with all the shit that he threw at you." He pointed at Vampire.

"Why is this my fault?" Vampire asked.

"It's always your fault," Cadet said, as they all laughed together.

The sun was setting.

"There it is," Seer told them. "Caarfu."

The road was now paved with white stones. A few miles back, they had started to see stones randomly appear in the road. Now they were able to see Caarfu.

The buildings of the city were completely white. The bone-white stones they found themselves walking upon led directly into the city and made up every avenue and alleyway. The doors of the buildings were the only structures that weren't white. Windows were adorned with white curtains. Even the flowers were white. The green stems and leaves were more pronounced.

Ironically, Caarfu was the spice capital of the world. The array of colors that made up the spices was almost overwhelming. To enter a kitchen meant that one's eyes would widen, as if starved of sensory feedback. The markets were even more intoxicating. The pristine whiteness of the city was a marketing technique of the merchants. Their colors popped even more against the white. People even said that the aromas were perceived to be stronger, as well.

The merchants of Caarfu had made their fortunes in the spice trade. AZ's uncle, Azurus, was one of these merchants. He held control over all the markets. He had bought his position years ago when he presented the orange Cez stone to the Spice Council. He offered its use for energy to supply the city with systems that modernized Caarfu and advanced its markets and port. However, it cost the rulers all their control and power.

As Azurus' lending of the stone gave him power and increased his riches, the other merchants also increased their share of Caarfu's profits. They wanted to back Azurus and share in his profits. It was social and political suicide to stand against Azurus: he and the Spice Council ruled Caarfu.

"Uncle Azurus lives in the house with the gold door," AZ told them.

"I thought that you were never here," Cadet reminded him.

"I remember my mother always talking about the gold door."

As they entered the city, AZ could not help but see how different Caarfu was from Mortua and Dellai, but mostly from Dremora. Every street in Caarfu appeared identical, except for the doors.

The color of the doors was a way to differentiate one home from another. No two buildings had the same color door. The color signified that that dwelling was owned by the merchant who traded in a particular spice. The other way to differentiate one home from another was by the size of the building. To no one's surprise, the house with the gold door was also the largest in the city.

The gold door was not the color of a spice. It was the color of the city's currency. Uncle Azurus owned not only the Cez stone that powered the city, but also the bank to which the other merchants were indebted through the loans that they had taken out over the years to increase their business or to compensate for a poor harvest.

Each merchant dealt only with one particular spice. If that spice did not grow well, that merchant would need to take a loan from the bank. The interest on the loan would keep the merchant in debt for a minimum of ten years.

It was once suggested that Uncle Azurus had a part in the fire that caused the destruction of the hottest peppers. That accuser was found dead from an alleged suicide and Uncle Azurus became the benefactor to the estate and now maintained that and several other spices under the bank's control. No one questioned his motives after that.

There were sometimes rumblings of discontent regarding Uncle Azurus' practices. However, the merchants, who were at this time all indebted, still maintained a more luxurious lifestyle than under the previous system. They were a greedy bunch, but they also accepted that they were still more profitable overall.

"And you think that he'll just give us the stone?" Cadet asked, with eyes wide in disbelief.

"We're family," AZ told her.

"AZ," Vampire said. "She may have a point."

Monk looked to Seer. He closed his eyes and AZ could see the crimson color which seemed even brighter amidst all that white.

Seer opened his eyes. "Yeah. I guess that I misspoke earlier. Yet, I do see success. Something is going on here. But it's too erratic for me to focus on."

They walked up a slight incline and turned. They exited the narrow street and found themselves standing in an open plaza. On the opposite side of the plaza was the largest building in Caarfu: the one with the gold door.

"Well," Monk said. "I guess we found it."

"Ghost!" Vampire yelled. Ghost appeared in front of him. "Go and let the others know that we are here," Vampire demanded. "Find out where they are and what progress they have made."

The sound of locks being undone echoed throughout the plaza. The gold door opened.

"AZ?" a rotund man asked. He had two armed guards at his sides.

"Uncle Azurus," AZ exclaimed and began to walk towards him.

"Shhh! You fool," Uncle Azurus scolded him. "Hurry! Inside! Who are these people?"

"They are with me. They are my…" he turned to Monk for the right words.

"We are in his service, sir," Monk said. "His parents asked for us to see him safely to you."

"Now is not a good time," Uncle Azurus told them. "But you—" he demanded of AZ, "inside."

AZ hesitated. "Not without them."

Vampire made his way forward. "Everything okay?" he asked.

"And this is. . ?" Uncle Azurus asked.

"Think of him as your savior, sir," Seer said. They all turned and gave him confused looks. "You see," Seer began, "your sister got wind of your troubles and sent AZ to assist in helping you back to your elevated position. We have been sent for his protection, as well as to use our particular skill sets to help you.”

“My sister heard of this?” Uncle Azurus asked.

Seer nodded to acknowledge that she had.

Uncle Azurus paused and thought. “Inside,” he demanded again. “All of you.”

“Where did that come from?” Monk asked Seer.

“It just made sense, so I went with it,” Seer told him.

CHAPTER 20
City of Bacaa

The sun was setting over the hills to the west. Sorcerer looked directly into it and closed his eyes. He allowed the last of sunlight to energize him. With his eyes closed, Sorcerer was listening to the playful banter amongst the Twins, Princess, and Tinker. He held a content expression on his face as he summoned a hawk and scribbled a note onto parchment. The hawk launched into flight, carrying the message back to the others to inform them that they had reached Bacaa.

"So how are we going to know who this guy is?" Axel asked.

"I have a feeling that we will just know," Princess told him.

"After all," Tinker added. "He is AZ's uncle."

Aldrick's attention was on Sorcerer and the majestic bird. "Are you okay?" Aldrick asked Sorcerer, while watching the bird spread its impressive wings, take flight, and turn south.

Sorcerer immediately snapped back to the present. "Yes, of course."

"It's just that, well…"

"You look like you just found treasure," Axel finished his brother's thought.

"No. No." Sorcerer continued to hold tight. "I was just thinking that when this is all over, I would like to get a farm."

"Okay…" Axel said, glancing at Aldrick and then the others.

"Anyway," Sorcerer decided to change the subject.

"AZ's uncle, here in Bacaa, has a red Cez stone," Sorcerer said, getting them all back on track. "Any ideas as to how we will be getting it from him?"

Axel offered the first idea. "Tell him that the Princess of Mortua wants it and if he doesn't give it up, the entirety of the Mortuan armed forces will be at his doorstep?"

"Umm, no," Princess said.

"You may want to think about using that line," he insisted.

Princess shook her head. "Tink?"

"The color of the Cez stone is connected to a character trait," Tinker said.

"A sin," Aldrick said.

"Monk has all these sins?" Axel asked. "Now, I'm impressed."

"Yeah, I didn't want to say it," Tinker said, ignoring Axel's comment. "And red…"

"Is wrath," Sorcerer finished. "So, you're worried that AZ's uncle is going to be one angry man."

"And that he will not be willing to give us the stone," Princess added.

"My idea is looking better and better, huh?" Axel said.

"Surely, if we explain the seriousness of the situation, he will be unable to refuse us," Princess said.

"Come on," Tinker said. "You don't really believe that."

"No," she replied. "But I was hoping that if I said it, someone would agree that it was a possibility."

The road was lined with colorful flowers. The volcanic soils were rich in nutrients that supported the most diverse plant life on the planet. The aromas were intoxicating.

"They're not as good as the ones from Quorca, but the wines from Bacaa are quite good," Aldrick said, pulling grapes from the vine.

"And strong," Axel added. "Maybe we can just get him drunk."

"So, you're the idea guy?" Princess joked.

"And I'm the muscle," Aldrick said, with a laugh.

"We'll have to drug him," Tinker said, as he plucked a flower from the nearest bush.

"Now, we're talking," Aldrick said.

"Is it us?" Axel asked Tinker. "Are we a bad influence?"

Tinker cracked a smile. "No. I've had to do things like this before," he confessed.

Axel and Aldrick looked at each other in shock.

"We both did," Princess added and high-fived Tinker.

"Wait? What?" Aldrick yelled.

"No questions," she told him. "Sorcerer? Do you have anything with you?"

"Yes," he said. "But for me to create what we need I will require magic. We will be caught with the first words of the incantation."

Aldrick picked a flower from the side of the road. "Axel," he yelled as he handed the bloom to his brother.

"Valerian," Axel said. "But that's not going to be enough."

"No," Aldrick agreed. "However, that's just the decoy."

"Yes," Tinker said, excitedly. He examined the plants on the side of the road and grabbed an assortment of colored flowers with their green stems. "This will definitely work." He turned to the Twins. "You are geniuses."

"Why, thank you, Tink," Axel said and shook his brother's hand.

"Tink," Sorcerer whispered as he pulled fruit from a tree.

"Bergamot," Tinker realized and inhaled the aroma of the yellowish-green fruit.

"Keep looking," Sorcerer ordered. He and Tinker rummaged through the vegetation, grabbing handfuls of herbs and flowers.

"Don't mix these with the other ones," Tinker ordered as he handed the plants to Aldrick and Axel. Princess smelled the fruit.

"This is what you used to hide us from the dragon," she deduced from the aroma of the bergamot.

"And we will be able to make more," Tinker told her. "Who's the genius now?" he joked to Aldrick and Axel.

They waited for night to fall before entering through the southern gates of the city. They'd agreed that the cover of night would allow the princess and her entourage to visit AZ's uncle without anyone in the city becoming aware of their presence.

The City of Bacaa was aglow. The buildings were all faced with volcanic rock which made for a very dramatic sight. The vibrant colors of the flowers contrasted sharply with the black buildings during the day. Yet, if the lights went out at night, the city would look as if it had disappeared behind a huge plot of wildflowers, vines and trees. There was a festive feel to the city; however, something about it was off.

"Why does it feel like everyone is being forced to be here?" Aldrick asked.

"Because they are," offered a chilling voice from the dark.

All of them reacted with weapons in hand and ready for an attack.

"Ghost…" Sorcerer said, as he exhaled.

"I was sent to see about your progress and to let you know that they have reached Caarfu. They are in the residence of AZ's uncle."

"So, I guess we made pretty good time," Sorcerer said, focusing on the first stars that twinkled in the sky.

"By the looks of things, it seems as if you just entered the city. Have you located the stone?" Ghost asked.

"No. Not yet," Princess told him.

"Is there a plan for obtaining the stone?" Ghost asked.

"As a matter of fact, there is," Axel told him with pride.

"Excellent," Ghost said, sounding unimpressed. "I will return to let them know."

"Ghost?" Princess asked.

"Yes, your highness," he replied, with a bit of softness in his voice.

"I'm sorry. But you said that these people are being forced to be at these festivities."

"Yes."

"Why?' Tinker asked.

"Who doesn't want to go to a party?" Aldrick asked.

Ghost turned and faced away. He returned his glance to Princess.

"AZ's uncle, Quahin, is a terrible man. He is abusive, ruthless—"

"Did you say Quahin?" Tinker asked.

"Yes," Ghost replied and floated over to where Tinker stood. "And yes, again: the same Quahin who scarred Monk all those years ago."

Tinker felt as though his stomach had just been punched hard. His eyes lost focus and he began to breathe rapidly through his mouth.

"Hold on," Sorcerer said. "Quahin is a monk? Monsignor Quahin of the Brothers of the Order of Naa?"

Ghost nodded.

"Tinker?" Axel asked. "Are you okay?"

"I know him," he said. "He is horribly abusive."

Tinker was lost in a painful memory of being beaten. He saw Monk intervene and cut Quahin's hand off. Monk carried it and Tinker out of the room while Quahin screamed in pain and anger.

Monk left a trail of blood that dripped from Quahin's severed hand, still in the metal glove. He walked with five-year-old Tinker in his other arm past the other monks, who were rushing to Quahin's aid. He casually walked down the hallways of the monastery and out the front door. Tinker saw someone jump and land in front of the door. The other monks stopped in fear and slammed the door closed.

"Vampire," Tinker said, realizing all these years later that it was he who had stopped the other brothers from coming after Monk and himself.

"What?" Princess asked.

"It was Vampire," he said, and watched Sorcerer.

Tinker looked up as if he had just awoken and was fully refreshed. "This man is awful," he told them. "There is no way he will give us the stone." They all gathered closer to Tinker. "He is forcing these people to be at this festival as a tribute to himself. People will be punished for whatever he decides is not a good enough offering."

Tinker observed the people and recognized the robes of the Brothers of the Order of Naa.

"Ghost!" he exclaimed. "You have to tell Monk about this. He needs to know that Quahin is here, that he is still alive and I'm sure as torturous as ever." Tinker turned to Axel and Aldrick. "We will need a very, very potent elixir. This man is the devil, himself."

CHAPTER 21
City of Caarfu

"Why are you really here?" Uncle Azurus yelled, as AZ rushed to keep up with him through the winding hallways of his grand home. "Your mother would never send you at a time like this."

"Well," AZ began, "my parents felt confident that I would be protected with my guards. They also wanted me to check on your business and to review your books so I could give them a full report. It seems that they might want to make you an offer and they want me to learn about your business, as well as theirs. They figured that I need to start on my own path of financial independence."

Uncle Azurus glared at him with a questioning expression. "They did, did they?"

He was still on the move. Servants rushed about in all directions. Men dressed in military uniforms were also moving quickly and speaking to each other in whispers.

"Out of my way," Uncle Azurus yelled to a servant passing in the opposite direction. "Well, this is not a good time for me. I have too many things going on. You will be given provisions but then you have to leave." He stopped and grabbed AZ by the shoulders. "And do not, under any circumstance, tell anyone in Caarfu that you are my nephew."

"Umm, okay," AZ stuttered. He glanced over at Monk and Vampire and then Seer. Cadet was lingering and sneaking trinkets into her pockets.

"And she will be frisked before you leave," Uncle Azurus yelled out and turned the corner.

"That went well," Monk joked.

"I would agree," Cadet said, as she was escorted by a guard to stand with the others.

"You saw it?" Vampire asked.

"Of course, I saw it," she whispered, noticing that the guards were preoccupied by whatever was going on and not listening.

"This way," demanded a servant. They were pushed forward by the guards.

"Seer?" Monk asked.

"I am getting many disturbances," he said, contorting his face in painful expressions. "The greed in the house is overwhelming.

There is a mob forming and going to attack. And…” He stopped and fell into the wall. He opened his eyes as the crimson light went out.

“Monk,” he said, breathlessly.

“What is it?”

“Quahin,” he whispered.

“In here,” ordered the guards.

“What?” Monk asked.

“In Bacaa,” Seer told him.

“Now,” the guards demanded.

Monk stared at Seer with growing anger. A guard pulled him by the arm. Monk responded with a counterattack that left the guard pinned up against the wall with Monk holding a knife between the man’s legs.

“Monk!” Vampire pulled him away.

Monk released the guard and allowed him to walk out of the room. The other guards looked at one another aggressively and then back at Monk, Vampire, and Seer. Cadet shut the door to the receiving room, where they had been led, with a flirtatious wink and smile.

“What is wrong with you?” Vampire demanded.

“We have to go to Bacaa,” Monk insisted.

“What?” Vampire asked.

“We need to get to Tinker,” Monk continued. “He’s in trouble.”

"And he has Sorcerer, the Twins, and Princess with him," Vampire added, trying to reason with Monk.

"You don't understand," Seer interjected. "Quahin was the head of the Brothers of the Order of Naa."

AZ watched Cadet shake her head.

"He's the one who did this." Monk moved his hand along the scar on his face. "Years later, he was torturing Tinker. The boy was just five-years old. He was so innocent. He had done nothing wrong. I had to intervene."

Monk continued, lost in his reverie. "His hand was in the air… It was in that torturous glove. Tinker just stared at it with wonder… My sword met his arm as he launched his attack on that boy." Vampire moved closer to Monk and put his hand on his shoulder. "I swung my sword," Monk continued. "Sliced right through his wrist."

Monk told them that that was when he brought Tinker to Mortua to be hidden in the palace.

"You stay and get the stone," Monk said. "And make good time." Monk moved about the room. "The plan is the same. We'll meet on the road two days from now."

"Monk," Vampire said, attempting to remain calm. "We don't have time."

"Cadet — we need a quick way to Bacaa," Monk said.

"I can do that," she said.

Vampire gave her a disconcerting look.

"A rainbow is not magic," she reminded him.

"Vampire," Monk said. "You and AZ will get the stone. We will meet as planned. You know that Tinker is in danger."

"Monk?"

"Danger from himself," Monk told him. "He has locked all of that away."

"You raised him, Monk. He is fine. He can handle it."

Monk stood silent. He dropped his stare to the ground, but his vision was inward. His thoughts were on Tinker.

"Maybe it's you who is still dealing with this," Vampire whispered.

"Monk," Seer said in a calm voice. He came and stood next to him. "Monk, I do see Tinker in the future. He will be changed," Seer said. "You've sent him into more dangerous situations before."

"But I was there with him," Monk shot back.

"Monk, I was there—" Vampire began but was interrupted by yelling from the other side of the door.

Cadet tried to open the door. "It's locked," she said.

Something slammed into the door and caused her to step back. "Well," she began, "it seems as though we have pressing matters of our own to deal with, anyway."

A second and then a third slam came, as the angry voices on the other side of the door became louder and more aggressive.

"Of course, there are no windows in this room," Vampire said, scanning around. AZ started moving about the room and moving random objects. "What are you doing?" Vampire asked. AZ continued feeling along the undersides of surfaces and pushing on details in the wooden inlay of the walls. "AZ!" Vampire yelled.

AZ felt the movement under his hand as a bookshelf unlatched itself from the wall, like a door opening.

CHAPTER 22
City of Bacaa

They stood in the shadows of an alley watching the reserved and false smiles on those who passed by.

Aldrick nodded towards the narrow-faced, bald, older monk. "And he has the stone?" Aldrick asked.

"Of course, he does," Tinker replied. "Did we really think that this would go off without a hitch?"

"Good point," Axel said.

"So how do we get close enough to drop the elixir into his drink?" Princess asked.

"We just walk up and introduce ourselves," Tinker said, confidently.

"What?" Princess said. "What if he recognizes you?"

"Oh, he will recognize me," Tinker replied. "I'm sure of that. As a matter of fact, I'm banking on it."

Princess glanced at Sorcerer and the Twins. "Is anyone following this?"

"Yeah," Axel said. "Sorcerer, your messenger, will announce that you are here and seek an audience with him. As you approach with your guards, Aldrick and me, he will receive you with appropriate protocol. You will call for your attendant to present the gift to him. He will recognize Tinker, who will cower and hide behind you and us—"

"And he will be thrown off," Aldrick added.

"That split second is what we need for Sorcerer to drop this into the drink, which he will take to welcome you," Axel stated.

"And no one will stop this?" Princess asked.

"They will all be thrown off by my presence," Tinker told her. "But one thing: I will not cower away. I will stare him down."

"Tink," Princess seemed about to talk him out of that danger.

"No," Tinker said. "It will distract all of them and buy us a few extra seconds." He paused and looked up at the stars. "And I will do this for Monk," he added, tearfully.

Princess held his arm in support.

"Monk will be very proud to hear of this when we meet again," Sorcerer told Tinker and placed his hand on his other shoulder.

"Well," Aldrick said. "Dry up and let's go. We have an evil monk to poison and a Cez stone to steal…"

"Before sunrise so that we can be out of here and on our way to Tebbs," Axel added.

Princess, Tinker, and Sorcerer exchanged looks.

"What?" the Twins asked in unison.

"We were born for this kind of stuff," Aldrick said, with a wink at Sorcerer.

"Quite the family we've assembled, huh?" Tinker joked. He then turned to Sorcerer. "Go on ahead and let them know that she is here for an audience."

Sorcerer nodded in agreement. "All good?" he asked. They all nodded. "Good," he said. "Let's go."

CHAPTER 23
City of Caarfu

Seer led the group through the hidden tunnel that ran between the rooms and even the floors of the expansive building.

Vampire kept a watchful eye on the tunnels behind them. They still heard screams and cheers coming from the other side of the walls.

"What's happening?" Cadet asked.

"Seems like a coup," Monk said, although he was still distracted with thoughts about Tinker.

"Against my uncle?" AZ asked. "That's not good."

"No wonder he told you not to mention that you are his nephew," Vampire said. He kept a watchful eye on Monk and his visible emotions. "Monk?"

"Yes," Monk answered, flatly.

"He's fine. I'm sure of it," Vampire said, attempting to reassure him.

"I know," he again said, flatly.

"You know, but you don't seem to believe it," AZ told him. AZ's words brought Monk's thoughts back to the group at hand. "You would be a terrible poker player," AZ added, with a laugh.

"That is true," Vampire admitted.

"It's behind this wall," Seer told them.

They all looked at one another and then along the wall for a way in.

"He's there, too," Seer added.

"Uncle Azurus?"

"And his guards," Seer continued to explain with his eyes aglow.

"They are after the Cez stone," Vampire told them.

"Seems that if they kill him, he won't have much of a choice," Cadet added.

"He has the door rigged to explode if they get in," Seer explained.

"Well," Monk said, "if we don't get through this wall, it may be for nothing. Seer, can you find the way in?"

"AZ?" Seer asked. "Have you ever played the game 'Hot or Cold'?"

"You mean the one where you hide an object, and the closer I get to it the 'hotter' I am?"

"Exactly that one," he said with excitement. "I will focus my energy on you and as you feel for the way in, it will reveal itself to me in proximity to you."

AZ started feverishly moving his hands along the surface of the wall.

"Slowly," Seer told him. "Move with purpose and definitely focus on trying to find it."

AZ did as he was told. He pressed against the individual bricks, sliding his hand along the mortar between them.

"Cold," Seer told him.

AZ, frustrated, leaned his hand against the opposite wall. The bricks seemed loose.

"Burning hot," Seer told him with a smile.

AZ pushed and then pulled at the bricks until one clicked and then protruded from the wall. A door opened on the other side and Vampire pushed it slowly. He saw the orange Cez stone under glass atop a gold table. As he stepped out, he was met with swords at his throat.

"No!" AZ yelled and pushed past.

"AZ?" Uncle Azurus said. "How did you—?"

"When the mob got in, one of your guards showed us through to the tunnels. He stayed back to hold them off," AZ lied.

"Thank goodness you are safe." Uncle Azurus pulled him in for a hug. "We will get you out of here and you must tell your mother that I saved you. Promise?"

"Yes, of course," AZ said.

"I will need her protection and assistance after this," he said, as if talking to himself.

"Don't worry, uncle," AZ told him. "We are getting you out of here. Is there anything that you must take with you? Anything that is of such high value that you cannot leave it behind?"

Uncle Azurus glanced at the Cez stone.

"This?" AZ asked.

"The orange rock?" Cadet added.

"It is much more than a rock, my dear," Uncle Azurus explained with an air of superiority.

"Looks like a rock to me," she said. "Let's have a feel."

Cadet moved towards the Cez stone. "Is there a key? Or do I just break the glass?"

Uncle Azurus did not answer. Cadet grabbed a candlestick and raised it as if to smash the glass.

"No!" he yelled. "AZ," Uncle Azurus pleaded. "You know what this is. Your parents have several others."

AZ's eyes widened. He glared at his uncle and the Cez stone with a sense of bewilderment.

"A Cez stone?"

"A Cez stone," Uncle Azurus told him. "Your parents gave it to me to buy my silence."

"And it worked," Seer told them.

"Buy your silence about what?" Vampire asked.

Uncle Azurus hesitated. He looked at Vampire and the rest of the group with an angry expression.

"AZ," he sighed. "You do not have a brother."

"He's dead," Vampire said.

"He never had a brother!" Azurus yelled. "AZ, your parents lied to you and bought both mine and your Uncle Quahin's silence by giving us each a Cez stone."

AZ stared at him, eager to hear more of the story. Vampire glanced at Monk who kept his expression flat at the name, *Quahin*. "They did it to protect you," Azurus added. "Do you know how valuable you are? You can find Cez stones," he added with excitement and placed his hands upon AZ's shoulders.

"Many with your gift are kidnapped, abused, beaten, and killed! It is a dangerous talent because of the greed that exists in this world."

"Not just this world, honey," Cadet told him.

"So, are you saying that my mother had to buy her brother's silence so that he wouldn't kidnap, abuse, beat, or kill her son?" AZ asked Uncle Azurus as he took his hands and pulled them from his shoulders. "Or sell me off?"

"And it seems your father's brother, as well," Seer reminded him.

Uncle Azurus' expression changed from one of superiority to worry, now that his lies had been exposed.

"You see Monk," AZ said, holding his uncle's arms. "That is the kind of face you need to win a poker game." He turned back to his uncle. "I already came to find that out. And yes, I am sure that they lied to protect me, probably from myself. But those are the things that led me to become a useless sloth. Until…" He looked at Vampire and Monk. "Until these two came into my favorite dive bar and made me believe that I can be something more." He smiled at Seer. "But what's sad to me is that my mother, your sister, had to bribe you to protect this secret. To protect herself, her husband, and her son."

Uncle Azurus lowered his eyes to the dizzying tiles on the floor.

"Cadet — please get the stone," AZ said.

She raised the candlestick.

"Wait!" Uncle Azurus demanded. "I'm sure we can work something out."

Something smashed into the door.

"No time for that," Cadet said and let the candlestick fall. The glass smashed and triggered an alarm. Sirens began to howl. The lights went out and emergency lights came on. The other side of the door was momentarily silent. Then the crowd cheered and pushed harder.

Vampire grabbed the Cez stone. Uncle Azurus gawked in amazement.

"He's a vampire," AZ told his uncle. "Seer," he demanded. "There has to be a way out through the secret passage. Get us out of here."

AZ let go of his uncle and turned to go back into the tunnels between the walls.

"Take me with you," Uncle Azurus pleaded.

"You can come," AZ told him. "You can even lead the way, since I expect you know how to get us out of here." Uncle Azurus hesitated. Then something slammed against the door again and the frame began to give way. "Or you can stay here and get blown up when that door opens," AZ said.

"Or worse," Monk added. "That crowd will torture you once they get their hands on you."

"Out of my way," Azurus demanded and walked into the tunnel.

CHAPTER 24
City of Bacaa

Sorcerer came around the corner with two of Monsignor Quahin's guards and a representative.

"Your majesty," he said and bowed to Princess. "These men will lead us to Monsignor Quahin."

"He eagerly awaits your majesty's company during this most festive of celebrations," said the representative, with giddy excitement. "The Princess of Mortua at our annual Purge celebration. How exciting!"

"Mortua has heard much of this celebration and wanted to send her support," Princess replied graciously.

"Please, your grace." The representative gestured towards the grandstand at the center of the festivities.

"A moment, my lady," Tinker said, and pulled her back. "Allow me to fix your make-up before gracing his eminence."

The representative respectfully gave them a moment.

"Tink?"

"Are you crazy?" he whispered. "Do you know what's going on here?"

"Yes, Tink. I do," she replied. "But we have to get them to believe that we are here for them, not the stone."

"Good point," he said.

"But seriously, how's my makeup?"

Tinker laughed. "Fine. But listen — he will be wearing the stone. It is not in contact with his skin, but its power has probably made him even more angry and horrible than before."

"Huh-hmm." Monsignor Quahin's representative cleared his throat.

"When he sees me, they will have very little time to poison him. Sorcerer has a potion ready for the distraction. You must snatch the stone from around his neck and the Twins will lead us out."

Princess nodded and turned to the awaiting escorts. "So sorry," Princess said. "The cost of being in such a position." She ran her fingers through her hair to make an effort at being more presentable.

The representative forced himself to smile as he escorted Princess to the grandstand for her introduction.

The festival appeared quite joyous. Dancers, jugglers, musicians, contortionists, and clowns were all performing before the grandstand. A double spiral staircase wound its way up to two mid-level observation platforms. The people on this level were pointing and nodding at some and shaking their heads in disappointment at others. On occasion, they would raise a red flag or a green flag as they pointed. If members from both platforms agreed on the flag color, that performer could be escorted to one of two places. If the flags were green, that performer would be brought up to one of the two, mid-level platforms to become part of the judging. If the flags were red, the performer would be weighed down in heavy chains and left on the ground of the performance space. It was expected that the other performers would use them as props, even if it caused them pain, injury, or even death.

At the top of the grandstand was Monsignor Quahin, along with his invited guests and other dignitaries. At the sight of the Princess of Mortua, he launched himself to his feet and leaned over the illuminated railing. He was in awe of the princess. She gazed at him and offered him a coy smile.

Sorcerer led her up the stairs. Tinker remained behind Princess and kept his head down. Aldrick and Axel looked across and saw that the members of the other platform were being pushed back to the performance space.

They realized that the staircase that Princess chose made that platform worthy, whereas the other was deemed unworthy and those who occupied that space were put back into the mix. She realized it, as well. A knot formed in her gut. However, she knew that for the plan to succeed, she would need to appear as though her choice was intentional.

"Your majesty," Monsignor Quahin greeted her with open arms and a convincing smile. His right hand was missing. His left hand was armored with a troll metal glove that had been forged to it. It glowed.

She did her best not to stare at either hand. She felt as though she was only looking between his hands, but he did not respond in a negative fashion.

Tinker was right. He was wearing the stone. The deep-ruby color appeared almost liquid beneath the light. Princess was captivated and understood how one could be consumed by possessing it.

"Your Holy Eminence," she said. "Thank you so much for receiving us at your annual Purge Festival. It is an honor to represent Mortua and her support of you, and the good work that you continue to do here."

"Thank you, Princess," he replied, sighing joyfully and placing his hand upon his chest. "There are some who feel my work is misguided."

"Well," Princess cautiously searched for the right words. "I believe that they are the misguided."

Monsignor Quahin smiled even more broadly and led her to an ostentatious chair beside him.

"Oh," Princess said. Monsignor Quahin peered at her with disdain. "Amazing how you matched my taste so perfectly," she added with a flirtatious posture and leaned into the monk. He was disarmed and laughing again.

"But please, Princess," he said and led her to the illuminated railing to oversee the festivities. "It looks as though your choice left us with a free platform."

"It looks that way," she agreed.

"Maybe we should have your people take up the charge to be the voice of our southern contingency.

"Sir?"

"Your men," he said, with a smile but a demanding tone. "You made your choice "Okwith the staircase. Let them have a little fun and decide how our festival concludes."

"I'm sorry, but I don't think—"

"No one asked you to think," he interrupted. "Your majesty. After all, you are only a princess…" He again peered at her with disdain. "And only a woman."

She matched his look. "I think it's time," she said.

"Excuse me?" Monsignor Quahin asked.

Tinker lifted his head and came to stand before him.

It took a second, but Quahin realized who stood before him. "You…" he whispered. It took all the air that he could muster. "Where is he?"

"He sends his regards," Tinker said, through clenched teeth. "They both do."

"Not the plan!" Sorcerer yelled. He smashed a vial onto the ground. The explosion threw the platform into a frenzy of confusion. Princess grabbed the chain from Monsignor Quahin's neck as the Twins came to stand in front of her with their swords drawn. The staircases were blocked by monks and Quahin's personal guards.

"Okay. Not exactly the escape that we expected," Aldrick said. Sorcerer came to stand with them as they circled Princess with their swords drawn. Princess pulled out Axel's other sword and held it aloft as well. The cover that Sorcerer had produced was clearing.

"Tink?" Princess said in a whisper as she saw him standing in opposition to Monsignor Quahin. Tinker had drawn his sword. However, he was holding it with the tip on the ground.

"You still haven't learned how to protect yourself," Quahin yelled from behind a line of guards.

"And you have?" Tinker yelled back. "You have a line of men fighting for you. Are you still afraid of little boys who are more than you will ever be?"

Monsignor Quahin's rage was palpable in the night air. The festivities had found themselves reversed. The action in the performance area had ceased and all attention was focused on the top platform for the standoff between Tinker and Quahin.

"Give me that!" Monsignor Quahin grabbed a sword from one of his guards. He started to sidestep towards Tinker. Tinker matched him in the other direction so that they remained in opposition. Quahin could not contain his anger. "You should be dead!" he yelled out and attacked.

"Probably," Tinker replied, blocking Quahin's blade with his own. "But not at your hand," he jested and motioned at Monsignor Quahin's missing right hand.

Quahin pushed Tinker with his full force and Tinker almost lost his balance. He attacked again. Tinker spun around to avoid the assault and came down hard on Quahin's upper back with the blunt end of his sword. The monk was forced to his knees from the force of the blow.

"I will give you the choice that you never gave anyone else," Tinker said to him. "You can admit defeat and walk away or meet your fate."

Monsignor Quahin glared at Tinker with hatred. "You were born a bastard, abandoned by your mother, and then taken in by my good graces. I can never be defeated by the likes of you."

"Not by me," Tinker said. "By them." He pointed to the crowd of people who had been gathered to be killed off in the Purge.

"You were nothing," Quahin said to Tinker while he felt the weight of the situation. "And you are nothing." Tinker walked towards Princess and the others. "You have nothing!" the monk yelled.

Tinker turned and raised his sword. Monsignor Quahin raised his arms in defense. Tinker lowered his sword with all his might and cut clear through the monk's left wrist. The metal glove dropped and rolled to a stop at Tinker's foot. He leaned over and picked up the armored hand as blood spilled all over the platform.

"Maybe I had nothing," Tinker said. "But now I have a matching pair." He walked back towards Princess, the Twins, and Sorcerer.

Quahin screamed in pain as the mob made its way up the stairs. The monks and the guards were conflicted. They had been taking orders for so long that they were now unable to decide for themselves whether to attack Tinker, come to the aid of Quahin, or fight off the angry mob.

Aldrick and Axel were quick to lead them down the other staircase and away from the mob.

CHAPTER 25
Road to the Palace of Tebbs

The road to the Palace of Tebbs was quiet aside from the calm chirping of the forest birds. The group from Caarfu waited. Monk was lost in his thoughts of recent events. Vampire was watching him from a respectful distance. Cadet was brushing Tinker's horse, who had been the first to arrive at the meeting spot.

"There they are!" she yelled, breaking the silence. The group from Bacaa came around a corner with Axel raising his arms in triumph. "We made it!"

Tinker ran up to his horse, who let out a joyous neigh. Nothing seemed disturbed in his attached cart. Tinker gave the beast a playful toss of his mane. Cadet hugged him with a relieved sparkle in her eyes. Tinker knew why. He knew that Monk was worried.

AZ ran to Princess. "You okay?" he asked.

"Yes. You?" she asked, smiling. He nodded. "AZ?" she began, cautiously. "Your uncle…"

"Horrible person," AZ stated. "Whatever you are going to tell me, I'm sure it was of his own making." He looked back to Monk who was smiling and greeting the other group.

"He did that," Princess said, pointing at Monk's scar.

AZ nodded. "And I bet far worse," he told her. "But I expect he will not be hurting people anymore."

Monk pulled Tinker in for a tight hug. Seer dropped his head to Tinker's shoulder. Seer, too, grabbed hold of Tinker's slender body in gratitude for his safety.

"A matching pair," Tinker told Monk and handed him the blood-soaked bag.

Monk and Seer stared as Tinker wiped a tear from his eye.

Vampire placed his hand on Monk's shoulder.

"Nice job, Tink," Vampire said.

"Thank you," Tinker replied, with a touch of embarrassment.

"He was worried," Vampire told him.

"He's always worried," Tinker joked. "And you?" he asked Vampire.

"Nah," Vampire said. "I know what you are made of."

Tinker laughed out of embarrassment and dropped his head.

"Yeah, man," Aldrick told AZ. "Tinker does not play around."

"I would not fuck with him when he's mad," Axel advised.

Princess looked back at him and smiled.

"Who are you?" Sorcerer asked the overweight man, who still appeared confused.

"Uncle Azurus," he replied nervously. "AZ's favorite uncle," he added. "I hosted them all in Caarfu, and … and I gave them a Cez stone for the cause."

Cadet rolled her eyes and walked away.

Uncle Azurus came over to Tinker who was rummaging through his cart. Some of Tinker's gadgets caught his eye.

"AZ!" Tinker yelled.

AZ and Princess ran to his side. Tinker motioned towards Uncle Azurus with his eyes.

"Come with us, uncle," AZ interceded. "The princess would like to speak to you."

Uncle Azurus seemed enchanted and immediately began asking Princess questions about the royal bank. Monk walked over to Tinker while Tinker adjusted dials and scanned back and forth from the sky to his device.

"Listen," Monk told them. "You have the red Cez stone?"

"Princess has it," Tinker said, still focusing on finding the cloud city.

"Here is the orange one," Monk said, handing it to him. It was wrapped in a blue gauze that he had torn from his robes. "Under no circumstance is anyone to know that you have this. No one."

Tinker turned his attention towards Monk as Seer walked up to them. Tinker nodded in agreement.

Vampire turned to Azurus and scared him with an evil stare. "I still don't trust you, but we need to get a message to AZ's parents. They need to guard their Cez stones until we get back to Mortua," he said, as his eyes turned to light, and he willed Uncle Azurus to do as he commanded. "He'll need a horse."

Vampire unstrapped the horse from Tinker's cart. "Sorry, Tink. We'll get him back to you later."

"Wait!" Tinker demanded. He walked over to his horse and lovingly stroked his mane. "I knew that you would have a part to play in this," he told the horse. Tinker pulled the blanket from the horse's torso and exposed a pair of free-flapping wings with a magnificent span of pure, shiny black.

"What the—?" AZ began.

"Yes," Tinker told them. "It'll be a faster trip. Without the cart attached, Halo will be able to avoid the dragon as he takes your uncle back to Mortua." Tinker turned back to the horse. "Be safe."

Halo neighed and lifted himself onto his hind legs.

"Amazing," Princess said.

"He certainly is," Tinker agreed.

Tinker watched as Halo began cantering and flapping his wings until his hooves left the ground and he rose higher and higher into the sky.

CHAPTER 26
The Palace of Tebbs

Vampire was quick to come back to the group with orders. "Hey! Now that he's gone, we need to get our heads back on track." He focused ahead. "The Palace of Tebbs," he pointed.

"We need a plan to get in," Monk said. He looked at Sorcerer who stared back with vengeful, squinted eyes. "You may need to stay hidden out here."

Vampire put his hand on Sorcerer's shoulder. "Yes. I agree."

Sorcerer said nothing but nodded his head in agreement.

"Princess," Vampire continued. "You are too recognizable. Your presence in this palace will only give us away. You too will stay behind with Sorcerer."

She too agreed with a silent nod.

"Cadet. You will use your Leprechaun trickery and get five uniforms for Monk, Tinker, Seer, and the Twins. The five of you will keep surveillance as AZ and I go in for the stone and the sword."

"But we don't know where they are," AZ reminded him.

Vampire cracked a smile. "Ghost?" He called again. "Ghost."

Ghost's greenish form appeared.

"You go ahead and find where the stone and the sword are kept, and report back to us." Ghost did not respond. "I will take that as a yes." Ghost disappeared from sight.

"I'm off too," Cadet said and ran, disappearing among the trees.

"Let's find a place for you to hide," Vampire said to Sorcerer and Princess.

The Palace of Tebbs stood six stories high and was two city-blocks long. It had a series of towers that extended into the clouds and were connected by bridges that spanned among them. The conical roofs of the towers glistened and were the source of energy for the palace and the grounds.

The group of Ambassadors was individually and collectively surprised that there was no barrier between them and the palace. They saw no wall or gates.

The birch forest that they had entered gave way to towering evergreens. The evergreens blocked the view of the sky and concealed the towers. Once they were past the forest and in the vast clearing, they were now standing in, the entirety of the palace was visible.

"Who needs guards when you have The Dark Sisters on your side?" Princess asked.

"Had," Sorcerer reminded her.

As if on cue, guards appeared from under rocks and piles of leaves. They descended from the trees. They encircled the group as they came from the front and behind.

The Twins drew their swords. AZ and Seer did the same.

"Wait!" Princess yelled and stood in front of them. "Stop," she demanded.

"Your majesty," one of the guardsmen said, with surprise.

"Hello," she graciously replied. "It's Georges, isn't it?"

"You remember me?" The strapping man smiled broadly.

"Of course," she flirted, while AZ tightened his grip on his sword. "It hasn't been that long. Has it?" she giggled.

Georges also giggled. He quickly realized that he was breaking protocol and changed his tone back to his military persona.

"You scared me, my friend," she whispered into his ear and then stood back and also changed her tone to match her regal purpose. "We are here to see the king," she demanded.

"Which king?" one of the other guards asked.

She hid her surprise at the question. "The King," she again demanded.

"Our apologies, my lady," Georges said. "It's just that with tonight's festivities and the heightened security, we seem to be a bit more on edge than usual."

"The festivities," she said with a nod. "Can't wait."

"The other dignitaries have already been shown to the tents that have been set up for them."

"Hence the confusion of 'which king', huh?" AZ interjected in an annoyed tone.

Georges came to stand in full military intimidation directly in front of him. He was a head above AZ in height, well-proportioned with a strong muscular build.

AZ tried not to, but he gulped.

"Georges," Princess said, putting her hand on his flexed biceps. "It has been a long journey for me and my party. We are in need of rest after such an arduous time. I'm sure that you are aware of what has been happening outside of the forest."

"I watched Gokyuzu fall from the sky," he said, with the sensitivity of an oversized teddy bear. "It brought tears to my eyes."

"I'm sure," she told him and put her hands around his lowered head to comfort him.

"Go ahead, AZ," Axel whispered.

"We dare you," Aldrick finished.

AZ held his position and kept his jealousy.

"Please follow me, your highness," Georges said to her. "I will alert his majesty of your arrival. I'm sure he will be most pleased."

"I'm sure you're right," she agreed.

"May I?" Georges asked as he held his arm with bent elbow, as if to escort the princess.

"Why, thank you," she said with a smile. "Of course." She took his arm and placed her other hand on his bulging muscles, which created a stronger contraction and caused a wide smile to break across his face.

CHAPTER 27
The Palace of Tebbs

"I'm going to need you to hold yourself together," Vampire warned Sorcerer. "You know who we will be meeting here."

"She destroyed my life," Sorcerer replied. Vampire waited. "But yes. I can wait until we get the stone and the sword."

As they approached the palace, the Twins continued to tease AZ.

"What does he have, huh?" Axel said into his ear.

"Aside from that smile and his intimidating size?" Aldrick continued. "Probably nothing."

"And we have a dragon on our side!" Axel reminded AZ. AZ gave him a confused look. "I mean, as long as Tinker can come up with plans to trick her into helping us," he said, shrugging.

They had reached the steps that led up to the exterior receiving area at the entrance to the palace.

A group was gathered to receive the guests. It was headed by the Queen of Tebbs, the Witch, Baltaan. She was tall and statuesque, her full lips and deep dark almond eyes adding to her allure. She was as inviting in her smile as she was cold in her eyes. Her hand was extended as if waiting to be kissed.

"Where is he?" Vampire asked her, disrespectfully.

She drew the most angered expression across her exquisite face, which gave her a different version of beauty, but quickly composed herself. "In bed," she replied, nonchalantly, purposefully avoiding looking at Sorcerer.

Baltaan shrugged her shoulders and turned away.

"Do we follow?" Tinker whispered, as he peeked his head up between Monk and Vampire.

"Just not too close," Monk answered.

Baltaan strutted her way to the oversized entrance and peered over her shoulder with a flirtatious grin as she continued through.

"Let's go," Vampire told them. He nodded at Sorcerer who was having a difficult time not reacting to seeing the Witch who had taken the life of his wife.

They made it to the door and turned right to follow where she had gone.

"I don't like—" Monk was quickly cut off by the vision of the royal temptress holding a rifle. She cocked the barrel and pointed it at them.

No one moved.

"That way," she demanded and made her way to them and then strode past, as they parted to let her through.

Baltaan stomped her heels down a corridor and through an open door onto the patio, where a celebration was being prepared. Servants were rushing around to ready tables and linens, dinnerware, silverware, crystal glasses, flowers, and strings of overhead lights. They were painting the royal seal onto the floor of the entrance for the evening's festivities. At the sight of the queen, the workers began rushing even faster and clumsily began to drop and break things.

"Ugh," Baltaan shook her head in disgust. "Guests will enter from there!" she yelled. "No one is to enter the palace. Is that clear?"

"Yes. Yes, my lady. Of course."

She made her way out past the temporary entrance and turned. She lifted her weapon into the air and pointed back towards the area being prepared.

A collective gasp fell over the servants. The Ambassadors faced one another in disbelief.

BANG!

The deafening sound echoed in the late morning air.

Servants dropped to the floor and the sound of breaking glass and porcelain followed. Vampire quickly stood in front of Monk, as if to shield him.

"Really?" Monk stepped out from behind Vampire. He walked towards Baltaan as she sent another shot into the air and forced everyone to duck for cover again.

"DUBAIR!" she screamed.

"Put down the gun!" replied the King of Tebbs as he stepped out from the palace. "Dear," he added with a sense of ease.

The king walked up with his arms outstretched and his hands palm down. He, too, expected that people would come forward and kiss his rings. The servants were still so frightened by Baltaan's actions that they could not think clearly. He sent a displeased look in their direction that quickly reminded them of their responsibilities. As several of them initiated the appropriate response, he refused their attempt with an angered glare. They froze, afraid to continue forward, towards him, yet afraid to go back and not give the proper greeting. King Dubair ignored them and looked to his stunning wife with a loving smile.

"I was sleeping, my love," he informed her and kissed her on her right cheek.

"Yes, my king," she said and then whispered as they kissed on the left cheek, "but you have unexpected guests."

"I never have uninvited guests. I have intruders who need to be dealt with properly."

The queen raised her eyebrow and looked over his shoulder.

His majesty turned and saw the Ambassadors staring. Their expressions ran the gamut of emotions. Tinker was still peering out from between Monk and Vampire with wide fearful eyes. Monk and Vampire looked annoyed. Seer kept his head down, as did Sorcerer, as if he were trying to solve a complicated puzzle. The Twins were focused on Baltaan, impressed by her beauty. AZ stood protectively close to Princess. Princess maintained her appropriately political air.

"Oh, my dear," the king held his hand to his heart, gazing at Princess. "You have become quite the beautiful woman, now, haven't you?" He walked forward, displeasing his wife by leaving her behind him.

"Your majesty," Princess returned with the appropriate curtsy.

"Is your mother here?" the king asked, displeasing the queen further.

"No," Princess apologized in her most charming tone. "Unfortunately, not. Nor my uncles. Due to pressing matters, they were unable to make the journey and have asked us to attend in their honor." She quickly added, "I'm sure you heard what happened in Dellai and of course, Gokyuzu."

"Yes. The dragon." King Dubair nodded as he spoke in a serious tone. "We have heard. We watched in horror as Gokyuzu fell from the sky."

"Yes. It was a shock to us all," Princess said, sadly.

"Terrible beast," he said, shaking his head.

"But they are safe," Princess continued. "And they send their best."

"Their best? Of course, they did — you are here, my child," he said, laughing obnoxiously.

The king took Princess by the hands and held her at arm's length.

"If he takes your girlfriend," Axel whispered into AZ's ear, "I'm taking his wife." He winked at Baltaan.

She returned the look.

"Not a good idea," Sorcerer let him know.

"Dubair?" Queen Baltaan questioned her enamored husband. "We need to start getting ready."

"Yes! Yes! Our anniversary party!" The king's eyes went wide with excitement. "I am happy to accept the gift sent from Mortua." He smiled at Princess. "To be in your beautiful presence."

Shaking her head, Princess lied and said, "Yes. Yes. We are here to represent the Royal Family of Mortua."

"You see, my dear!" King Dubair spoke to his queen. "I told you that the RSVP must have been intercepted."

"Yes, you did," Baltaan agreed, smiling suspiciously at Princess. "Yes, you did."

"We'll need another table… Near ours!"

"No, your majesty," Princess said. "Please don't go to any trouble on our behalf. You were obviously not expecting us, and our finer wardrobes had been sent with the response. We have nothing to wear. We would not want to draw any attention and would definitely not want to be the reason for a blemish on this most spectacular… *spectacle*. We will speak tomorrow."

"Nonsense. You will be our guests and give no thought to your attire. I'm sure that we have the perfect pieces and sizes for you and your entourage. Your servant and guards will, of course, be given lodging in our stables."

"Servant and guards?" she asked.

"Yes, my love. Those three," he said, pointing to the Twins and AZ. "Vampire's manservant can serve as your waiter," he added, pointing to Tinker, who again ducked behind Vampire and Monk. "Hello, Monk. Always nice to have you here," Dubair continued. "He will have to have his back to the crowd. I don't want him scaring the other guests with that face," he whispered to Princess. "Sorcerer, my friend. I must remind you that magic is illegal here," he yelled.

"And I will not tolerate any form of retaliation for days gone by." He again whispered to Princess. "We will discuss your need to have that mage in your party. I want him in the open so that if he gets fidgety with those fingers and spells, my people can stop him before he lights something on fire or poisons the food."

"I understand. I vouch for your security."

"Yes, my child. I know."

Princess noticed Georges, who returned the look with his perfect smile. "And your own guard detail is, as always, top notch," she told him.

Baltaan had been listening to their exchange with growing interest. But she maintained her cold facial expression.

"Oh, I am so happy to have you here," the king said. "Now this party is worth having!"

Baltaan's eyes widened in disbelief. "*Now* this is worth having?"

"Oh, my dear. You know what I mean. Family is here. And here to celebrate us. To celebrate you," he told her in his jovial way. King Dubair leaned in for a loving hug with his wife.

"Yes. Such a reunion is so welcomed," Baltaan lied as she gave Princess a death stare.

Princess stood her ground and maintained her stoic facial expression.

CHAPTER 28
The Palace of Tebbs

Princess walked back to conference with the others. The king and Baltaan had turned their backs and were gliding back into the palace.

"So that we are all on the same page," Princess whispered as she met with the Ambassadors. "There was no invitation. Agreed?" Princess asked.

"Oh God no," Vampire whispered back. "These two would never willingly allow any member of the Royal Family of Mortua inside these palace grounds. We need to exercise great caution."

"Regardless, we are going to a party tonight," Princess told them, with her body language moving as if giving orders.

"Yes!" said Axel, just loud enough to stop Dubair and Baltaan from walking back into the palace. But when he grew silent, they continued into their royal home.

"No, not you," Princess told him. "Nor you, and sorry — but not you either," she told Aldrick and AZ. "My guards and servant will be staying in the stables."

They stared at her in disbelief.

"And Tinker, you will be our personal waiter. That also means that you have to taste the food before handing it to us."

"So, I may die," Tinker stated, offended by the idea.

"Sorry," she said.

"Why him?" AZ demanded.

Princess replied, "The king thinks Tinker is Vampire's manservant."

"What?" Tinker yelled back.

"So, Vampire, Monk, Sorcerer, Seer, and I will be guests at their anniversary party with Tinker as our server."

"Can I go to the stables?" Sorcerer asked.

"No. He doesn't trust you not to do magic and wants you close," Princess informed him. "Remember, magic is illegal here. He doesn't trust that you won't light the place on fire or poison the food."

Sorcerer gave her a look of disbelief.

"His words, not mine," Princess told him. "Just be careful with your hand movements."

"What's that supposed to mean?"

"Just keep your hands on the table."

"We need to get that sword," Monk reminded everyone. "And the green Cez stone."

"Well, walking in and asking for it was never going to work," Vampire said sarcastically, as he faced Princess.

"You still don't know that for sure," she argued, but then backed down. "But you're probably right. The good thing is that he did not mention The Dark Sisters. Plan?"

Everyone glimpsed around and to the ground and sky and then to each other.

"Ah-hmmm…" sounded from behind Princess. The Twins drew their swords.

"Excuse me, your highness," begged a frightened servant.

"Oh. I'm sorry," Princess said.

"Thank you. Can you please have your men lower their swords? It's already been a very harrowing day and we still have the rest of the preparations and the event tonight," he continued, as if he were just one emotional breakdown away from permanent insanity.

"Yes, of course." Princess motioned for the Twins to put away their swords.

"I have been tasked to take you and your party inside to get ready," the servant said, his voice shaking.

"And Kungs will take your servant and guards to the stables."

"Thank you, Kungs," Princess said to the beastly looking ogre with his excessive underbite and fang-like lower incisors sticking up to the sides of his nose.

Kungs said nothing as he turned and walked away. The Twins and AZ glanced at each other. Kungs continued to walk from the palace without any regard to the fact that they had not followed.

Princess hit AZ in the back of the head. He looked at her in shock, but then spied the servant's shocked expression.

"Oh sorry!" AZ said. "Yes. Yes. We go with Kungs."

He turned away as ordered, but she pulled him back with concern in her eyes.

"AZ. Trust no one. They are separating us with intent. Get whatever information you can but be careful."

AZ nodded and listened to his orders. This was uncharacteristic for AZ. Vampire overheard the exchange and nodded to Princess as AZ moved away.

AZ hit the Twins on the shoulders, and they all rushed after Kungs, who was far into the field.

Princess turned back and saw the servant, still looking shocked. "Good help — you know," she attempted to joke. "Hard to find."

"I would have lost my eye for that," he said, his voice quivering.

"Too much to do," she replied. "Maybe tomorrow. You know, after the party." He stood shaking. "Shall we go?" she asked, trying to change the topic. He turned and although he continued shaking, led them into the palace.

The servant walked with an even pace as Princess, Monk, Vampire, Sorcerer, Seer, and Tinker lingered back.

Tinker was studying every elaborate detail as they walked down the hallway that ran the length of the palace.

"What are you looking for?" Sorcerer asked him.

"Places to set up surveillance equipment and some distractions, just in case," he replied, his gaze turning in all directions like a squirrel searching for a nut.

"Good idea," Monk said. "But be a bit more conspicuous, please," he added, sarcastically.

"Ah, yes." Tinker apologized and stopped fidgeting. He began to drop what seemed like sand from his pocket. The grains were immediately hidden in the carpet.

They arrived at the far end of the palace hallway.

"Your rooms have been prepared for you at the top of the staircase," the servant told them.

"Are we to go alone?" Vampire asked, his brow furrowing with suspicion.

"Yes. My service area is restricted to this floor. But worry not, if you trip and fall, I will be here to catch you," he attempted his joke with a neutral tone of voice.

No one laughed.

"Okay, then. Thank you," Monk nodded at the servant. "Shall we?" he said to the others.

They began ascending the red-carpeted, wide staircase that split at the mid floor landing and curved out on both sides to continue up to the second floor.

CHAPTER 29
The Palace of Tebbs

AZ and the Twins continued to follow Kungs. They had purposely caught up with him and attempted to befriend him. AZ wondered why an ogre like Kungs would be subservient willingly. He began to think that someone had something over him.

AZ ran through scenarios in his mind. *Could you have killed someone, and this is your punishment? No: you would fight that. Did they destroy your village and kill everyone you knew and loved? No: you would have nothing to live for and would fight against—* AZ stopped and thought the saddest thought.

"They are keeping your family imprisoned. Aren't they?" he said out loud.

Kungs stopped but did not turn. The Twins continued their attempts to coax Kungs into their trust. He stood silent and motionless. AZ knew that that was the reason. His loved ones were imprisoned with the promise of their torture and even death if Kungs did not do what was demanded of him. The Twins realized that Kungs had stopped and turned back at AZ. They saw the tortured look on AZ's face. They focused back on Kungs and saw the sadness in his eyes.

"Well," Axel began, "maybe—"

"We can help," concluded Aldrick.

Kungs answered them with silence.

AZ walked up to them and faced Kungs. "The Princess of Mortua will hear of this. She will—"

"She will do nothing. She will hear nothing," Kungs said. "You will be staying here."

He pointed to the impressive looking stables.

"These are the stables?" asked Aldrick.

Although the stables were beautifully maintained, they were out of sight of the palace. They were in a valley with a river rushing behind them. The white and copper birch forest through which they had entered continued on the other side of the river. The evergreen forest was on the side of the river with the stables. However, the trees were more spread out in this area and allowed for more sunlight. On the other side of the river was another building. The building appeared dilapidated and in ruin.

"Kungs — what is that building?" asked Axel.

"The old stables. It houses the fireworks for tonight's festivities and will be destroyed when they are set off."

"I could see why," Axel acknowledged.

Kungs said nothing. He turned to walk away.

"Kungs?" AZ begged. Kungs stopped but did not turn. "Thank you," he said.

"Thank you," Kungs replied and began his walk up the hill off the road.

AZ watched as Kungs walked away. His posture assured AZ that what he thought was true. He turned to discuss it with the Twins, but they were making their way to the river.

"Where are you going?" he asked and began running towards them so that they were not overheard.

"To the old stables, obviously," Aldrick told him.

"Wait! We don't even know who's here… and who is watching us," AZ pleaded.

"We are tired, and we smell. The river is our excuse," Axel said.

"Bathing in the river?"

"Yup."

"That river?" AZ pointed to the violently rushing river in front of them.

"I see your point," Axel said.

"But yup," Aldrick said.

"Let's at least see the stables. Someone is here. I'm sure of it. Someone has to be. Maybe there's another way over," AZ pleaded.

The Twins continued walking towards the river.

"We're going to get caught!" AZ yelled to them.

"Then you can be our lookout!" they shouted back, but the sound of the river drowned out their voices.

"Idiots," AZ said to himself.

AZ refused to follow the Twins to the rushing river that separated the new stables from the old ones. He entered the new stables, which he found to be quite lovely. Inside, it smelled of flowers and sweet fruits. These stables were not the sloppy, smelly barns that he expected to find, but quite accommodating. However, he did remember that his purpose was not to be comfortable, but rather to get the Sword of Sansit and the green Cez stone and get back on track with the quest before them.

As AZ searched around the stables, he found familiar structures for animals such as horses, and possibly cows, and also wider pens that he thought would be for goats and sheep. There were fenced-in areas outside of the wider pens and he also spied an area that looked perfect for chickens. There was a large fenced-in area that appeared to be for training horses, and an open field for cows and sheep.

The interesting thing was that there were no animals; not a single horse nor any chickens clucking in the afternoon breeze. The sound of the river was a hypnotic white noise that encouraged sleep. AZ thought that maybe the animals were being housed elsewhere as the stables looked as if they'd just been completed.

No one was present in the stables. There was not a single worker: No carpenter finishing the building. No servant or attendant cleaning and readying the pens. No trainer for the missing animals. AZ spied outside towards the river and saw that the Twins had made their way across.

"*How the...?*" he questioned, as he watched the rushing white water smashing against boulders that were too far apart to step across and too slippery to jump and successfully make one's way across. AZ turned to go out and get to the river. He was stopped in his tracks and frightened by the sight of the ogre standing directly in front of him. The sound of the river had silenced his approach.

"Kungs? Hey!" He attempted to seem jovial through his fear. "Sorry. I didn't hear you coming." Kungs stood with his brooding posture but said nothing.

"Hey. I'm going to go and bathe in the river with the Twins," he added. "We smell from the journey."

AZ motioned as if he would like to go around Kungs. But Kungs maintained his position in the way of AZ's exit.

"Kungs? Excuse me. I'm going to the river to bathe."

"You were told not to go to the old stables," Kungs reminded him.

"Well, as you can see, I am not in the old stables. I am here in front of you." Kungs said nothing. "And smelling like a pig too ugly for slaughter. So… if you don't mind…"

"They are in the old stables," Kungs stated with a robotic tone.

"Okay. Then, let's go and see what's going on so that you can scold them. Believe me. They can use a good ass-kicking. Poor parenting, I guess."

Kungs did not move.

"You were told not to go to the old stables," Kung repeated.

AZ tried to contain his nervousness. "And I didn't. Kungs? I am going to demand that you get out of my way. Otherwise, the princess will hear of this and I don't think that-"

Without warning, Kungs grabbed AZ and hoisted him over his head.

AZ screamed out and attempted a pointless struggle. "Kungs! I demand that you put me down!"

Kungs pulled back and then launched AZ into the wall. The force was so hard that AZ felt the pain of crashing into the wall and smashing it and then the second offense of landing on the hard ground, which knocked the air from his lungs.

The smash was so loud that despite the noise of the river, the Twins heard it from the other side.

"Oh shit!" Aldrick yelled out.

AZ made feeble attempts to move. He was in serious pain and unable to catch his breath. Kungs walked slowly towards him. AZ was in too much pain to attempt a quick escape.

"Kungs?" AZ tried to force out. "Please — no…"

Kungs reached where AZ lay and lifted him by the throat with his left hand. With his right hand, he punched him in the face and sent him flying through the air for the second time. However, this time, he flew out of a window and landed in the river. The rush of the water immediately took him. AZ continued his feeble attempts to control his body. He was unable to breathe and was now drowning in the rushing river. His body made contact with the boulders that lined the river. He felt as though he was starting to break apart as he bobbed up and down and tried to take in air through his mouth.

Princess, he thought, as water entered his lungs. Yet he was too weak, and his body was too broken to cough the words out. AZ's limp body was pulled out of sight over a waterfall by the violent river current.

CHAPTER 30
The Palace of Tebbs

AZ struggled for air. His bones were broken. His right lung was punctured. He was bleeding from the mouth, and he definitely had a concussion. Yet his single thought was still the same. Princess…

He could not feel, and he did not know if he was dead or alive. If alive, he was out of the water and survived the drowning. If dead, it did not matter. His right eye was swollen shut and his left was closed. He was too weak to open it, but he tried.

Alive, he thought.

He figured that if he were dead, he would be able to open his eyes and he would not be so weak. Then he began to feel something. It was pain. He was definitely alive. The pain was severe, yet he was too weak to scream.

He started to experience light. The blackness behind his closed eyes was now turning red. He was able to sense light the same way that one would experience facing the sun with closed eyes. The light was now turning white. The pain was increasing. Then he heard the sound of his own screaming. The pain was overwhelming, but he was now able to muster the strength to make audible sounds. Although still labored, his breathing was deeper. He felt his lungs being able to increase their volume and actively inhale. Exhalation was still involuntary, but it now came with a cough. The cough caused muscle contractions that increased the pain. AZ began to focus on all the changes in his functions. He began to feel his body move with erratic convulsions.

"This is it," he said, softly. "I died."

"Almost," he heard someone say. "But we got to you in time."

The voice was familiar but still distant. AZ felt that his body was spread out. He was on his back. The white light began to flicker. He felt the warmth of a fire. He felt the cold of his wet clothes. He took his first deep breath. It forced him to cough and caused painful contractions throughout his body. Slowly, he was able to control his exhalations.

"Alive," he mouthed.

"Yes, AZ. Alive."

The familiar voice was Sorcerer.

"It was a damn good thing that Seer was able to tell you about this," Axel said to his father.

"And that you were able to get here without being missed," Aldrick added.

"They are keeping a tight watch on me so that I do not perform any magic but your mother had taught me an invisibility spell that leaves no magical trace, the same one that kept me safe for all those years."

AZ was able to open his left eye and saw that he was staring at Sorcerer's relieved face. He felt the warmth of a fire and smelled a series of herbs. They smelled awful and he wrinkled his face.

"Yeah, well, just be glad that I had them," Sorcerer joked and moved away. "And that the spell had been prepared before getting here in anticipation of something like this along the way."

"Welcome back, AZ," Axel said with a big smile.

"I'd hug you, but you'd probably break," added Aldrick.

"Okay. I have to get back," Sorcerer told them. "This shit-show of a party is going to be starting in a little while, and if I'm not there, they will come looking for me. He needs to rest a bit longer, but when he starts to get anxious and tries to get up—"

"Knock him out?" Axel hoped.

"No. Let him move. He needs to start moving as soon as possible. His body will let him know when it is ready."

"All right," Axel agreed, pretending to be disappointed.

"And then, you know where to meet."

"Yes," Aldrick assured him.

"Good luck."

"Yes. You too. AZ? You're in good hands."

AZ coughed.

"Not sure he agrees," Aldrick joked.

"But not like he has a choice," Axel added and gave his brother a fist bump.

"True," Sorcerer said as he faded from view.

CHAPTER 31
The Palace of Tebbs

Princess found herself in a large bedroom suite with an assortment of gowns and accessories.

"Oooh," cooed a voice from behind a rack of ball gowns.

"Hello?" Princess attempted to find the source of the sound.

"Boo!"

Princess jumped back with a bit of shock at the frivolity.

"Ummm," she attempted a greeting. "Hello?"

A child-sized woman with wide, shimmering eyes came through the rack of gowns and began to make orgasmic sounds as she rubbed herself against the fabrics that she touched.

"Was I escorted to the wrong—"

"Petitious LaGare," the woman said, offering her outstretched hand. Princess met her hand with a gracious, palm-down gesture.

Petitious grabbed Princess forcefully and began to shake her hand as if she would rip her shoulder from its socket.

"May I say, you are as exquisite as I've heard!" She continued her physical assault on Princess' right arm.

"Why… why, thank you," Princess stammered. "May I have that back please?" She glanced at her arm.

"Oh, I am so sorry, my lady," Petitious apologized. "It's just that—" She scanned around to see that they were alone. "And I did not say this…" She spied again. "But your beauty rivals even hers. I mean, if this is Mermaid beauty, no wonder men dive to their deaths just to get one chance at— you know…"

"Yes. I know," Princess said cautiously. "And thank you. Can I help you with something?"

Petitious laughed so hard that she fell back into the rack. "Can you help me?" she said and continued laughing. "No. No… I am here to help you." Petitious pulled herself upright again and fussed with her hair and clothes to make sure that they were in order. She produced a hand mirror and saw her heavily made-up face. "You see, I am your royal dresser for the evening. My team and I will be providing your beauty for the festivities."

"Oh, thank you but—"

"No. Thank you! The queen has asked me and my team to assist with your wardrobe, hair, and…" She waved her hands through her hair and then lowered them to frame her face. "Makeup."

"Oh. Again, thank you," Princess said, graciously. "But I am simple in my presentation—"

"Yes. Natural beauty. I hear ya!" Petitious rummaged through the rack of gowns. "But we can all use a little help for a special occasion, right?" she said with a wink.

"Right. But… I'm actually allergic…" Princess lied.

"Hypoallergenic," Petitious insisted as she continued to search through the fashions.

"And I'm used to a simple palette…"

"Lips and eyes, my dear. Lips and eyes must be accentuated."

"But…"

"Listen, my lady. I understand. You may not feel as though you could pull this off." Petitious playfully acknowledged her own look. "But let's see what you can offer as 'the best you'."

Princess was stunned. "Ummm… Okay," was all she could muster. And then she thought, *I can always wipe it off before heading down.*

"Great!" Petitious screamed with excitement. "Gals! Let's go! We are full on for glamor."

Petitious began to circle Princess as her assistants came into view. They came from under tables, from behind curtains, from under the sheets on the bed and one even descended from the chandelier.

"WOW!" Princess exclaimed. "Quite the entrance."

"And quite the Glam Squad!" Petitious bragged.

"Do you work with the queen as well?" Princess asked.

"No. No. No," Petitious whispered as the others held their tongues and gasped. "She has a very… particular group of dressers and assistants.

"She has a certain look," one of the others added.

"She is quite beautiful," Princess admitted.

Princess was positioned in front of the mirror. Two of the women carried a step ladder and placed it behind her. They opened it and one ascended to the top rung. Two of the other ladies began to bring the gowns and climb halfway up the ladder to hand them to the woman on the top. She threw the gowns, one at a time, over the front of Princess to see how they looked against her. Petitious was sitting and drinking a cup of tea and nodding or shaking her head to say either 'yes' or 'no' to the potential gown for the evening's event.

Princess tried to ask questions but was frequently interrupted by feathers and collars blocking her mouth.

The gowns were a full onslaught of color, fabric and fit. The ones that got a 'yes' response were hung on the rack to the right and the 'no' gowns were thrown into a bin on the left to be taken away. Sixteen gowns made the cut.

"Color down," Petitious said. "Now for texture and fit." She waved her fingers to demand that Princess begin to try on each gown for comparison and for further eliminations.

Princess was actually enjoying herself with all of this. It was not something that she would regularly agree to do. However, since she was fishing for information, she felt as though she needed to comply with Petitious' demands.

"So, tell me more about the queen," Princess said from behind the dressing mirror. "I know that she's beautiful, but how did she come to marry the king? How is she received by the people? How—" Princess cut herself off when she came out from behind the dressing mirror in the first gown and saw Baltaan towering over the dressers.

Petitious was making wide eyes at Princess as if warning her.

"Your majesty?" Princess said with a bow. "I'm sorry. I did not realize you were here."

"Obviously," she said in an annoyed tone. "Otherwise, you would not be questioning this lower class of servants about me." She peered with distaste at the ladies of Petitious' team. Her nose twitched with anger.

"Oh no, my lady," Princess quickly apologized. "I just wanted to make sure that I would make a good impression on you this evening." Princess offered a full apology. "I am sorry if I offended you, but I meant nothing like that."

Baltaan forced a half smile. "Oh, my child," she began and reached out to stroke Princess' hair. "That dress is definitely not your color."

She turned and exited with a slamming of the door.

Princess looked to Petitious. Petitious shook her head.

"Back to work ladies," she said, all business now. "Lots to do and not much time."

The ladies performed their tasks with caution and kept quiet while doing so.

CHAPTER 32
The Palace of Tebbs

Petitious continued with her detailing of Princess' styling.

"Petitious?" Princess asked while she was finishing her makeup.

"My lady?"

"Did I cause a problem for you and the ladies?"

"Oh, my dear," Petitious spied to see that no one was close enough to hear. "Life here is a constant problem." Princess gave her a look of pity. "We are sent to dress and do the makeup of female dignitaries so that they will be embarrassed by the queen. No dignitary who is wanting to gain favor would dare question her. They go along with it for political reasons. Everyone has a personal agenda. Ours is just to survive."

Princess looked to the floor with sorrow. "Petitious. I owe you an apology."

"No, you don't."

"Yes. Yes, I do. I told a member of my party that no one here can be trusted. No one is a friend." She glanced up at Petitious' heavily made-up face. "I was wrong."

Petitious smiled.

"You are my friend."

Petitious began to cry.

"And I humbly thank you and your team for giving me such special attention."

She leaned in for a hug. Petitious pulled back.

"Oh, I'm sorry. I just thought…"

"No. No, my dear," Petitious cried out. "It's just that you caught me off guard. Usually, the women are horrified at what we do to them. They beat us. They hold us responsible. In a way, they are right. We are the ones who do it to them, but we have no choice."

Petitious was crying effusively. Her make-up ran down her face, streaking in garish colors from her eyes to her chin. Princess pulled her in for a hug and this time, Petitious did not pull back. She cried every tear that she had in her onto Princess and the shoulder and chest of that ball gown. Princess held her there until Petitious felt as though she was dried out. She sat back and laughed at herself.

"You are not like any royal I've ever met," she joked. But then, she stopped, horrified. "Oh, Princess! The gown!"

Princess peered down at herself and began to laugh. "It looks better now."

She laughed harder. Petitious followed suit and laughed as well. She stared at the make-up stains on the gown.

"Petitious — why do you say that you have no choice?"

"No, my lady. Please. It is too dangerous to talk about. These walls have ears… Very fearful ears but ears nonetheless."

"I understand."

Petitious sighed in relief.

"I understand that the queen makes her guests alter their appearance so as not to take away from her own beauty."

Petitious' eyes widened in fear at Princess' whispered words. She looked around in horror. "My lady?"

"I understand. I do not believe that her beauty is threatened, but it's not me who has her beauty."

"Oh, but you do," Petitious could not help but admit. She quickly held her hand to her mouth as if she had let out a foul sound.

"Thank you, Petitious."

Petitious observed the girl with curiosity as Princess stood and looked at herself in the mirror. Princess considered how to make the best of Petitious' offensive styling while also respecting her political position and needs.

"No," Petitious spoke. "You are not like any other royal I've ever met." Princess shook her head and smiled at the reflection of Petitious in the mirror. "And I do not believe Mermaid, either," Petitious added, sniffing the air.

"Excuse me?"

"You do not smell like a Mermaid," Petitious continued, moving closer and took whiffs from the air uncomfortably close to Princess. "Your scent is different... Somewhat like hers."

"Excuse me?" Princess repeated, but this time with a bit of offense.

"Oh, don't get all sensitive on me now." Petitious began milling about the dressing room and gathering various accessories. "It's not like Mermaids smell like dead foul fish or salty dried seaweed," she continued, scrunching up her face. "Just the opposite." She smiled and stared away in reverie. "Mermaids smell like sunshine and a fresh breeze. They smell like everything that makes you smile."

"I do believe that I am equally offended for not smelling like that," Princess joked, while still looking in the mirror at Petitious' joy.

"Oh, my dear," Petitious laughed as she took Princess by the hand and brought her to stand on the elevated block that was set up for alterations in front of angled mirrors. "Your beauty surpasses even that of the Mermaids. More like a... Witch."

"A Witch?" Princess laughed. "No, Petitious. My mother comes from the original line of the first Mermaid queen of Mortua."

"Yes. I know the legend."

"Legend? No. It's the truth," Princess said, getting a bit defensive.

"Oh, your majesty. No. Please don't be angered at me. I mean no disrespect." Princess continued her gently offended glare. Petitious looked around and leaned in. "I am Fae…"

Princess quickly pulled back. She had heard stories about the Fairies of the Forest and the trickster ways that made them untrustworthy.

"I should say, reformed Fae," Petitious added, with her right hand over her heart and her left hand in the air as if swearing to a cause. "You would be right to not trust the Fae. It's not our fault. We had to learn to protect ourselves and stay hidden. Unfortunately, over generations, our self-protection through trickery created the stereotype that we are not to be trusted."

"Oh Petitious, I am sorry," Princess began to apologize.

"Oh, no. The stereotype is there for a reason. It is true. Fae are not to be trusted. It's just that, initially…" she looked around the room to be sure that no one had snuck in, "my present situation confirmed that the Fae would always be abused by others. We were captured and brought here. At first, they were stripping our wings from us."

"You mean—"

"Yes. They would go and brutally cut them off. But you see the essence of a fairy is in the wings. To separate the wings from the fairy would result in death and death with no afterlife."

"They realized that this procedure was not going to aid them, so they then started to snip areas throughout the wings. The wings were made useless for flight and the Fae would have no means of escape. But this aged us too quickly to be of any use to them. And then this added to the sadness of the Fae."

Princess felt every bit of the pain that was being described by the fairy.

"Petitious?" Princess asked.

"Yes. Yes," Petitious returned to the present and continued with her story. "But then finally, they got it right. They locked our wings to our bodies."

Petitious undid her petticoat and exposed the metal corset that concealed her fairy wings. Even beneath the corset, the wings twinkled as if ready for use. Princess reached out to touch them, but then pulled her hand back.

"Now that story is not true," Petitious said. Princess glanced at her quizzically. "You can touch the wings of the Fae. It will not hurt us, and it will not hurt you. It will not transfer any powers to you, either. If I had an apple for every pair of wings I've touched, I would have— six apples."

She turned and looked excitedly at Princess. She pulled her top back on and buttoned it.

Princess was still staring at her new friend with pity.

"Please wipe that look right off your face," Petitious said. "Being here has shown me the error of the ways of the Fae. We have been living in fear and that is no way to live. Afraid of coming out of hiding. Believing that anyone who is not Fae will take advantage of us." She caught Princess' expression. "Yes. I can see that that is more likely, but not always," Petitious added, walking back to Princess, and grabbing her hands. "Not everyone is trying to take advantage."

Princess smiled modestly and squeezed her hands.

"I did find love while I was here," Petitious beamed, but then grew sad again. "But he was taken away. I was told he was dead."

Princess felt as though her heart was continuously being ripped out of her chest listening to the journey of love and loss that was the life of Petitious.

"But at least I felt love," Petitious said, with false cheer. She looked at Princess, who seemed to have the most comforting and giving spirit Petitious had ever encountered. "We just have to search for the right ones and bring love back into the world."

Princess leaned over and pulled Petitious in for another tight hug. "Agreed."

"I have an idea," Petitious said, holding Princess at arm's length as her eyes shimmered again. She pulled Princess up and behind the dressing mirror.

CHAPTER 33
The Palace of Tebbs

It was less than an hour since Sorcerer left the stables. AZ was on his feet and able to move independently. AZ, Axel, and Aldrick were moving at a quick but cautious pace. They stuck to the cover of the trees to avoid being seen walking through the open field.

"The old stables," Axel told AZ.

Sorcerer's elixir had taken effect and aside from a slight swelling of his eye, AZ showed no signs of Kung's assault.

They kept to a path deep in the woods

"And how did you get over the river, anyway?"

"Why, Tinker, of course," Aldrick said, laughing.

"Tinker? He wasn't with us," AZ said.

"Oh, but some of his toys were. He made the mistake of telling us how some of them worked and we guessed which ones might serve us the best."

"They seemed to—" Aldrick searched for the words.

"Somehow…" Axel added.

"Somehow make their way into our pockets," Aldrick said, finishing their combined thought. "Including this invisible bridge that expands upon contact with water."

"Although not exactly sturdy," Axel added, rotating his hand in the air.

"It got us across."

"Yes. Yes, it did."

"Invisible bridge, huh?" AZ wasn't sure if he was more impressed with them for having the sense to steal and use it or with Tinker for inventing it in the first place.

CHAPTER 34
The Palace of Tebbs

Princess and Petitious rushed down the staircase. Princess was late. Petitious would be punished. Her assistants might even be put to death in front of her for her disregard of protocol.

"But it is all worth it," Petitious said to herself. "We will be oppressed no more."

Petitious had reworked everything: the dress, the makeup. Petitious had styled Princess to enhance her natural beauty rather than cover it up the way the queen demanded. Princess would shine as the beacon of hope and love that she was. This was to serve as the beginning of the revolution. The Fae would rise from the slavery and tyranny that they had been forced into. Petitious would lead the revolution and Princess would stand beside her, providing the hope that her people needed in order to trust that they had allies and that their time to rise was now.

They were halfway down the middle hallway of the palace when they heard, "Princess!"

They turned to the familiar voice.

"Tink!" Princess said, excitedly.

"You're gorgeous. I mean, you are always gorgeous, but…"

"This is not *him,* is it?" Petitious asked, wondering at Tinker's awkwardness.

Tinker went silent.

"No. This is my best friend, Tinker," Princess told Petitious. "What's going on?" she asked Tinker.

"I'm trying to bring out drinks and fighting with the staff," Tinker told her. He realized the Petitious was one of them. "Sorry."

"Sounds about right," Petitious spoke without surprise. "The kitchen staff is mostly human and does not take to newcomers."

Tinker looked questioningly at the smart-mouthed fairy.

Servants rushed past them in all directions, carrying all sorts of trays with food and drink and pushing carts and carrying furniture and linens.

Groups of guards were heading in the other direction. Tinker turned his back and tried to not be seen.

"Come on, Tink. Come with us. We are heading out to the party. And my dear friend, Petitious, is about to lead a revolution. She and her people—"

"And others too; not just Fae," Petitious interrupted.

"The time is now, Tink."

Princess grabbed his hand and pulled him quickly down the rest of the red-carpeted hallway. She held Petitious' hand in her left and Tinker's hand in her right. And then she stopped dead in her tracks and turned to Tinker.

"Tink? By any chance, do you have anything on you that can get through a metal restraint?" Princess flashed Petitious a sneaky grin.

Petitious returned the look with a wink.

"Magical or non-magical?" Tinker asked, as he held two different keys with malleable ends that could conform to any lock.

"Magical," Princess answered to Petitious' surprise. "That would be the only way to limit the spirit of the Fae."

Petitious nodded in proud agreement. Petitious and Tinker ran off to release her from the restraint. Princess continued charging to the end of the palace and entered the cool night air.

CHAPTER 35
The Palace of Tebbs

The festivities were in high gear. Regalia adorned the area of the palace grounds that had been decorated for the anniversary celebration. Princess stood at the top of the staircase and scanned the crowd. She caught the infuriated eye of Baltaan. She nodded with a simple smile and descended the staircase with a dramatic posture that she knew would catch the attention of the other guests.

Baltaan's face began to twitch at the left side of her nose and the right side of her mouth. All eyes were on Princess. No one, not even King Dubair, was aware of Baltaan's displeasure… Except Princess.

Princess saw Monk and Vampire in a back corner and nodded to them. Sorcerer came running up to them, a bit out of breath. Princess knew that all eyes were on her and so she did not allow her reaction to show itself on her face. She did not want to draw any attention to the conversation happening among Monk, Vampire, and Sorcerer. Seer walked up to them with his mouth gaping in awe.

"She is stunning," he said, looking up at Princess.

Sorcerer was caught up in the sight of Princess, too. He lost all concern while watching the vision of beauty that descended the palace staircase.

Sorcerer sighed. "Like her mother."

Princess graciously accepted the compliments offered by the other dignitaries as she made her way through the crowd.

"They made the right choice in sending the princess," Vampire overheard one nearby noble comment to another. "Her beauty rivals even that of the queen."

"I agree," Vampire leaned in to acknowledge.

The nobles turned in fear, worried that they'd insulted the queen and would have to buy the silence of the one who had overheard them. They were met with the smiling face of Vampire and the scowls of Monk and Sorcerer.

"Lord Just," Princess greeted the noble, as she was now within an earshot of the group. "And Lady Just," she said gracefully, leaning in for a double air-kiss. She held her gloved and bejeweled hand out to Lord Just, who gave it a kiss.

"That ring," Sorcerer demanded. He pushed Lord Just to the side.

"Please excuse my ambassador," she begged, as the Lord and Lady walked off.

"What are you doing?" she asked Sorcerer.

"Where did you get that ring?" he again demanded.

"My dresser gave it to me to wear," she replied, pulling her hand from his grip to admire the green jewel.

She immediately understood what was on her finger.

"And what were you thinking with that entrance?" Monk asked. "Subtle? I think not."

"Definitely not," she agreed. "Now, enough with this bickering. I found Tinker," she whispered, but maintained a posture that made it seem like they were not sharing secrets.

"Found? Was he more 'lost' than usual?" Vampire joked.

"There is a lot more going on here than we thought," Princess informed them.

"Yes. We too found that out," Sorcerer told her. "AZ was attacked and thrown over a waterfall."

Princess gasped in fear.

"No!" Sorcerer quickly reassured her. "He is fine! I just left him with— with the Twins. They are making their way to us."

Princess furrowed her brow.

Sorcerer, Monk, Seer, and Vampire leaned in as she spoke to them over her shoulder while continuing to graciously accept the nods and curtsies offered to her from the other party guests.

"My dresser and her team are Fae. The Fae have been kidnapped and forced into submission. Tinker is assisting with releasing them from their confinements."

"And not just Fae," Sorcerer added. "Ogres, and probably others."

"Fae have been tortured and murdered by the king and queen in order to keep them under control-"

"How dare you insinuate that," demanded Baltaan, walking by on the arm of King Dubair.

"Really, my child," he added, lightly. "From whom did you hear that? Fae? You know that they are very clever liars. Their deception is their key to survival. It's the only weapon that they have."

"And a very good weapon it is," came a voice behind the king and queen. "But not the only weapon," added Petitious, who hovered in the air with her fluttering wings moving at a dizzying pace. Also in the air were the other dressers, and several gardeners who had also doubled as lawn ornaments earlier in the day.

King Dubair looked at them in horror.

"Love is our greatest weapon," Petitious added, turning to Baltaan. "And you took mine." Her pain and anger were obvious in her voice.

CHAPTER 36
The Palace of Tebbs

Baltaan shielded herself with a magical spell as Petitious lifted an iron hammer and attempted to smash it over her head. Upon contact with the magical shield of light, the hammer turned to embers and the sparks immediately died out. Baltaan maneuvered her hands to elicit a spell that called forth a purple light that hit Petitious and sent her backwards through the air until she smashed into a table full of glasses at the far side of the party area.

"Petitious!" Princess screamed.

Baltaan grabbed Princess as the party goers began to run for cover. "Go ahead and try it," she said to Sorcerer, who had begun to cast a spell.

Baltaan held a dagger to Princess' throat while her other hand was sparking with a spell, ready to annihilate her rival. "You're coming with me," the queen said to Princess. She grabbed Dubair by the wrist and the three of them turned into a flame that swirled away in the night air.

The guests were still running senselessly around one another. Fae were flying through the air and smashing everything in sight.

"Sorcerer!" Tinker yelled, pointing towards Petitious.

Sorcerer pulled a vial from his belt loop and threw it to him. Tinker turned to Monk.

"Find us," Monk demanded.

"I will," Tinker promised, and ran off to the table where Petitious had landed.

"The ring!" Sorcerer yelled to them as he began running towards the palace. "It contains the green Cez stone."

Monk and Vampire looked at one another. "I can feel the ring," Monk said. "Why?"

"The stone," Sorcerer told them. "Envy is the sin that you are least connected to. The smallest stone."

"So I will feel them in order?" Monk asked.

"Yes," Vampire told him. "It will also let us know that we have the right stones. And exactly how sinful you are," he added, with a wink.

Sorcerer began maneuvering his fingers, and then wrists. The movements were small at first but grew as he began to move his elbows and shoulders. He rotated his trunk to the left and then pushed himself forcefully back to facing forward, and a void opened in front of him and anyone who touched its sides was sent flying away as if a bomb had gone off.

Monk ran into the swirling void and was quickly followed by Sorcerer and Vampire. As the three men entered the emptiness, it closed, leaving the chaos behind.

Tinker ran through the panicking crowd, and over to Petitious, while being pushed and shoved in all directions. Her dressers were already with her and hovering at her side. Tinker hurtled the ones on the ground and dodged the ones in the air. He uncorked the vial and held it to her nose.

"No!" yelled one of the dressers. "He'll kill her!" the dresser screamed, as the essence of the vial entered Petitious' nostrils. The smell of grass after a Spring rain came into the air.

The Fae attacked Tinker and pulled him back and away from Petitious. They were beating on him hard and all he could do was to attempt defending himself by curling into a fetal position.

But then the attack stopped.

Tinker cautiously opened his eyes and slowly lowered his clenched fists from his head. The Fae stood and hovered over him but were looking slightly away. Before him stood a defiant Petitious.

"You may need a sniff of this," she told him, as she held the vial out to him.

"Yeah," he agreed. He hesitated, but then took the vial and held it to his nose. The rush was immediate. The pain was gone, and he too was on his feet and ready to fight.

CHAPTER 37
The Palace of Tebbs

Sorcerer, Monk, and Vampire came through the portal in the palace ballroom. They looked around but saw no one. The sound of Baltaan's laughter echoed through the air.

"Sorcerer?" Vampire said. "We will get her back."

Sorcerer immediately threw an orange powder onto the ballroom floor.

"Damn it!" Vampire exclaimed.

Upon contact with the black and white harlequin tile surface, the powder immediately filled the room with a dense orange smoke. Monk reached out and grabbed hold of Vampire's outstretched hand. The smoke rising into the air made it impossible for any mortal to open his or her eyes. Vampire was able to keep his eyes open, but they were of no use. The smoke was too thick to see through. However, the magical powder allowed Vampire to sense heat. He closed his eyes and turned his head to the hand that held Monk's. He saw the heat that was generated from Monk's body and also saw that Monk's contact brought heat into Vampire's hand and arm. He looked at himself and saw that this contact was adding heat to his whole body. He turned and saw Sorcerer's heat. His register was warmer than Monk's even temper. Vampire grabbed him by the hand. Sorcerer immediately went into a defensive crouch.

"It's me," Vampire whispered. "Take my shoulder and do not let go."

Vampire took Monk's hand and placed it on his other shoulder. The three men walked cautiously. Monk and Sorcerer looked like they were outstretched wings attached to Vampire as they slowly made their way forward.

Sorcerer's spell was working. Vampire began to see the warmer cores of figures in the room. He knew by the intensity of the heat and the posturing that showed itself as the heat image became clear, that it was Baltaan restraining Princess. The king had no presence. Vampire continued his slow approach through the orange fog. Monk and Sorcerer, trusting every step that Vampire took, moved in time with him.

Baltaan's form was full and burning hot, even more intense than Sorcerer's. However, it was constantly shifting. It was as if there were more than one entity held within that form. Princess was singular and surprisingly calm, given her situation. Vampire turned to look at

Monk's essence again and saw that his own shoulder, where Monk was holding on, held a full sense of warmth. And then he was able to start making out Monk's hand through the smoke. He turned and was also able to make out Sorcerer's hand on his other shoulder. Vampire took their hands from his shoulders and stood between them. Monk and Sorcerer again followed his lead without hesitation.

The three men stood en garde. Baltaan was standing in front of them and continued turning, in an attempt to be ready for any attack. She was now panicked and continued to hold the dagger to Princess' throat.

Vampire felt Monk squeeze his shoulder. He turned and saw that Monk was able to see him. Monk nodded but maintained his silence. Sorcerer followed suit. They were close to one another but still too far from Baltaan and Princess.

Vampire saw that Baltaan's panic had begun to subside. She stood facing him with Princess as her shield. Baltaan released a sinister laugh as the smoke cleared enough for everyone to come into view. She drew the edge of the dagger deep enough against Princess' flesh to pierce it.

"I needed Mermaid blood to finish the spell. And now—"

"And now, she still needs Mermaid blood to finish that spell," said Vampire to Monk, with his usual playfulness.

A sudden explosion at a distance made the palace shake. Princess took advantage of the moment and pulled herself free from Baltaan's grasp.

Monk and Vampire glanced at one another. "Tinker," they said in unison.

Baltaan continued to stare at Vampire with an air of superiority. She took the dagger that still held the drops of blood and used it to cut a lock of her own hair. She spoke the words of a spell that made fire erupt.

"It's all right, my girl," Sorcerer whispered to Princess, holding pressure on her neck wound.

With a dramatic flourish, Baltaan spoke the final words of the spell and dropped the lock of blood-tinged hair into the burning cauldron. She began to laugh in the same eerie way again, as yellow smoke started to rise. She brought her face over the smoke and inhaled. Immediately, she knew by the sweet aroma that the spell was not cast properly.

"I don't understand," Baltaan said her thought aloud.

"The flame should be red," Sorcerer told her. "And it should have a pepper-like smell. It should make you sneeze."

A warm breeze blew in from behind them. Vampire wondered at the hauntingly familiar aroma of orange and vanilla.

Baltaan stared at Sorcerer and then focused behind him. She fought to maintain her disposition. Something was distracting her.

The king stood and grabbed Baltaan by the arm to stop her. She looked at him in surprise as he stared beyond the Ambassadors. Something at the end of the dark hall was now drawing his attention.

CHAPTER 38
The Palace of Tebbs

The silence was broken by the slow, rhythmic tapping of heels on the marble floor. Each point of contact created an echo that filled the moonlit throne room. The scent of orange and vanilla became stronger and more fragrant in the air.

The evenly spread crystal chandeliers extended in all directions and appeared like branches covered in icicles. The moonlight reflected on the floor as a breeze blew in and began turning the chandeliers. The crystals captured the moonlight in ever-changing patterns that reflected off everything in the room. As the crystals moved, their gentle clinking became louder and harsher. The candles blew out. The eerie cast of moonlight and its fractured reflections caused the room to fall silent.

No one spoke. Each wondered what was happening. The taps became louder, but the rhythm stayed the same. There was no sense of rushing. Whoever it was approached with confidence and a strength that commanded attention.

Vampire looked at Monk. He returned the stare and nodded his head in the direction of Sorcerer. Sorcerer was held in a tense reverie. He gazed at the moonlit reflections on the ceiling. His breath was short and his eyes almost tearful. Monk turned his attention towards Baltaan; although she maintained her powerful stance, she had lost control of her expression. Her nose and mouth quivered involuntarily, and her eyes squinted just slightly with each footstep that emanated from the hallway. Vampire saw that King Dubair continued to hold his wife's arm but seemed entranced. Princess' gaze lingered on Sorcerer and his tension. As she stared at him, she began to experience visions. She felt a familiarity in the footsteps, the weight, and the timing. It seemed as if she knew the sounds like a long-lost song.

"Sorcerer?" Vampire asked.

"It must be…" Sorcerer spoke almost inaudibly. "But — how?"

"Sorcerer?" Vampire reached out to him but was interrupted by Monk.

"Vampire. Look."

Vampire turned and watched as a striking female silhouette sauntered into the moonlit ballroom. She walked in and out of the natural light through the windows, displaying a robin's-egg-blue gown with a seductive fit. Her chainmail face covering moved in rhythm with her gait. The metal veil glistened as it captured the moonlight and gave intermittent hints as to the identity of who it concealed. The sound of the heels hitting the marble was now almost musical.

"No…" Baltaan whispered in disbelief. "It can't be."

"Oh, but it is," the stranger said confidently and casually leaned against a nearby column. "Hello, Baltaan."

"Ileana?"

Sorcerer gasped but kept his gaze at the ceiling.

"Surprised?"

"Shocked," Baltaan replied, losing her dignity.

"You thought I was dead?"

"I certainly did," Sorcerer replied, as he turned to see Ileana.

"I'll get to you when I am done here," she told him.

Monk noticed his nervous friend staring at the ceiling with added worry. He looked to Vampire, who was already staring back at him and shaking his head.

Ileana started her slow approach towards Baltaan. But then she began to run and moved her hands to create intricate patterns of pink light as she built up speed.

Baltaan held her position, but she too began to maneuver her arms and hands into patterns to create crimson-colored forms in the air. But she was too late. Baltaan was struck with a burst of white light that held her suspended in place.

"Who is that?" Princess asked with admiration.

"That is your mother," Sorcerer answered.

Princess focused back and forth from Monk to Vampire and then to Sorcerer, then to the action that was taking place between Ileana and Baltaan. She was unable to take her eyes off the enchanting woman who had entered the situation with full control and power.

Baltaan let out a painful scream. Her form began to morph. Her solid figure fluctuated in size, shape, color, styling, and form. Her screams grew louder and more intense. She fell to her knees and crawled over to her throne to pull herself up.

Ileana had slowed the speed of her assault but continued her approach and her hand movements.

King Dubair looked at Baltaan in horror. "My dear?"

"Get back!" she demanded.

He immediately obliged, mainly because he thought that she was about to explode.

Baltaan forced her attention back to Ileana. But her hands were too busy keeping her from falling face down on the floor. She was unable to retaliate. She let out one, last, bone-curdling scream as she turned into a white light.

Ileana's face and posture showed her strength as she continued her magical strikes.

The white light began to move. It separated into three parts of equal intensity, although one was slightly warmer, one slighter cooler, and the third a true bright white. The lights began to dim and what remained were three female figures.

The white lights were gone. Three women were left. Baltaan was down on the floor unable to physically recover. The other two looked around with confusion and fear. They struggled to balance, and their hands kept feeling all over their naked bodies as if it were the first time that they had sensed touch. The light was completely gone, and the three physical forms were solid. Baltaan was face-down and crying on the floor. She panted heavily as Ileana strolled forward and ascended the steps, staring at the shocked king.

"Sire," Ileana said, with contempt.

"I can't believe it," he begged.

"Too late for that," she replied, and reached down to grab Baltaan by the hair. Ileana pulled her to her feet. "Get something to cover them," she demanded of the onlookers, as she acknowledged the two nude beauties who had seemed to form from the light.

"That explains what I saw in the smoke," Vampire realized.

Dubair and Princess quickly grabbed tapestries to cover the two women. As the king covered the first beauty, she looked at him with the greatest sense of gratitude. Princess threw the tapestry around the second who began to do the same. She reached for Princess' hand. She immediately screamed as their hands touched.

"What? What is it?" Princess asked.

Ileana let go of Baltaan, who balanced herself on her throne. She glanced at Sorcerer who continued to stare at the movement of the chandeliers. She turned her attention to Vampire who held his gaze.

Tinker rushed into the throne room accompanied by the now rebellious flying Fae.

Ileana turned. "Tinker," she acknowledged, with a coy smile.

CHAPTER 39
The Palace of Tebbs

Tinker appeared shocked. He glanced at Monk, who was staring at him quizzically. And then to Vampire, who did the same. He turned quickly back to Ileana.

"Nice to see you again," she said, laughing as she noticed Vampire and Monk's confusion.

Tinker looked at Princess, and then at Sorcerer, who stared intensely at Tinker, Monk and Vampire.

"I'm sorry. I— I…" Tinker began. "She's getting away!" He pointed at Baltaan, who was now running out of the ballroom.

Ileana gazed back at Sorcerer. "You've looked better." Without waiting for him to respond to her insult, she pulled Baltaan back and threw her onto her throne.

Princess was still attempting to comfort the woman she'd wrapped in a tapestry, but the woman cowered away from her.

"Here. Let me," Tinker offered. He gently lifted the woman back to her feet and helped her walk over to the other woman who'd appeared in the light.

"Sorcerer," Vampire said. "Help Tinker. Those women need to be reoriented."

Sorcerer seemed to be fighting some internal battle.

"And so do you," Vampire added. "You'll only be in the way right now."

Sorcerer looked deep into Vampire's eyes.

The Fae assisted the two weakened Witches and snarled while cornering King Dubair with weapons fashioned from broken glass and table legs.

"Let me help you," Sorcerer said to the king, so that the Fae would not yet kill him for his crimes against them. He turned to see that Tinker had things under control with the two ladies who were seated on the floor, still wearing the tapestries. The Fae offered them each water.

"Tinker!" he yelled angrily. "We will talk!"

Tinker said nothing and focused on attending to the two women.

The king pushed himself up from the floor and refused any assistance. "I saved you misbegotten lot from extinction!" he yelled at the Fae.

"With slavery," yelled back one of the Fae, spitting anger.

"I don't care about you." The king seemed to weaken, and he sat on the marble steps.

Sorcerer walked over to Tinker and the two ladies who were now giggling and flirting. "That didn't take long."

"Hello, Sorcerer," said one of the women.

"Esmeralda," Sorcerer said to Tinker's surprise.

"You know her?"

"And this is Ariel."

Tinker stared in disbelief.

"I see that you ladies have met our Tinker."

Esmeralda and Ariel giggled and touched Tinker flirtatiously. He giggled, too.

"It seems that Tinker has played a part in all of this," Sorcerer said, angrily.

CHAPTER 40
The Palace of Tebbs

"You were supposed to be destroyed," Baltaan said to Ileana.

"Well, apparently that did not work out the way you planned," Ileana said, holding her arms aloft and admiring her own physical form.

"I was doing what was best for our kind," Baltaan screamed. "This one is a Witch, a powerful Witch. And now we can be five again."

"Yes. We are five again," Ileana said, kindly. "But you would be one too many."

Just then, light came crashing through the windows on either side of the room. Axel and Aldrick came swashbuckling through the southern windows and then the door to the north was flung open as AZ and Seer burst in with a slew of Fae.

Baltaan conjured a fiery ball as a threat to not come any closer.

"No, Baltaan," Ileana spoke in a comforting voice. "Don't do this."

Baltaan was crying. Her grip had weakened. Ileana was close enough to take her hand and dismiss the spell.

Ileana held her sister Witch who was now completely unraveled on the floor. Ileana rocked her to calm her.

"It was him," Baltaan spoke through her tears. "I had no choice but to keep them safe. I could not do it for the rest. I am so sorry," she added and cried harder as she looked at the Fae and the other creatures who had entered the room.

Tinker turned and saw Petitious flying. Kungs climbed through the broken window in the east. Petitious caught sight of the beastly man.

"Kungs?" she said, as if dreaming. "But no. It cannot be. Kungs is dead." She turned and screamed at Baltaan. "You told me that Kungs was dead!"

"Petitious?" Kungs questioned. "You're flying," he added, joyfully.

Petitious flew fast towards him and threw her little arms around the ogre's head. She kissed him repeatedly all over. Kungs laughed joyfully and gently held her in his massive hands. They stared at each other with obvious happiness. Then Petitious turned back to the queen.

"You told me he was dead!" she screamed.

"I had to," Baltaan shouted back through her tears. "You would never have stopped and then you would both be dead."

"They told me that you would be tortured if I fought," Kungs told Petitious.

"The king would have ordered your death, but I could not have that," Baltaan insisted. "He wanted to punish love."

"I'm not sure that I believe you," Ileana told her and faced Vampire.

"I'm not sure that I believe you either," Vampire confessed back to Ileana.

She ignored his comment and looked at her sister with pity.

"The king conspires with The Dark Sisters," Baltaan whispered, "as did I."

"Well, he will conspire no more," riposted Ileana. "The Dark Sisters are no longer."

"What do you mean?"

"I have destroyed The Dark Sisters. They are officially gone."

"And the blade?" Baltaan asked. "The Sword of Sansit?"

Ileana shook her head. "I did not find it."

"Then where is it?" Tinker asked. "I thought it was here."

"It was," Baltaan said. "But Dubair said that he destroyed it."

"That had better be a lie," Vampire said with concern as he looked at Monk's horrified expression.

Sorcerer entered the room.

"Ileana," Baltaan pulled her in for a hug. "You did what I could not."

"It took some time, and I had some help," she admitted, winking at Tinker. "But yes, I did it."

"Twenty-three years, to be exact," Sorcerer said.

Ileana helped Baltaan to stand and the two shared a look of understanding. Vampire escorted Baltaan to Monk and they both stood over her protectively. Ileana maintained eye contact with Sorcerer. The room grew quiet, as if they were the only ones in it.

"Well," Sorcerer began. "You are still quite striking."

"You've looked better."

"You already said that."

She tried not to giggle. She glanced at the Twins. "And you've done the most embarrassing job," she continued.

The Twins turned to one other in confusion.

Ileana gestured at their neck tattoos. "Any other questionable life choices that I should be aware of?"

"And who the hell is this bitch?" Axel asked, frustrated at being insulted.

"Boys — this 'bitch' is your mother," Sorcerer said.

"Well, that explains our good looks," Aldrick said. "We knew they didn't come from you."

The silence was broken by a sudden loud pop. Everyone ducked and searched to see what had happened. The Fae were uncorking champagne bottles. The corks hit the chandeliers, making them clink as they moved.

"No reason to waste it all," Axel said, as he and his brother joined the celebration.

Petitious and Kungs were holding each other tight and dancing, even though there was no music playing. The joy and laughter of the crowd set a mood that was light enough to lift their spirits into a gentle sway. They looked almost ridiculous, as if he were an oversized child squeezing his doll. Yet, their obvious love for one another made it look right.

Ileana nodded to Vampire, signaling that she wanted to meet with him privately. He walked out towards the gardens. She followed at a distance. Her gait was cautious. She and Vampire did not trust one another.

CHAPTER 41
Gardens of the Palace of Tebbs

The garden was illuminated but more dimly than the terraces that hosted the party. Ileana watched as Vampire turned back to make sure that she was following. He saw her out of the corner of his eye and turned behind a tall hedge. She grew cautious and removed her chainmail cape. It fell to the ground at the entrance to the garden maze. Vampire was leading her deeper into a garden maze.

She'd always enjoyed puzzles, especially since she completed them faster than anyone else. However, this one was different. Those were for her ego. This one could end up being for her life.

Ileana had known Vampire for centuries. They did not trust one another. They had worked for the same and for different causes. She knew his tricks, or at least, some of them. And although this did not feel like one, she hesitated. She needed to quickly come up with an escape plan.

"Up?" She looked to the sky.

Her attention was quickly pulled back to the hedges as she heard a rustling of the leaves and branches, as if a strong wind were blowing. However, she did not feel a breeze. Instead, she felt the magic.

"Damn you, Baltaan," she whispered just loud enough.

"To be fair," Vampire came into view as the hedges moved to expose his position by a fountain, "she had nothing to do with this."

"She had everything to do with this," Ileana argued, with a wave of her hand. The hedges stopped moving and seemed they had always been in their new positions.

"Well, yes. What I meant was that she had nothing to do with me guiding you here."

"Only in that she told you about the tricks of the maze," Ileana argued.

"I figured that out for myself."

"I felt it, too. But I guess I'm a bit rusty after being focused only on the destruction of The Dark Sisters for so many years."

"Or maybe you've learned to trust me," Vampire said, with sincerity.

"Yeah. That's not it." Vampire laughed. "Why did you lead me in here?" she asked.

"To see if you would follow."

"That was stupid."

"Why?"

"Because we are on the same team now, Vampire."

"Are we?"

"Yes."

"And Baltaan?" Vampire asked. "Do you believe her? That she has been protecting your sisters and those other creatures?"

"To be determined," Ileana admitted.

Vampire gazed into the fountain.

"What do you see?" he asked Ileana and motioned for her to look into the fountain.

"Flowing water?"

"Ileana."

She paused. "The future."

Ileana looked again and saw things more clearly. She saw death. She saw pain and fear ruling over love. She saw the destruction of everything.

Ileana glanced back at Vampire with concern. "You know as well as I that this is only a possibility," she told him.

"Yes. But the most likely possibility."

"And Seer? He's said nothing?"

"This deals with Immortals," Vampire said, reminding her of a seer's limited skills.

"The Jeweled Dragon."

"The image is not available to him."

"Can't you do something? After all, your purpose was destruction."

"My purpose was much less grand than this beast's. I was sent by the Enlightenment to destroy mankind. Ironic that the Enlightenment created and now aims to destroy humanity. Again and again."

"But you made a choice not to do that. Maybe the dragon… "

"That will not happen. I made the choice because of—"

"Love. How's that going for you? Eight deaths so far?" she joked about Monk's lifetimes.

"We're working through some things."

"Ah, good. Very therapeutic."

"My failure has brought that beast here."

"It was not a failure. It was a choice."

"Whatever you want to call it, the stakes are higher this time. And it is because of me."

"You are such an egomaniac," Ileana shook her head. Vampire looked at Ileana with surprise. "Your pride is what keeps telling you that," she continued. "It's not true. You made a choice. Mankind was spared by you, and you have spent the rest of your time making good on that choice to understand mankind. To feel… human. To feel love." Vampire stood and turned. He held his lower lip as he paced around the fountain. "All of this is to save him," she reminded Vampire. Vampire stopped and glanced back at her. "To save love. There is no greater cause. There was no other choice," Ileana said, with a kind smile.

"This beast has been sent to destroy all of space and time," Vampire pronounced. "Everything that ever was or is or will be in every plane of existence."

"All because you—"

"Failed."

"Made a choice."

"I caused a chain of events that has now led to the beginning of the end."

"Again, that's your pride talking. That beast would have been sent, anyway. Humanity has been destroyed in the past and come back."

"I would have ended humankind completely," Vampire argued.

"Evolution would have brought them back."

"I would have been left here to keep that from happening."

"So then, yes. This is all your fault!" she yelled. "You are a terrible creature and in need of very skilled counseling, but it will not be from me. If you want to sit here and whine about your choice, well then — do it with someone else. I am busy right now!" Vampire was silent. "Who else knows this? Monk?" Ileana asked.

"Yes, but he would never allow me to take on this responsibility. He blames himself."

"Ironic. Love is the destroyer of everything."

"Or the savior," Vampire whispered, thinking of Monk.

"So, we're going with *savior?*"

"Yes," Vampire said, with the hint of a smile. "I just needed to say it all aloud."

"Then you had better move these hedges so that I can go and reintroduce myself to my family. They will have a lot of questions."

"And Sorcerer is very pissed off."

"Very."

Vampire waved his hand and the hedges in front of them moved to the side. They opened wide enough to display the palace and the continued celebration.

"He never stopped loving you, Ileana."

"I know. Nor I him."

"He knows. It's just a shock. You hid well — well enough for even him to think you dead."

"He never thought I was dead, just… gone."

Ileana smirked as she turned and walked back towards the palace. "You've assembled a good team, Vampire. But we have a lot of work to do."

Vampire cocked his head and smiled proudly. He knew that there was a limited chance of success, but he also knew that his love for Monk gave them their greatest hope.

"And it looks like you have a visitor!" Ileana yelled, still walking swiftly towards the palace.

Vampire smiled. He knew that Monk was around the hedge.

When Monk appeared, he was holding two glasses of champagne.

CHAPTER 42
The Palace of Tebbs

Princess was alone as she entered the room where Sorcerer and Ileana were talking. They did not acknowledge her presence as they were focused on their own whispered discussion. Princess closed her eyes and took in a deep breath through her nose. The smell of orange and vanilla filled her senses. It was familiar. Yet, there was cinnamon, as well. That was not expected. She began to walk over to them. She became more confident with each step. The smell of orange and vanilla became more familiar, yet as a child she had always thought it came from the palace orchards.

As she came nearer to them, Ileana looked up at her and smiled. She walked past Sorcerer and wrapped her arms lovingly around the girl's neck to pull her in and squeeze her tight. Princess returned the gesture. It felt familiar. Ileana held tight and it seemed like she did not want to let go. Princess opened her eyes as a tear fell. She saw Sorcerer smiling.

"So, I guess this answers your question," Sorcerer said to her, referring to her question in that Palace of Mortua.

"I guess it does," she answered, as Ileana released her hug and held her by the hands to look into her daughter's face.

"I am so sorry," Ileana said.

"I know that scent. I always imagined that it was the orchard. And even though the vanilla would not have been in the air, nor would the orange at certain times of the year, I just let myself accept it. But now I know that it was you."

Ileana smiled as she brushed the hair from Princess' face. "Yes."

"Ileana?" Sorcerer asked.

"I needed to be sure that she was all right." Ileana turned and faced Sorcerer. "You had the boys and they had each other." She turned back to Princess. "And Queen Sharon has been a perfect mother, better than I would have been, but I still needed to make sure. I even made sure to enchant your appearance so you would look more like her than me. The fewer the questions, the better."

Princess smiled. "Thank you for looking out for me. And yes, she gave me everything. She loves me as if…"

"As if you were her own daughter? You are. She is your mother, as am I. It's unconventional, but it is yours to own. And he…" Ileana motioned to Sorcerer. "He is your father. He did what he had to do to protect you. And the sacrifice paid off."

"So, I am a Witch," Princess said, her tone somewhere between a statement and a question.

"One of the most powerful, as you will find out," her mother told her.

"You and your brothers are the Three of Legend," Sorcerer said.

"Another reason we had to protect you," Ileana confirmed.

"The Three of Legend?"

"From the prophecy," Sorcerer told her.

"Your elemental gifts will add to the weapons required to save mankind." Ileana explained. "We knew from birth that it referred to you, Axel, and Aldrick."

"Do my brothers know?" Princess asked.

"They know of their connections to Fire and Earth. But we have not yet discussed it all with them. When they sober up, we will tell them," Sorcerer told her.

"Maybe it will be better with them drunk," Ileana joked.

"It is a lot to take in," Princess said, laughing.

Princess did not deny her parents' story because she felt the truth in it. She quietly nodded as she turned to the light of a candle and watched it flicker in the gentle breeze. She willed the flame to hold still and surprised herself that it did.

"Air," Ileana told her. "That is your gift. That is the element to which you are champion."

Princess looked at her with a questioning expression. "Air. Fire. Earth," Princess said aloud. "That leaves Water."

Sorcerer and Ileana glanced at one another and smiled.

"Water chose a…" Sorcerer hesitated, searching for the right words.

"A different type of champion," Ileana concluded.

"Who?"

"Time will tell," Ileana told her.

Sorcerer pulled up his sleeve to expose the marks on his forearm. He'd already shown Axel and Aldrick the symbols of Fire and Earth. But now he pulled the sleeve higher and exposed the circular mark which was the symbol for Air.

Princess turned her wrist over and showed them the matching mark on her forearm. She smiled.

"Shall we join the others?" Sorcerer asked. "After all, this is a celebration, and we need to figure out our next step."

Ileana gently placed her arm around her daughter and held her forehead to the princess.

"I think, yes," Ileana said. "And I need to see about that boy."

"What boy?" Princess asked.

"Don't lie to your mother," she joked.

"Oh, *that* boy."

"Yes," Ileana giggled with Princess. "That boy."

CHAPTER 43
The Palace of Tebbs

The following morning found AZ and Tinker with pounding headaches. They were seated in a room of mirrors and saw their ragged reflections.

"I don't get it," AZ said, just above a whisper.

"Shhh," Tinker told him, with his hands to his head.

AZ was watching at Axel and Aldrick. They were laughing it up and continued flirting with some of the women that they had met at the celebration the night before.

"They drank at least as much—" AZ groaned.

"More," Tinker corrected him. "Definitely more."

"More than we did and look at them. Totally fine."

"Cadet!" Vampire screamed into the air.

"Ouch," Tinker and AZ said, collectively. They also noticed that he did not cast a reflection.

"Calm yourself," Cadet said as she appeared from behind a column. "I'm right here."

"Where have you been?" Vampire demanded as the others gathered close.

"There's a lot of crazy shit happening here," she told him.

"We have to go," he told her.

"Really?" Cadet replied, sarcastically.

"Did you find it?" Monk asked her.

"No," she said, with disappointment. "It's not here."

"You trusted her to get the Sword of Sansit?" Vampire asked, his anger growing with every word. He began to frisk her.

Cadet scanned the group over and then caught sight of Ileana. She gasped with excitement. "Your majesty." She pushed Vampire away and curtsied.

"Please, no," Ileana said, graciously helping her up. "Thank you, Cadet. For everything that you did for me. Your assistance helped to get the Book of Spells to a safe hiding place."

"Funny you should say that," Sorcerer added. He looked at Vampire.

"Lucifer does not have the Book of Spells," Vampire told her.

Ileana cautiously spoke. "He was supposed to hide it-"

"Oh, he hid it," Vampire continued. "But not in Hell." Ileana looked at Cadet who shook her head, appearing to not know what they were talking about. "He hid it in the library at the Monastery of the Order of the Brothers of Naa… Randomly among the shelves,"

Ileana cracked a smile. "I have the book."

"Monk has the book," Vampire told her.

"No I don't," he argued.

"I smelled your scent at the monastery," he raised his eyebrow. "The first night of the Blood Moon?"

"Nope. Not me."

"You were there," Vampire argued.

"I was there," Monk confessed. "But once you appeared, I apparently had a meltdown and Seer got me out of there."

Monk and Seer glanced at one another. "Tinker," they said in unison.

"It's not his fault," Ileana told them. "I hired Tinker to attend to certain things for me. That included getting me the Book of Spells. He did not know what it was of course, just to bring to me the book with the rose gold binder."

Tinker's ego got the better of him as he confessed. "I made a copy," he said, wishing immediately that he could take back his words.

"How?" Sorcerer asked. "Only a Witch can call forth the writings within that text."

Ileana laughed. "Men. So predictable." She looked at Cadet who nodded in agreement. "I knew that Tinker would be curious. So,

I gave him an enchanted necklace that allowed him to expose what was in that book." They awaited further explanation. "He would have lost himself trying to access it and possibly would have destroyed it."

"Not on purpose," Tinker argued.

Ileana put her hand protectively on his shoulder. "This way, he felt empowered and I got the book back."

Everyone waited for someone else to break the silence.

"So," Axel began. "Where is the book?"

"In the City of Witches," Ileana said at the same time as Tinker saying, "Here. On my cart."

Everyone looked at Tinker. "I mean, my copy is here… on my cart."

"So then why were you there that night?" Vampire asked.

"Tinker told us that there was something that we needed to get," Seer told him.

"You mean *steal*," Vampire argued.

"Okay. Steal." Monk walked over to Tinker and smiled. "You sly fox," he joked. "Nicely done." He turned to Vampire. "We have the Book of Spells and the green Cez stone," he said pointing to the ring still on Princess' finger.

"The Three of Legend," Sorcerer continued, noting his children.

"We need to go back to Mortua and get the rest of the stones," Monk added, looking at AZ.

"And Mavi said that the shield is Gnim's shield," Vampire told them. "She said that it is in Istanbul…Part of it, at least."

"With that, all we need to find is the yellow Cez stone, and then we will have gotten all the weapons," Seer said with a rare sense of optimism.

"Time is definitely of the essence now," Vampire warned. "The dragon has already attacked three times."

"We'll have to split up," Ileana told them.

"Monk should go to Istanbul with me so that he is not exposed," Vampire told them. "We will travel through the Mirror Realm," Vampire told them.

"How?" Ileana asked. "He's a mortal."

"Ghost!" Vampire yelled.

Ghost showed himself directly in front of Vampire.

"Good," Ileana said. "And since I know *exactly* where to find the shield, I too will be going. Ghost can shroud both of us."

Vampire shook his head, but knew that she was right. "Cadet. You will take the others by the Rainbow Express to AZ's home in Mortua. We will meet you there."

They all nodded in agreement to their assignments.

Cadet began counting heads. She pulled everyone into position and then began to reposition them several times.

"What are you doing?" Axel asked.

"Balancing the energies so that no one gets spliced," she replied, pulling Aldrick to the back of the line. Then she pulled him back and placed him next to his brother. "This isn't working," she said, turning from Vampire to Sorcerer and then shaking her head at Ileana. "There are too many energies. Someone else will have to go with you through the Mirror Realm."

"I may have an idea," Ileana told her as Vampire and Monk walked around the room to find the right mirror. Ileana pulled Axel from the line-up. Cadet looked over the crowd.

"Yes! That will do it. The lower energies will give enough space for the added… guests." Cadet smiled and she and Ileana nodded respectfully at each other. "You still are the most gifted." Ileana respectfully accepted the compliment. "Okay," Cadet said. "We are ready."

"Wait," Axel demanded. "And us?"

"You're coming with us through the Mirror Realm," she told him.

He stared at Aldrick who shared a slight concern at being separated from his brother.

"Don't worry, Aldrick," Ileana joked. "You and I will catch up when we get back."

"Go. We will meet you in Mortua," Ileana told Cadet.

Cadet immediately began the incantation and used the prism dust to intensify the rainbow.

Cadet curtsied to Ileana as the air became more humid and the water particles began to vibrate into a prism of colors. Tinker could not help but smile. The colored lights came over those who stood in the line.

"Here we go," Cadet said, as the colored light began to extend over the line in order of frequency and wavelength. The colors reflected off all the mirrors and then out a window as the rainbow rose into the sky.

Ileana and Axel met Vampire and Monk and stood in front of the chosen mirror.

"Now Ghost," Vampire demanded. Ghost took a visible form but was still transparent. "We are ready," Vampire told him.

"I did not agree to this," Ghost said, with an air of snobbery.

"You also don't have a choice," Monk told him. "We have to get there, and this is the only way."

Ghost snarled at Monk. Monk took no offense.

Ileana stepped forward and met Ghost eye to eye. She said nothing, but her action and stare told him that he did not have a choice.

She turned and extended her hands to Monk and Axel. They stepped closer and held her hands. Ghost shook his head as he expanded his form to surround the three of them.

"Excellent," Vampire said.

"What happens when you enter the Mirror Realm?" asked Axel.

Axel stared at his reflection with curiosity. He attempted to see what Vampire saw. He wanted to see the world on the other side.

Vampire watched as a tower appeared, and its lights ignited his interest. The lights were electric. He was unfamiliar with this city in this time. However, he had been there with Monk in one of Monk's previous lives.

Vampire said to Axel, "You cannot enter the Mirror Realm on your own. The paths are clear, fixed from mirror to mirror. But you still need to know how to see through it to be able to navigate a path. It's a place where up and down are exactly alike. Left is the same as right. It makes no sense and yet makes perfect sense at the same time."

"Sounds drunk," Axel said.

"Yes. It seems as though it does," Vampire agreed.

"But you know how to get through it?"

"Yes," Vampire replied, still curious about the goings-on on the other side of the mirror. "Too many questions," Vampire said, dismissively.

"So, it doesn't matter how old the mirror is," Axel said. Vampire glared back at him, annoyed. "That wasn't a question. It was a statement," Axel told him. His voice echoed as Ghost's form descended over him, Monk, and Ileana.

"No, " Vampire added, as he pulled himself back.

Axel looked into the mirror but saw only his own reflection.

"Another plane of existence," Axel concluded, rolling his eyes. "If I have to hear that phrase again, I may just fling myself into the mirror to end my misery."

"A bit dramatic, but okay," Vampire told him, grabbing hold of him and rushing into the mirror.

"What are you doing!" Axel yelled in horror. "Are you—"

And with that, they were gone.

CHAPTER 44
Mirror Realm

Axel was amazed that he had just gone through a mirror and was walking on an illuminated path. The glow of the path seemed to pulse to the steps that he took. He, Monk, and Ileana were shrouded by Ghost's form which felt physically limiting, if not, suffocating. The feeling was contrasted with the vastness of the space that surrounded them. As he looked around, he saw what appeared to be shooting stars traveling above, below and to the sides of them.

"Those are other mirror paths," Vampire told him. Vampire looked ahead to the opening and smiled. "Monk!" Vampire yelled.

"Yes?"

"I'm taking you on a date. This is one of your favorite places ever!" Vampire screamed over the whooshing sound that flew past them in the Mirror Realm.

He pointed to the distant opening. Colored lights flew by them. Vampire shielded his eyes from the brightness and focused on the end point. Through the olive-colored hue of Ghost's form, Monk saw the tower illuminated through what seemed like a doorway. It felt familiar but he had no true reference.

"When was the last time that you had *simit?*" Vampire asked as they neared the other end.

"You tell me," Monk said with a laugh.

Vampire felt the breeze through the opening. He reached his free hand out and felt a filmy thickness as his hand exited the Mirror Realm. He stepped out into the cool air and pulled the others through. Axel closed his eyes in fear of the glass breaking and blinding him, but also felt as though he needed to have this experience. He was robbed of being fully conscious when entering the Mirror Realm due to the forceful surprise of being pulled into the mirror. He watched as the others disappeared in front of him at the mirror's surface. They continued to pull him towards it. He felt the pressure of Ghost's form pushing him through the mirror and into the ancient city.

Once they were all through, Ghost retracted himself and diminished his visibility. He appeared as a ripple in the air and his presence was easily dismissible.

"Seems like no one saw us come out," Ileana said as they scanned around to check for any surprised expressions.

"Good," Vampire told them. "No time to deal with that."

"Istanbul? Where is Istanbul?" Axel asked. "Never heard of it."

"You should be asking *when*," Ileana told him. "Where is less relevant."

"*When* are we?" Axel asked, with sarcasm.

"2016," Vampire told him as he looked at the poster on the jazz club. "This guy is really good," Vampire told them, as he recognized the headlining performer's name.

"Vampire," Ileana called, pointing up to the top of the Galata Tower. "The shield is there," she said.

"Where? How do we get it?" Axel asked.

"Monk?" Vampire said. "Maybe he's not as bright as I thought."

Axel aimed his middle finger at Vampire's back.

"Okay. Let's make it quick," Monk said. He began to walk up to the Galata Tower.

"Monk?"

Monk stopped and turned to Vampire.

"Simit?" Vampire asked, pointing to the vendor with his cart of hot sesame-encrusted bread.

"Really?" Monk asked.

"I said that I was taking you on a date," Vampire reminded him, and extended his hand.

"It just gets more ridiculous," Axel whispered to Ileana.

"Give it a minute," she said.

Vampire led Monk to the cart in the middle of the milling evening crowd. Axel started to follow them but was halted by Ileana. She shook her head.

"Just watch," she said.

Vampire had his arm around Monk's shoulder. He leaned in and whispered, "Do you trust me?"

Monk knew that Vampire was about to put him in a precarious situation. However, he also knew that it would lead to success. Vampire looked back at Ileana and nodded.

"Stay here," she said to Axel. Ileana pulled her hood up over her head and seemed to disappear. "Ghost," she said. The voice from her invisible form scared Axel.

"I will meet you there," Ghost said.

Axel watched as the air seemed to ripple in an upward direction towards the top of the tower. He also saw some leaves get caught up in a circular wind that raised them to the top of the tower.

"Witches are cool," Axel said, with a smile.

Axel glanced over and saw Monk and Vampire eating the warm bread. The smell wafted through the air. He realized that he was hungry and walked over to Vampire and Monk. "Hey," he demanded. "I'm starved."

"Excuse me!" Vampire yelled. "We have rights, too."

Axel was taken aback.

"Let the show begin," Monk said to himself, while he kept eating the simit, unaffected by Vampire's angry display.

"You think that you can just come over here and say that to us. My boyfriend and I are just having a nice evening out, and you think that you have the right to insult us with your foul words?"

"What are you doing?" Axel asked, embarrassed.

"Boyfriend?" Monk asked. "Really? That's my title?" he continued his jest.

The attention of everyone in the plaza was drawn to the altercation taking place by the simit vendor. It was so loud that the tourists atop the tower looked over the edge to see the cause of the excitement. Axel turned to Monk for help. Monk continued to eat the warm, sesame-crusted bread as if nothing was happening.

"Really?" Axel asked him.

"It is so good. If I were able to remember everything from my previous lives, I'd be able to tell you that it's just as good as the last time, but…" he ended with a shrug of the shoulders.

On the roof of the tower, Ileana cast a spell to have all of the visitors go back inside. She lowered her hood as she reappeared. "Small problem," she said to Ghost. "This is only the frame of the shield. We are missing the center, the ruby." She looked over the tower at Vampire, Monk, and Axel. Ileana began singing an enchantment, as she poured drops of a silvery liquid onto the circular-shaped metal that bordered the top of the tower. The liquid was placed on the north, south, east, and west points and then she pulled each drop down to the base so that a silver line marked the four directions.

Ghost covered the top of the tower as he expanded his visible form. He pushed the door to the observation platform closed and sealed it. His greenish form was transparent enough to blend into the night sky.

Ileana continued the enchantment. The silver lines on the metal turned to ice. She flicked each of them with her index finger and the vibration from the sound broke the metal into four equal pieces. "So much easier to carry through the mirror," she said.

Her spell changed and the four pieces began to shrink until each was as long as a forearm. Their weight matched their size as she lifted all four pieces and placed them in her hands.

"Done," she told Ghost.

She pulled her hood back over her head and disappeared. Ghost dimmed his form and was now completely transparent. The door opened again, and the tourists and locals came back out to the observation level atop the tower. Ileana and Ghost both descended to the ground. She removed her hood and appeared in the back of the crowd. She pushed her way through.

"There you are," she said to Axel. "What's going on here?" she asked Vampire.

"Your child—"

"Child? He is my lover!" she exclaimed. The crowd let out gasps and catcalls. "I am so sorry," she said, reaching out to place a piece of the ring into Vampire and Monk's hands. They allowed the metal to twist itself up their forearms under their sleeves.

"Well, put him back on his leash and keep him out of public places. If I see him again, it won't end well," Vampire said, as he stepped forward and snarled at Axel. "Come on," he said to Monk, who still seemed unaffected by what was going on.

"Thank you," Monk said to the vendor.

"Was that really necessary?" Axel asked Ileana.

"We needed a distraction," she told him. "Take this."

"What is it?"

"The shield," she told him. "Part of it at least."

Axel seemed confused.

"Magic. It's in four pieces. We each have one. If anyone else gets a hold of this, we will be in even more trouble than we already are." Ileana looked around and saw that the crowd was no longer paying them any attention. She motioned for Axel to hold the metal to his forearm. It began to bend itself and snake up to his elbow. It was lighter than he anticipated. Ileana did the same with her metal piece and motioned with her hand. "This way. We have to meet them in the Spice Market."

Axel was mesmerized as he watched the metal twist its way up his forearm. "Amazing!"

Ileana led Axel down the cobblestone street which led from the tower to the Bosphorus River. Axel admired the illuminated mosques that were scattered throughout the city.

"This place is beautiful," he said in awe.

"It is," Ileana agreed. "So, tell me." Axel looked at her eagerly. "Tell me about your life." Axel gulped. "Good response," she laughed, as she held him by the arm. "You have to know that your father and I did what we did to protect you, Aldrick, and your sister."

Axel tried to muster up the right words as he focused on the tapping of her heels on the cobblestones.

"I do," he said with a slight nodding of his head. "We do," he rushed. "But all Aldrick and I know is the life that we had to struggle through."

"You learned how to survive," she told him. "It was a hard lesson, but the only one that could have prepared you for those times and for what lies ahead of us. The three of you are listed in this prophecy. And although I do not know what exactly it is, you have a very important part to play in defeating the Jeweled Dragon. The three of you will need to master your power and work together."

"We have no idea how to do that," Axel confessed.

"By mastering your element." Ileana laughed. "You're just like your father."

"Sorcerer? How's that?"

"He used to lack confidence, too. Cute. Very cute," she said as she stopped walking and faced at AZ. "But he too needed a push to get on the right path. Once he was there, he was unstoppable. Oh, don't get me wrong. He's brilliant. And cocky as anyone can possibly be. He will teach you. We will teach you."

Ileana glanced at Axel and smiled. She appreciated his simple honesty, his lack of agenda.

They had reached the Galata Bridge. They walked past the fishermen crowding the railings of the bridge to collect their night's haul.

They walked towards the illuminated structure that housed the Spice Market. "Now let's find those two. Ghost? Are you with us?"

"I will lead you to them, my lady," he whispered into her ear.

CHAPTER 45
Istanbul, 2016

"How often have you used that on me?" Monk asked Vampire, watching him glam the vendors into giving them whatever they wanted.

"Never," Vampire told him. Monk gave him a look of disbelief. "I've never had to," Vampire insisted. "You do whatever I want without me even asking."

Monk laughed. "Yeah. I probably do," he admitted, "Has it always been like this?"

Vampire hesitated, thinking of Monk's past lives.

"Yes," he said, turning away. "You have always seen through my selfishness and called me out on it." He looked at Monk. "You can be extremely annoying."

"You're a better you because of it," Monk said with a soft laugh. "Come on. You have a great fear that you will be seen as the villain."

"We've worked that one out already."

"Did we? Are you sure?" Monk joked.

"More than once," Vampire said, laughing.

"Maybe this time it will stick."

"Phin, I'm a vampire who was sent to destroy all of humanity. I *am* the bad guy."

Monk smiled, thinking that he liked when Vampire used his real name, *Phineas*. "But what exactly did you do wrong?" Monk asked, his expression making it clear that he refused to accept Vampire's evil nature.

"In your memories, I killed you," Vampire admitted with shame.

"Yeah, more than once," Monk joked and took another sip of Turkish coffee before holding it up in salute. "But it didn't take," Monk continued to joke. "Not yet, at least."

Monk saw that Vampire was struggling to continue this conversation. "No, Thaddeus. You did not kill me. You ended my life. You did not allow my suffering."

"That is the truth," Vampire admitted. "I just need you to know that it is."

Monk gazed into Vampire's eyes. "When I first saw you, at the monastery, I knew who you were. "It felt like you were the other side of my soul."

"Even though I am Immortal?" Vampire questioned in disbelief. "I have no soul. Remember?"

"The Mermaids were once Immortals, with no souls," Monk reminded him.

"So, I'm going to get a soul for my selfishness? Vampire joked.

"Well," Monk said. "Only because your selfishness will help to save everything… And only if it works."

Vampire leaned in and kissed him hard. It felt as if the entire world, all the worlds, and all their problems, went away in that one moment.

They finally softened but maintained contact with their foreheads. Vampire's eyes were still closed, and they were both catching their breath. They both felt an adrenaline rush, but Monk took control of himself first and calmed himself enough to speak.

"The first time that you took my life, you killed me out of fear. You were afraid to love me, so you had to push me away and killing me was your only solution. But then you marked me and spent every subsequent moment trying to find me… to convince me to love you again."

Vampire nodded although his eyes were still closed. He knew that what Monk said was true. He opened his eyes and looked at Monk. "Yes," was all he could say.

"The only reason you ended up on that path of destruction is because evil got to you first. If you'd met me before you were chosen, you never would have taken it."

"I'm not sure about that, Monk. It is my nature."

"Was your nature, but only because I wasn't there for you to love. You filled an empty void with emptiness. You were the bad guy. You were the villain," Monk said, putting his arm around Vampire's shoulder. "Now, you're just a do-gooder who has assembled the greatest team of misfits and time travelers to save not only humanity but all of time and space. You're the leader of heroes, Thaddeus."

Vampire smiled. "I like when you call me Thaddeus."

"You called me by my name, so I called you by yours," Monk told him and leaned in for a kiss.

Monk gazed deep into Vampire's eyes. "You're a good guy. It just took me this long to mold you the right way," he said, laughing.

Ileana and Axel followed the subtle ripple in the air and found Vampire and Monk surrounded by vendors and tourists taking in the sensory overload of the Spice Market. The aromas were overwhelming. Axel had never smelled so much at once.

"Why don't we have these smells?" he gasped.

"Most of the plants that create these spices have gone extinct in our time. Take it in. It's about to be nothing more than a memory," Ileana told him as they walked up to Vampire and Monk.

"All good?" Monk asked, as he was eating a piece of something that he held in a napkin. "Here, Axel. Try this," he said as he handed him a decadent dessert.

Axel's face glowed with joy. "This is so good," he mumbled, with his mouth full of the nutty sweetness. "We need to take some of this back."

"We have more pressing matters at hand, Axel," Vampire reminded him.

Monk nodded at Axel and motioned to his oversized pockets and the bag over his shoulder. Axel saw the bags of spices and gave him a big smile, which he quickly hid as he looked to Vampire to make sure that they would not get caught.

"We have to go to the other part of the market. There is an area that is all mirrors. Stay together and don't talk to anyone," Vampire told them. He turned back at Axel. "Anyone," he emphasized.

"Keep feeding me and I won't be able to talk anyway." Vampire looked at him with an intimidating stare. "No way, man. Kill me right now and I die happy."

Ileana and Monk laughed.

"His bravado is expanding," she said.

"It's a phase," Vampire said, maintaining his stare. "He'll grow out of it."

Axel continued eating and stared back at Vampire with joy in his face.

"It's the sugar," Monk said. "Be careful Axel. It's like a drug. And you crash when it wears off."

"Says the guy who is eating as much as me."

Monk laughed.

"Come on," Vampire told them. "This way."

CHAPTER 46
The Rainbow Network

Princess felt the energy of the light as a sense of weightlessness pulled her along the path of the rainbow. It felt as if she were actively moving but without actually taking a step. She turned to Tinker and saw, from the look on his face, that he was thinking.

His face wrinkled into the same varied expressions that he always made when he was in an argument that he knew how to win but didn't want to waste his time. His mouth would pull from one side to the other. His eyes would widen and then close. His forehead would wrinkle and flatten. The base of his nose would twitch. It seemed he was upset. However, he was figuring something out in his mind, something other than what was happening in front of him.

Tinker was trying to understand this process of travel. He was aware that some of the group were bathed in a particular color of light and others, a combination. He saw Cadet. It appeared as though she was actually generating the light and directing it. He was covered in a yellow light, Sorcerer orange, and Seer red.

Warmth, he thought. *Lower frequencies.*

Aldrick was orange but combined with red. His colors seemed to mix together, but then separate.

Orange and red are next to one another on the color scale so that makes sense, but why are they combining and retreating? Tinker thought. *And AZ… light blue.*

He glanced at Princess, who had a different kind of light entirely. It seemed to glow from deep within her. It was varied, however; it was not a distinct color of the rainbow. Silver and gold covered her like armor. She, like Cadet, seemed to generate her own light.

Tinker continued thinking. Princess noticed the way he concentrated and looked around at the others. She saw the same things that Tinker had observed.

Aldrick and AZ were laughing at the adrenaline rush that came from the leaps and drops of the rainbow's path. Sorcerer kept a watchful eye on Princess and smiled. Seer stayed quiet and reserved. Cadet felt like she controlled the universe with the joy and confidence that came from her making the rainbow.

Princess looked back at her own hands and noticed the silver and gold. She knew her experience, but not yet that of the others. She knew the power that was rushing through her. Aldrick and AZ were joyous; Sorcerer content; Seer withdrawn; Tinker eager for more. Cadet, like herself, demonstrated a power from within.

"We're almost there," Cadet yelled back to the others.

"Oh, too bad," Aldrick yelled. "This ride is incredible!"

AZ nodded and laughed in what was almost a drunken agreement. Princess looked at Tinker and laughed. He did the same with a shrug of his shoulders. Sorcerer, too, was smiling with an almost proud grin. Seer maintained a stoic expression. Princess caught Tinker's attention and motioned towards the clairvoyant.

"Is that look for us or the others?" Tinker asked Seer.

"Possibly all of the above," Seer replied.

CHAPTER 47
Istanbul, 2016

"Please! Please! Yes! Looking is free, my friends," the chubby vendor in the bazaar said, excitedly. Vampire was pushing through the busy crowd in the Spice Market and leading the others into the section that housed the mirror vendors. "This beautiful woman should never be without a mirror. She should be able to see what we see," he insisted.

"I couldn't agree more," Ileana said.

Vampire was ignoring the shopkeeper and searching from one mirror to the next. Monk and Axel were continuing to eat.

"Monk?" Axel asked, through a mouthful of food. "How are you eating so much?"

"How are you?"

"I'm a growing boy," Axel said.

Vampire did not seem to be having an easy time with the mirrors. Ileana continued to enchant the shopkeeper but was growing bored.

"Time is still of the essence," Monk told him. "But as long as we are all still here, we know that past, present, and future are all in play."

"Until the dragon destroys everything, and we get stuck somewhere," Axel pointed out.

"We won't be stuck anywhere. There won't be anywhere," Monk reminded him.

Axel stared at him with a disgusted expression. "Thanks for that. Now my stomach hurts," he said, trying to contain a belch.

"No worries. You'll digest on the way."

"Or vomit right now," Vampire said.

"Or that."

Ileana came over to them.

"Where is the shopkeeper?" Monk asked.

"Making tea," she said with frustration. "Can we please go?"

"Yes. This one," Vampire said.

"Let's go," Ileana demanded.

The greenish mist descended over Ileana, Monk, and Axel. They all grabbed hands and Vampire's thumb massaged the webspace between Monk's thumb and index finger.

"That's familiar," Monk told him.

"Good," Vampire told him as they stepped through the mirror.

The shopkeeper came back with the silver tray and the tea. He was unsure if he was more upset about losing the sale or losing the beautiful woman who seemed so enamored by his conversation about goats.

CHAPTER 48
Mortua - The Perculfilus Estate

"We're here," Cadet announced.

Simultaneously, they all felt the softness of the ground becoming a comfortable sensation under their feet. They were each caught off balance.

The light of the rainbow quickly diminished.

"That certainly didn't wait, huh?" Aldrick asked.

The sun was high, and the heat was intense. It seemed hotter than it should be. AZ led the way into his parents' estate.

"We are here for the stones," Sorcerer reminded him. "And to wait for the others."

"And the truth," AZ replied.

AZ rushed through the house looking for his parents. He did his best to keep his voice to a low volume until he found them.

"AZ," his mother rushed. "Thank goodness you are safe," she added and hugged him tight.

AZ turned to his parents. "Mother. Father. We need the stones."

"Stones?" Mr. Perfulcilus questioned.

"The Cez stones," he told him. "All of them."

AZ's parents glanced at one another with concern.

"I know the truth. I know that Saric never existed and that you made him up to protect me. The Cez stones may have secured our family's fortune, but they fell for a different reason. We already collected the orange and red ones from your brothers. And we found the green one at the Palace of Tebbs. But if we don't get them all, this dragon will destroy everything and those stones will have no value at all. We will be destroyed."

His parents looked at one another.

"Everything will be destroyed," AZ added to his plead.

"This way," Mr. Perculfilus told them and led the others through the villa to where the stones were kept.

A guard came rushing in. "Sir! The dragon attacked the city again."

"The palace!" Princess worried. The rest of the group ran outside to see what was happening.

Mrs. Perculfilus nodded for AZ and her husband to continue as she comforted the princess. "Magic has been protecting the palace and all of Mortua. I'm sure that your family is fine."

Cadet stepped out of the villa and watched a billow of smoke rise from the city. "What about you?" she asked Tinker. "Anything in your bag of tricks?"

He shook his head and looked apologetically at Princess who followed them out to see the attack. "The rest of my stuff is on my cart. Halo is supposed to meet us here." Tinker worried that the Jeweled Dragon may have caught and destroyed Halo.

Tinker pulled out a pair of tinted sunglasses and turned towards the sun. "No," he said, as his breath was knocked from his chest.

"What is it?" Sorcerer asked.

Tinker handed him the glasses and shielded his eyes.

"The dragon?" asked Aldrick.

"Hurry. Inside," Sorcerer ordered. "And stay quiet."

"What? How?" Seer questioned.

"I don't know," Sorcerer told him. "Maybe she saw the rainbow as we arrived," Sorcerer said. "As soon as she spots us—"

"We are fucked," Aldrick finished his thought.

"Not exactly my words, but yes."

Princess turned to Sorcerer with horror. "We need to lead her away from the city."

"Yes," Cadet agreed. "But where?"

"The caves!" AZ exclaimed as he joined them carrying a satchel with the stones.

Aldrick was looking up at the sky. "We need to be quick and draw her attention."

"Then, another rainbow should do the trick," Cadet said. "Where exactly are these caves?"

CHAPTER 49
The Caves of Waku

The rainbow took them from the Perculfilus estate to the Caves of Waku. Cadet was sure to create a strong enough surge to increase its height and visibility to draw the attention of the Jeweled Dragon.

As they arrived in the crater that made up the Valley of Kaar, they looked around at the mounds of packed sand and rock that comprised the entrances to the Caves of Waku. Tinker warned everyone not to rush forward because the ground was unpredictable. AZ, Aldrick, and Cadet kept an eye on the sky.

"She's coming!" Aldrick yelled as he watched the dragon flying towards them. "Wait! She's gone."

"She's hiding in the sunlight," AZ yelled out.

"Damn it," Tinker said through his frustration as he rummaged through his bag. "I need the rest of my stuff."

"There," Princess yelled, pointing to the black stallion flapping its wings and pulling Tinker's cart from behind a cave entrance.

"Halo!" Tinker yelled to the horse, "Do not take flight." He turned to the others. "The Holocator is in the cart. Without it, we risk falling through the ground and into the caves."

Seer surveyed the area between them and Halo. "I can guide you," he said. Seer's eyes began to glow. "Step *exactly* where I step."

Seer began to take a step and then pause. He occasionally shifted back before committing his foot placement. One by one, the others followed his footprints in the sand, making sure to step exactly where he stepped.

Tinker was the first to follow him. They both made it across and faced back as Princess, Sorcerer, Cadet, AZ, and Aldrick followed. Tinker led Halo and his cart into the nearest cave entrance as the others made their way under cover.

"Sorcerer?" Tinker asked. "Do you still have the ingredients for the potion to hide us from the dragon?"

Sorcerer rummaged in his backpack and then back to Tinker with a smile, but his feeling of hope was quickly diminished as the smell of bergamot filled the air. Princess was aware of it as well.

"What was that?" Cadet asked, as the ground began to come loose.

"Everyone go deeper into the entrance… All the way to the gates," Tinker ordered as he rummaged through his gadgets. "Sorcerer! Change of plans! I'm going to need an incredibly hot source of energy."

"We're on it," Sorcerer said and immediately began moving his arms, hands, and fingers in varied patterns until a visible light began to form.

"Bigger," Tinker demanded. The ground continued to move as if something were coming through the sand. "Wait," Tinker demanded. The sand was flowing faster. "Wait," he continued to hold him.

"Tink? It's gotta happen soon," Sorcerer said, struggling to control the spell.

"Wait!"

"Tink!"

"Wait!"

"Tinker!" Princess demanded.

"Now!" he shouted, as the Jeweled Dragon thrashed out from the sandy ground and exposed one of the caves below.

Sorcerer pushed his arms forward and the shield of light he produced clashed into the mountain of sand that surrounded the dragon. The heat of the light immediately liquified the sand into a shell of thick glass that hardened around the dragon's body.

The dragon was trapped in it and dropped into the exposed cave, but her head was still exposed. Her body had fallen in but her head was still at the surface level. She howled her rage with a high-pitched squeal.

Tinker and Sorcerer ran back to the cave where the others awaited.

"We trapped her." Sorcerer announced.

"Sort of," Tinker clarified "Her head is free, and we're within range of her fire."

"We need to get out of here now!" Aldrick exclaimed.

"I better get started with that potion," Sorcerer told them.

CHAPTER 50
Mortua - Perculfilus estate

Vampire led the others through a mirror that opened into the Perculfilus estate. He found the path when he recognized the painting of Saric that still remained hung above the fireplace. Ghost pulled his greenish covering from Monk, Ileana, and Axel. Axel responded with a shiver from the chill of Ghost moving through him.

"Where are they?" Ileana asked.

AZ's parents entered the room with a fireplace poker held aloft.

"Oh, thank goodness," Mr. Perculfilus sighed with relief. "It's you."

"Where are AZ and the others?" Monk rushed.

"The dragon was attacking the city," Mrs. Perculfilus told them. "They led her away to the Caves of Waku."

"And the Cez stones?" Vampire asked.

"They have them," Mr. Perculfilus said and pulled his wife in. "You must hurry!"

"Ileana?"

Ileana maneuvered her arms and opened a portal. She and the others ran into it and it immediately closed behind them.

CHAPTER 51
Caves of Waku

Sorcerer was working quickly to prepare the invisibility potion. Aldrick and Seer were at the cave entrance monitoring the dragon.

"Can you see any clear path out of here?" Seer asked.

"What's that?" Aldrick questioned as he saw sparks in the air near the high grasses.

"A portal," Seer told them. "They're here."

The others gathered nearer to the cave entrance and looked beyond the struggling dragon to see Ileana, Axel, Monk, and Vampire come through the void. The portal closed immediately as they stepped out.

"We need to get to them and then out of here," Aldrick said.

"The potion is ready," Sorcerer told them and showed them the corked container. "Those ingredients really reduce down once combined. We'll have to be quick to get past her." He uncorked the vial and sprinkled it all over them, including Halo.

"Still smells awful," AZ commented.

"Remember to stay close," Tinker told them. "She won't see us as long as we are a single unit."

"Let's go," Sorcerer ordered.

"Did they trap the dragon?" Monk asked.

"Looks like they did, but where are they? Can you see them?" Axel questioned.

They watched as the trapped dragon fought the confines of the hardened glass. She was randomly shooting fire and wriggling her body as much as possible. Her head was exposed and the high-pitched sounds were painful to the ear.

The group stepped in time with one another as Sorcerer led them past the dragon.

"My *Dazer* is on my cart," Tinker told Sorcerer. "I can stun her like I did in Dellai."

They stepped with caution to not disturb the rocks that made up the surface near the cave. AZ tapped Princess and pointed out that they were leaving tracks. Princess glanced back at the dragon who was still focused on trying to escape.

Aldrick saw her angst and turned back as well. His foot came down on some loose stones which caused him to trip and fall behind the group. The sound of the rocks being disturbed grabbed the dragon's attention.

Princess went to help Aldrick up. However, as she moved back towards him, the dragon noticed the three missing spots in her vision.

Aldrick had twisted his ankle and Princess assisted him into the nearest cave entrance. The dragon let out another roar as the smell of bergamot filled the air.

"No!" Axel exclaimed and threw his hands upward. A wall of sand and rock rose between the dragon and his siblings. Princess shielded Aldrick as the dragon let loose a flame. The wall of earth protected them from the fire and Princess was able to get Aldrick deeper into the cave.

Axel looked at his hands with complete shock.

"Your powers are innate," Ileana told her son. "Your protective instincts took over. Stay focused," she demanded. He nodded his head.

Vampire heard the sound of cracking glass. "She's breaking free," he yelled and pointed to the top of the hardened casing that began to shatter.

"Hurry!" Cadet called out to the group.

Tinker broke away from the others and ran back to the cave. The dragon pulled herself out of the collapsed cave and focused on him as she shook the broken glass off her back. She began to chase after Tinker with a roar that concealed the sound of other, deeper caves collapsing under her weight.

"No!" Monk exclaimed.

The Jeweled Dragon gave no caution to the unstable surface. She again fell through and out of sight. They heard a crashing sound as she hit the floor of the cave.

Tinker reached his cart as the disturbance began to collapse the cave entrance that he was in. He rummaged through the items and found his *Dazer*. Next to it was the orb given to him by Ileana. "This might be useful," he said, stashing it in his pocket. He grabbed a backpack with a set of retractable wings to fly out of the deep entrance as the sand and rock began falling in on him.

The dragon flew out of the ground and took flight high above them. Again, the smell of bergamot was in the air. The high-pitched sound came at a noxious volume as the Jeweled Dragon flew towards the Ambassadors. Monk knew he had to draw her away from the others and ran towards the nearest cave entrance without attention to the crumbling surface below him. His steps were crashing through and exposed the caves below.

"Monk!" Vampire yelled out. Ileana grabbed his sleeve.

"You know what has to happen," she told him. Vampire tore himself from her and ran after Monk.

Tinker had taken to flight and came out of the cave when he saw Monk running with the dragon and Vampire in pursuit.

Ileana maneuvered her arms and hands and spoke the incantation for a portal opening. Tinker's pocket began to glow; he was too focused on the dragon to notice. The Jeweled Dragon flew past Vampire as he chased after Monk. She shot flames back at him to slow his approach.

Ileana finished the spell and a portal opened directly in front of where the Jeweled Dragon was flying. The beast was distracted by her attack on Vampire and did not see the opening. The portal closed immediately once she was through.

Everyone cheered as Sorcerer hugged Ileana tight. "You did it," he told her.

"For now," she said. "Who knows when and where she will return."

"But we know that she will," Seer added.

"Monk!" Vampire yelled out. The rest of the Ambassadors froze as they heard the panic in his voice.

Monk had stopped running and turned around to face Vampire when the ground crumbled beneath him. He grasped onto anything to prevent from falling into the opening but felt himself sliding. Monk could not gain stability as he was blinded by the sands and the hot air blowing up from within the abyss. He was pulled further over the edge.

Vampire leapt with all his might and reached him. He peered beyond Monk and saw the swirling portal below him. Monk looked down and saw it as well. He felt the outline of the tattoo on his back begin to throb. Monk looked up and saw the fear in Vampire's eyes.

Vampire screamed. "Monk! I have you!" Vampire's voice was panicked. "I will not let go."

"Vampire," Monk said, as a sense of peace came over him.

"No," Vampire demanded. "I can't do this again."

"You have to let go," Monk told him. "You're the only one who can stop the dragon."

Monk felt the throbbing become burning and then excruciating pain. He twisted in agony and lost his grip on Vampire.

"Monk! No!"

Monk was falling.

Vampire lost control. He remembered this pain. He remembered this anguish. Three tears of blood welled up in his eyes and fell.

Tinker flew past Vampire and followed Monk into the portal as it closed immediately.

The Ambassadors stood in uneasy silence as they waited for Vampire and Tinker to bring Monk out of the opening. Seer had dropped to his knees, looking deeply into the future. He let out a painful gasp as the crimson light in his eyes diminished, "They're gone…"

ABOUT THE AUTHOR
James Voorhees

James Voorhees is the author of The Ambassador Chronicles, a character-driven series of shorts that introduces the main players of The Dragon Constellation, the first book of The Ambassador Chronicles trilogy.

Voorhees began writing through sleepless nights during the COVID-19 pandemic. He was working as a physical therapist in a Miami-based hospital and needed a quiet outlet. Little did he know that his random thoughts would come together to create an epic fantasy adventure, pitting love and darkness into desperate conflict.

Voorhees was raised in Secaucus, NJ. He has spent his lifetime immersed in music, fashion, travel, art, and with people who bring him joy and laughter as his greatest forms of inspiration. He currently resides in Miami Beach, FL.

www.ingramcontent.com/pod-product-compliance
Lightning Source LLC
Chambersburg PA
CBHW061106310726
48974CB00002B/417